D1188396

SQUARE 1

DATE DUE

KATIE Z. HARTMAN

SQUARE 1

A NOVEL

VBC Library
289 Factory RD
Clinton, AR 72031
501-745-2100 www.fcl.org
223003

TATE PUBLISHING
AND ENTERPRISES, LLC

Transformers littered my bedroom floor instead of tea sets and Barbie dolls. Looking back, I guess the friction came because we were more alike than I'd like to admit. Independent. Strong willed. And hopelessly driven to be people pleasers.

One big difference was in our appearance. I didn't look a thing like her. Even when I dug up photos of her from when she was a teenager, I didn't see much of a resemblance. Her tall frame, jet-black hair wound up into a classic beehive, and hazel eyes were the exact opposite of my features. I'm short. Five foot four in flip-flops. Blond hair and round blue eyes. Pretty average. On a scale between Jessica Rabbit and Olive Oyl, I fall somewhere in the middle. But Mom would say I look like Jessica Rabbit (just to make me feel better, even if she didn't have a clue who she was) and my brothers would say I look more like Olive Oyl (just because they love to harass me).

I grabbed my carry-on along with one large piece of luggage and made my way to the driveway. I was only going to be gone a week and I figured I'd be shopping for clothes while I was there.

"Be sure to let me know when you make it there, okay? Don't forget!" Mom ordered as I threw the suitcase in the back of my SUV with a growl.

"Mom, chill out. I'll be fine!" I glanced at my phone. Already running ten minutes behind. "I've gotta go. I'll call you soon," I promised as I gave her a hug and climbed into my new, black Chevrolet Trailblazer. She stood there, as always, waving till I was out of sight.

I enjoyed the ride to Oklahoma City. It was about an hour and fifteen minutes to get from Mom's house in Cordell to my house in Yukon. Then about fifteen minutes more to get to the airport. I was running a little behind, so when I decided that I didn't have time to go by and check on my house, I didn't feel as bad. I could always do it when I came back. I still hadn't been there since Josh died. I quickly let that thought dissipate as I got lost in the music blowing through the speakers—my random mix of songs that blurred my senses into a livable numbness.

As engrossed as I was in my singing, I couldn't help but realize when I was driving through Yukon and passed my house. My house was in an addition right off I-40, the major interstate that divides Yukon. The backyard actually backs right up to the interstate. If I'd had a rock, I could have rolled down the window and hit the house from the road. I recognized the top of my house and just kept right on driving. I took several deep breaths to calm myself and to get in the right frame of mind.

"Square one." I sighed heavily. I just had to start all over again. That's what I'd been trying to do for the past three years, without much success. That's one of the reasons I managed to convince myself to go on this trip. I still thought it was ridiculous, going on a trip by myself. No matter how crowded New York City was, I'm sure it was not going to be enough to keep me from feeling all alone. But perhaps the constant hum of people, cars, and street noise would be enough to drown out the misery long enough to have a little fun. Maybe, but not likely.

I made it to Will Rogers World Airport without incident twenty minutes later. I made short work of parking my SUV, catching a shuttle, and making my way through security. I had barely parked my behind in a chair at my gate before the boarding announcement was made. Nothing like cutting it close. One cramped seat and some stale cabin air later and I was airborne for the first time in years. I settled in with a sigh and re-checked my connecting flight information for when we landed in Denver.

I was already a little peeved that I couldn't find a more direct flight to New York. I had to go from Oklahoma City to Denver to get to New York. Made no sense, but it's what I get for planning a last-minute trip. So having to practically run to catch my connection wasn't making the start of my vacation any better. And on top of that, in an effort to give this trip a shot, I had gotten all dressed up to ride on a grimy plane all day. Dressed up for me anyway. A new form-fitting top, a pair of cute low-riding jeans, and some black patent, open-toed high heels. The shoes were the part I was really kicking myself for right now. But this morning it seemed like a good idea. I had gotten all "glammed" up before my trip and wanted to show off my pedicure. Well, as "glam" as I could get in a town with only one stoplight. A mani-cure, pedicure, a trim and color. Wow. Glam.

I was out of breath by the time I got to my gate in Denver. I was there just in time to check in; apparently I was the only one from my flight from Oklahoma City to get on this plane. I was greeted by a pixi-like brunette flight attendant. I noticed her name badge said Tina.

"You made it." She winked. "Boarding pass?"

I handed her my ticket, and she smiled as she waved for me to follow her. Tina slid back the black fabric curtain that sepa-rated the first-class area from the rest of the plane. I figured if I had to take a vacation by myself, then there was no need to be squished up next to some stranger for this longer leg of the trip. I glanced over my shoulder at the poor souls sitting in coach. Some seemed irritated that we were obviously waiting to depart, probably because of me. As I walked through the first class cabin, I looked over my shoulder and saw the poor coach passengers peeking through the open curtain. Suckers.

It was nice—roomy. Big leather chairs that had a lot more head and foot room. But no obvious bells or whistles. No cham-pagne fountains or personal masseuses. The attendant led me to a row that was completely empty on the right side of the plane. Sensing everyone's eyes on me, I sat quickly in the aisle seat, and a loud sigh automatically escaped my body. Great. Just in case there was someone who missed my late entrance, I had officially made myself known. Yeesh.

I tried not to look up to see if anyone was looking at me. I just grabbed my phone out of my purse (which I had already stowed under the seat in front of me, along with my carry-on) to make sure my phone was off.

I rested my head on the back of my seat, closed my eyes, and stretched out my legs a little toward the empty couple of seats to my right. No need to stick my legs out in the aisle and trip someone. Don't need any more attention. I heard the common, monotone monologue from the flight attendants telling us what to do in case of an emergency. Yeah, yeah yeah—seat belts, flotation device—got it. Like it would make a difference... I shook my head quickly from side to side. *Get a grip*, I told myself. *You're supposed to be enjoying yourself.*

It didn't seem like it was much longer till we were in the air and the attendants were walking around serving drinks. I thought it was cool that the champagne was free (even if it wasn't served from an ice fountain), so I took them up on it. I also took advantage of my iPod, once we were cleared to use electronic devices. There was a family in the row right behind me, and their son was in the seat directly behind mine chattering away, gently rapping his feet on the back of my chair.

It was a pretty long flight, and it was in the middle of the afternoon when we took off. We had the chance to order some food if we wanted. I ordered a little half sandwich. The two glasses of champagne I had were already going to my head since I hadn't eaten much that day. I was such a light weight. The thought of me stumbling off the plane was too embarrassing. Not that I was *that* affected by the alcohol. But the alcohol, my klutzy-ness, and my sore feet in these stupid heels were more than enough to cause concern.

Since I didn't feel any eyes on me, I took the liberty of glancing around the first-class part of the cabin. People were finishing up their meals, reading books, or listening to music. It was pretty quiet. Even behind me. Maybe the little munchkin was asleep. I noticed the friendly attendant, Tina, the one who greeted me as I entered the plane, chatting with one of the passengers. I couldn't really see him; he was in the very front row, in the middle seat, all by himself. I could only discern that he was male. Tina seemed almost giddy—smiling and hair flipping. Oh-kay…

But my rubbernecking was interrupted by a weird sound behind me. A faint sound. Choking and gagging. Confused, I craned my neck toward the row behind me. "Billy? Billy? Are you okay," a woman asked anxiously but in a hushed tone. "Honey, *do something!*" She went from anxious to frantic in three seconds.

I turned my head a little to the left to try to hear better. My heart was pounding now, and I couldn't quite figure out why. I could see a few more people angling themselves to get a better idea of what was going on. I could hear some light thudding. It had only been a few seconds since the woman's frantic plea, but the time seemed sluggish.

Finally curiosity won out over discretion, and I turned all the way around. The man and woman were both grasping onto the boy—who was probably eleven or twelve. The boy's eyes were wide and teary. His hands were around his neck.

That was it. I was up and out of my chair in one swift move-ment. The man, the dad I guessed, scanned my face as I stood up. "He's choking—help him!" he said helplessly.

For half a second I wondered why in the world this person thought I was able to help his son (especially if he couldn't!), and it only took another half second to realize I didn't have a choice. I grabbed the boy under his arms and tried to yank him out of his chair but I was met with resistance and grunted. *What in the world*, I thought. *Oh yeah, seatbelt.* I fumbled with the release and got the boy to his feet. The adrenaline was coursing through my veins, keeping me calm and giving me physical strength. The boy could have been Chewbacca, and I still would have been able to get him up and out of the chair with ease. (Okay, maybe not *Chewbacca*, but still…)

He still had his hands around his neck and was gasping for air between muffled coughs. Once I had him in the aisle, I turned

10

him so that his back was pressed against my chest. I pulled his hands away from his neck and wrapped my arms around him, clasping my hands together in a fist and placing them under his rib cage.

The entire first-class area had turned their attention to us at this point. I could hear gasping coming from the boy as well as most of the other people. The two flight attendants were making their way through the aisle trying to get to where we were. People were getting up to get out of their way, and I could hear the mom beside me starting to cry. My brain seemed to be processing anything and everything. People huddled closer to me; several bodies claimed the small space as I took my stance.

I struggled to get my balance. Again, these stupid heels were causing me grief. With a grunt I pushed forcefully into the boy's abdomen. Nothing. Again, harder this time. Nothing.

"Come on," I groaned as I forced my fist even deeper into his diaphragm with enough force to pick him up off the ground.

A large whoosh of air was followed by whatever object, which was now clear of his airway, flew forward and landed a few feet in front of him. Billy doubled over to catch his breath; I turned him so he was facing me. A sudden wave of anxiety replaced the surge of adrenaline.

"Are you okay? Did I hurt you?" I crouched down to eye level and took inventory. The color was back in his face, and he wasn't complaining about any broken ribs. So far, so good.

He was taking wheezy, deep breaths. The mom knocked her husband out of the way to reach him while the rest of the passengers sighed in collective relief. The whole experience probably only lasted thirty seconds, but I could have sworn it lasted minutes. The mom wrapped her arms around her son as she sobbed. I felt a large hand on my shoulder. The dad was wiping tears away from his eyes with his free hand, shaking his head.

"T-t-thank you so much," he finally stuttered. "You saved his life."

"He's okay," I said as peacefully as I could, but my voice was a little shaky. All of the adrenaline was wearing off, and the severity of the moment had suddenly caught up with me. "I'm glad I could help." It was all I could come up with. I'd never done anything like that before. That first aid/CPR class I took last year was just supposed to be something I did to keep my mind off things. And now, it seemed as if it had helped me keep these two strangers from going through the same immeasurable amount of pain that I had been through.

Tina huddled around us, ensuring the boy was really okay as the other flight attendant tried to calm the rest of the passengers. I just stood there, catching my breath, trying, again, to not notice everyone's eyes on me. I glanced toward the front of the cabin and made eye contact with the man who Tina was talking with earlier. He was turned around backwards in his seat, sitting on his knees. I blinked twice to see if he would still be there when my eyes re-opened. And he was. Holy crap! Was that? No—it couldn't be…

"Ma'am, are you okay," Tina asked while shaking my shoulder, interrupting my staring.

"Huh? Oh, yeah—I'm fine," I replied automatically as I turned my attention to the boy and his mom in front of me.

"Thank you, thank you, thank you," the mom recited over and over as she hugged me, very tightly, with the boy still attached to her hip.

When she finally released me, all I could do was manage a smile and a weak "You're welcome." I patted the boy's blond head. "You okay?"

He just bobbed his head up and down as Tina informed us that we needed to take our seats; then she turned to leave.

"I'm Nancy, and this is Billy," the woman said as she pointed down to the boy as they took their seats behind.

I took my seat then turned my body around to look back at them, "I'm Evie," I said with a big smile. "It's nice to meet you."

"No, it's great to meet you. I'm Everett, by the way," the man said as he extended his hand to shake mine. He was in the seat behind mine now, with Billy in between him and his wife. One big happy family.

"Nice to meet you too, Everett. And Nancy and Billy," I added earnestly. "Do me a favor, Billy, and stick with liquids for the rest of the flight!" I suggested with a laugh.

They all laughed heartily. It seemed as though the intensity of the moment had worn off. The other passengers were quietly back to their in-flight activities.

I hadn't noticed Tina, who was now beside me in the aisle.

"Ma'am, the pilot asked me to pass along his gratitude for your heroic effort." Her eyes were beaming—as if she were the one who just saved the boy from choking. "He would like to know your name too," she added.

"Oh, wow. Evie—Evie Castner. It was nothing really," I blurted out. "I just happened to take a CPR class last year, so everything was still fresh in my mind I guess."

When I faced forward again, I glanced at the seat at the front of the plane, to the gentleman who had caught my attention just a few moments ago. All I could see was the back of his head now.

"Well, thank you again, Ms. Castner. We are all deeply appreciative of your assistance," she cheerfully declared.

"Really, it was nothing." I felt a rush of blood gather in my cheeks. I had to ask her before she went back to her duties. I had to know for sure, know that my eyes weren't just playing tricks on me before. "Uh, Tina," I motioned with my finger to come closer to me. "Is *that*"—I motioned with my head to the front and left—"who I *think* it is?"

She didn't turn around but seemed to know who I was talking about. She pressed her lips in a hard line to keep from smiling—at least that's what it looked like. "I'm not at liberty to say." Her tone was very flat, professional. But then her eyes twinkled as she let a smile break the tight line of her lips.

13

"Wow..." I said as my eyebrows lifted in surprise. It really was him—Bradley Matthews. Wow...what were the odds? I instantly recalled the conversation I'd had with Mom just a few nights ago. How she was trying to think of reasons for me to go on a trip—like how I could run into a celebrity. She'd get a kick out of this. Even though I hadn't technically *met* him, it's still pretty cool that we're on the same plane.

"Is there anything I can get you? We still have about an hour before we begin our descent," she asked, interrupting my obvious stupor.

"Uh, no. I'm good, thanks."

"Just buzz if you need anything." She smiled again as she turned to assist another passenger.

I got myself situated back in my seat after I retrieved my iPod. I was shuffling through the songs, trying to find the right one to calm my nerves after the flurry of emotions that had just quaked through me. A few songs later, Tom Petty was finishing up "Running Down a Dream" when I noticed someone standing next to me in the aisle. I looked up sharply, expecting it to be Tina, again.

"Hi. I hope I'm not interrupting," *Bradley friggin' Matthews* whispered in my direction.

I blinked a couple of times while I tugged the earphones away from my ears. "Uh, no, no. Can I help you?" I'm sure my tone and bewildered expression was the catalyst for the smug smile that was now on his face. Okay, I don't know why I went into "can I help you" mode; he just caught me off guard. I felt a flush creep up my neck.

"May I?" he asked while eying the empty chair next to me.

"Sure." I shrugged. Okay, that seemed pretty nonchalant. Nonchalant was good.

He wedged his tall body between my legs and the row of seats in front of us and then plopped down next to me.

"I just had to meet the woman of the hour." He smiled and then nodded his head back to motion to the happy family behind us. To say he had a killer smile would be the understatement of the decade.

"Oh, yeah—that's me," I replied as I rolled my eyes. I was still uncomfortable with all this nonsense about my being a "heroine."

"Oh, so this is something you do on a daily basis? Because you sure are acting like it's nothing." He seemed a little surprised by my apathy, or maybe it was because I wasn't ogling him with ga-ga eyes. Good thing he didn't have a clue what was going on inside my head. I'm sure he was used to the more normal reaction to his presence. A big movie star like him couldn't so much as go to the grocery store without being attacked by paparazzi and obsessed fans clamoring over each other for just a glimpse of him.

"No." I chuckled. "I've never done anything like that before. But it's not like I performed open-heart surgery. I just did the same thing that I'm sure more than a half dozen other people here coulda done."

"Well, you're still the lady of the hour though," he reminded me.

"Until another passenger has a near-death experience, and in that case, I'll let somebody *else* be the hero."

He laughed, a low, sexy sound that rumbled through the air around us. Good, he got my sense of humor. I actually seemed to be entertaining him. How odd…

I was eerily calm. You'd think my heart would be pounding right about now. I mean, I don't think that I would react so differently to somebody just because they're famous, but he was really attractive. But now that I've had time to get over the initial shock of seeing and talking to him I felt oddly comfortable. I could remember back to what seemed to be eons ago—to when I'd get all giddy and nervous any time a hot guy got within a hundred feet of me. Now I have what was probably the hottest male celebrity of the decade right next to me and—nothing. Well, not *noth-*

ing, but I was able to be myself. The years of numbing loss and antisocial behavior must have affected me more than I thought.

"Texas?" His one-word question came out of nowhere, it seemed, while I sat there thinking about my situation.

I just raised my eyebrow and cocked my head to one side in response. "Is the second biggest state in the Union…?"

"No." He laughed. "Your accent…are you from Texas?"

"Oh, nope. Close. Oklahoma." I quickly replayed our thirty-second encounter. I hadn't even said "howdy," my still standard greeting.

"Oklahoma. Never been there."

"Not missing much."

"So are you staying in New York City, or is it just a stop?" His big blue eyes were locked on mine. I noticed the way they turned a little green toward the middle and rims and how they were surrounded by long, inky lashes. I've never been to the ocean, but I couldn't imagine the Caribbean Sea being any more alluring or beautiful than his eyes. His eyes were clear, deep, and at the moment—amused.

"No, I'm staying in New York. First vacation in years." I was able to look back at him without blushing. Eye contact usually made me pretty uncomfortable, celebrity or not. No staring contest winner here.

"By yourself?" he asked, seeming genuinely surprised.

"Yup, all by my lonesome. It was kind of a spur of the moment thing." I noticed how my "accent" seemed a little heavier now. He must have too because he chuckled, just once, under his breath.

"Don't have any big plans then?"

"Not really. Didn't really have time to plan anything. I have no clue what I'm going to do for a week." Why was he so interested? And why was I answering his questions with more detail than what was needed?

"Well, I'm meeting a few friends after we land, for a late dinner. I'd love for you to accompany me." His grin turned cocky.

"They'll never believe me if I tell them that some dainty little woman saved somebody's life during the flight." I noticed how perfectly balanced his features were, like he was made to be gawked at. I shook my head to clear my thoughts.

"I'm sure they will if you tell them the *whole* story…that I did abdominal thrusts on a young *boy*."

"Doesn't sound that impressive when you put it that way," he said as he furrowed his brow in amusement.

"Told ya."

"So, you don't want to come?" he teased.

"Oh, no, I'd love to. I'd enjoy a tour guide." I flashed him an innocent smile.

He laughed again. He was obviously amused by the fact that it seemed as if I had no clue who he was. Like he was just some normal, very attractive, very charming guy.

"All right then," he answered.

His attention was abruptly diverted to the rows behind us. I turned slightly and could just hear whispering and see a lot of curious faces looking in our direction. His face hardened and the amusement in his eyes was replaced with annoyance. By moving through the cabin and approaching me he had given up any pretense anonymity.

"Have anything to write on?" he asked in a low whisper.

I dug through my purse and found the little notepad and pen I always had on me. I offered it to him without asking why he wanted it. Like it mattered…

He scrawled something quickly. I tried not to be nosey in case it was something I wasn't supposed to see.

"Where are you staying?" he asked, still writing.

"The Plaza." His head snapped up. "You rich?"

I felt myself bristle instinctively. Was I supposed to shack up at a Motel 6 since I was from Oklahoma? Maybe there was a little spark left in me after all. Not the fire there once was, but at least it was good to know I wasn't as dead inside as I sometimes felt.

"No, I just work a lot and don't have anything to spend money on," I said, a little defensively. "Besides, it's the smallest room they have and I got a good deal 'cause it was last minute. Plus, since I'd never been to the Big Apple, I wanted to ensure I stayed at a nice place, in a nice part of town. Don't wanna take up space in *The New York Times* obituary section: 'Poor Oklahoma Girl Murdered While on First Trip to the Big City,'" I said, as I mimicked the headline with my hands, visualizing the headline.

He laughed again as he handed me the page he'd been writing on. He leaned a little closer to me to whisper, "Here's my number. After you get your luggage, go to the second set of exit doors to the left of the baggage claim. I'll be there waiting outside in a black Range Rover. Call me as you're walking out," he instructed. "Can you get all your luggage by yourself?"

"I managed to get it *to* the airport all by myself," I quipped.

"Funny." He smirked. "Write down your number just in case," he added as he handed me the pad and pen.

I started to write down my number. "Do you want to know my name too?" I asked as I tore the page off to hand it to him.

"I already know. Evie, right?"

I nodded.

"Tina," he acknowledged with a chuckle. He folded up the piece of paper and put it in the front pocket of his shirt. He was dressed very nicely of course. Dark washed jeans and a black long-sleeved dress shirt, with the sleeves rolled up to his elbows. Just enough of his forearm was visible to tell that his tall frame was covered with a nice layer of sinewy muscle.

He started to get up from his seat. "Don't you want to know my name?" he joked.

"I already know. Bradley, right?" I grinned. "Tina."

He scooted past me again and bent down, incredibly close to my face. "Try to be as quick as you can. I don't have any luggage, so I'm going to rush out to get the car, trying not to get noticed along the way. See you soon," he whispered in my ear.

I just nodded as he pulled away. He walked gracefully through the first-class cabin, back to his seat. Half the eyes in the small space were on him, the other half were trained on me. No doubt wanting to know the substance of our brief interlude.

"Oh my goodness, was that Bradley Matthews?" I heard Nancy gasp behind me.

"I think so," answered her husband.

"Wow!" Nancy said. She seemed to have the more appropriate reaction to an encounter with a celebrity.

I sank back into my comfy chair, and my mind started to travel backward…

CHAPTER 2

I can't tell you for sure whether it was cloudy or sunny the Saturday after my eighth birthday, but when I force that day into my mind it's always overcast. Only a few images from that day are certain. Our bodies, our memory, as a way to self-protect, tend to naturally suppress certain things in an effort to help us cope. This phenomenon ticks me off a little. I fight daily to remember, in detail, every moment that I can of my youth—or my dad.

I do remember sitting on the front pew of a church auditorium that was full of mourners. I remember the velvet-covered folding chairs lined up under a flapping green canopy that did little to ward off the March chill. I remember not quite understanding what was going on, but knowing just enough to feel sadness and loss. I remember a preacher saying nice things about my dad. I remember the little American flag on a stick that I took from the inside of my dad's casket.

But I don't remember Dad's favorite color. I don't know what his favorite food, or song, or movie was. It seems so awkward to love and miss a man I know so little about. Only tiny pieces of a man, that's all I remember. How he smelled of Old Spice. His warm hugs and gravelly laugh. Dad standing over the stove as he cooked his specialty—fried potatoes and onions. What I do remember, I miss. What I don't, I lament.

By the time I graduated from high school, I had already survived my fair share of heartaches. Or at least that is what I thought. My parents divorced when I was very young, and my dad passed away just a few days after my eighth birthday. Even though I knew I wasn't the only girl in the world who had lost a parent, it sometimes felt that way. I threw myself a pity party sometimes. And it was definitely a party of one. But in my defense, I was young and didn't know how to process what was going on. I knew my family loved me, but it did little to fill the part of my heart that would always be missing.

My dad's early death seemed to set the stage for the way I would feel about certain things in my life. I grew up knowing that my dad would be absent, physically at least, from the most important moments in my life. Getting my first car, going out on my first date, graduating from high school and college, and—gulp—of course, my wedding and everything that would follow after that. A lot of firsts. I always focused on the fact that *he* wouldn't be there instead of counting my blessings for the wonderful family I still had. Maybe that's the reason I turned out to be a bit of a loner. A little reluctant to be too close to anyone because I knew firsthand how awful it would be when they weren't there anymore. Okay, so I wasn't all doom and gloom. I didn't walk around wearing all black, but I wouldn't say I was a happy-go-lucky teen. I used sarcasm and self-deprecating humor as a shield and often cried myself to sleep at night after looking over what few mementos I had of my dad.

Along with being a morose loner at times, I often questioned things that nobody else even considered. Like why we could manage to send a man to the moon but still can't make a household cleaner that couldn't kill more than 99.9 percent of all germs. Was that last remaining tenth of a percent of germs just that stubborn? Or why is it that we can supposedly clone a sheep, but if you have a zit, forget about it? That pesky little anomaly that seems to come around at the most inopportune time can't seem to be stopped. And come on, are you telling me that nobody ever figured out that Clark Kent always disappeared *right* before Superman came to the rescue? Puh-lease. No one else seemed bothered by these things, but I always figured there had to be some kind of conspiracy involved.

I didn't think much of my upbringing either. Okay, I grew up in Oklahoma, but I didn't grow up on a farm. I never owned a pair of cowboy boots. I never really liked the rodeo—I liked football better. I guess I wasn't what one would think of if they were trying to conjure up an image of your stereotypical Oklahoman. As a teen I was more interested in clothes by Abercrombie and Fitch than pearl snap shirts. I figured I grew up just the same as anyone else did, in any other town or state. Lucky even. I had a roof over my head, three square meals a day, and a large family to keep me irritated and loved. More than what some get in a lifetime.

Oklahoma seemed boring to me, and I always secretly longed to get out; couldn't wait to leave for college even if it wasn't out of state. For one thing, we have peculiar weather here. March is an odd month for instance. Kind of caught in the middle of things. It wouldn't be strange at all for several different weather elements to take place in that space of thirty-one days. A tornado siren would more than likely call into the howling wind at least a couple of times, warning us that this was only the beginning of the storm season. Old Man Winter would prove his ability to chill our bones regardless of what Punxsutawney Phil did or didn't see, signaling that winter may not be over just because spring has "officially" begun. And of course, there were those days that seemed perfect. That made everyone long for the spring and summer days ahead. Seventy-five degrees. A slight southwesterly breeze. And a light blue sky feathered with white, wispy clouds that would shield the sun's intense rays at random points during the day.

Those were the days that the parks were crowded and you saw your neighbors starting to battle those weeds in the front lawn. Even the Bradford pears would show their eagerness for the spring by blossoming. Large clusters of dainty white flowers would fill out the baron brown limbs into the standard pear shape. On those days, you forgot all your troubles.

So, growing up, I had never given much thought to what kind of love story life had planned out for me. I grew up in a small town, and for the most part we found our "soul mate" early and married young, settled down, and had a few kids. After all, in Small Town, USA, this life pattern was the most easily accepted. So I began to wonder what was in store for me when I was one of the few girls in my tiny senior class that hadn't ever had a steady boyfriend. I was interested in a couple of the boys in my class, but since I grew up with them, they felt more like brothers to me.

When I left for college, I was a little closer to the town where my dad grew up and where he was also buried. I would sometimes go there on certain dates: his birthday, Veterans Day, my birthday. I would just sit there in front of his headstone and talk to him as if he were there. I knew it was kinda creepy. I knew he wasn't *really* there, but it was just symbolic. I would tell him what was going on with my life, crying most of the time. I found it hard to talk about my dad without crying—even if I was trying to describe some long suppressed happy memory of him to someone. It annoyed me.

So there I was—young, full of energy and skepticism—ready to go out into the world, the real world. Something had to be beyond Cordell; this tiny little town of only a few thousand people where I had spent all of my life. This stupid little town that only has one stoplight... And with such a weary outlook on life—how in the world would I expect my love life to be simple, normal?

■   ■   ■   ■   ■

"I got it," I yelled from the back of the small, cluttered workroom of the flower shop where I worked. I had gotten an academic scholarship to Oklahoma State University, and I was enjoying the end of my third year. Stillwater was two and half hours from Cordell, but I felt a world away. And I'm not saying that as a bad thing.

I walked through the threshold that separated the back workroom from the front "showroom" and set the colorful spring arrangement I had just finished on the table in the middle of the room. "Here ya go."

"Thanks, newbie," joked my boss, Randy. Even though I had worked at the flower shop for almost a year, I was still considered a "newbie." Randy was middle-aged with a medium build. He always wore the same OSU hat to cover his receding hairline and always, always had a smile plastered on his face.

I sprinted back toward the workroom. As I jumped over a box of flowers, I caught my toe, and the racket that ensued was normal, for me. "Son of a goat roper!"

"You break anything?" Randy chuckled.

I have always been something of a klutz. *Graceful* would never be a word that someone would use to describe me. How I hadn't impaled myself on scissors or broken something while working there surprised us both!

"Ugh." I groaned getting back on my feet. "Nope, I'm good!"

"Back to work then."

Randy was also the owner of the shop, but he somehow had taken on another role, almost like a father figure. One of his daughters had been good friends with one of my older brothers in college. That's how I got the job. Randy wasn't what you'd normally think of when you thought of the stereotypical male owner of a flower shop. He was all male—he wore camo on most days (usually because he had been out hunting with his trusty Weimaraner, Dover, early that morning), snapped the stems of flowers with his bare hands (or hunting knife), and always had some kind of semi-misogynistic joke to throw our way. The shop was run by all women, of course...

I loved working in the flower shop. It was laid back. It allowed me to tap my creative side and was a window into the lives of others. From weddings to funerals. Birthdays to graduations. Prom to hospital visits. People sent flowers for a bunch of reasons or for no reason at all. And the arrangements they chose and the cards they sent would often bolster my confidence that maybe the world wasn't quite as sucky as I sometimes thought. But not always...

I was lost in thought later when Randy snuck up behind me. "Too monochromatic."

I just shot him an evil eye, another "woman thing" that ticked him off. "That's kinda what I'm going for here."

"Oh, well—don't."

I groaned. I grabbed the order ticket and shoved it in his face.

He glanced at it then rolled his eyes. I knew that I was following the customer's orders. All shades of blue, which is kind of hard to do with flowers. The arrangement seemed odd to me too when I was taking the order over the phone. Until the gentleman told me what to put on the card: *Your life will be all blue, now that I've dumped you. Mike.*

"Brutal, right?"

"Well, it's creative."

"Oh come on! I had to bite my tongue to keep from telling him off! What a jerkwad. Be a man—break up with her in person...or at least on the phone."

Randy just shrugged, obviously less riled up about it than I was. "So have you sent your latest boy-toy packing yet?" he asked with a snicker.

I had sort of slipped into a pattern, with guys that is—and I thought it had gone unnoticed. After about a month, I'd send whomever it was I was "seeing" down the road. I wasn't being harsh. He had either already started to bore me, or he only wanted one thing. I wasn't *that* kind of girl, so I really didn't have any other choice at that point. There were only a couple more weeks of my third year left—so I had been in this new, larger town swimming with guys for a few years and had already "dated" about a dozen guys. It wasn't depressing me or anything. Since I hadn't really dated in high school, I felt like I was just catching up.

"Ah, well he's probably got about a week left unless he surprises me or something, but not likely. Bedsides, I think he's going back home for the summer, and I'll be trapped here of course." I spun around with my arms out indicating that "here" meant working at the shop. I had already planned on taking a couple of summer courses and would still work at the shop too. I definitely had no intention of going back home, to Cordell, for the summer. Yikes.

"Mmm humm" is all he managed as he stuck his hands into his front pockets and rocked back on his heels.

"What?" I demanded, with hands on hips. I tried to keep from acting defensive since I knew that he was just picking on me. "What do you have to complain about? If I had a serious boyfriend, then I may have to cut back my hours and then where would you be?" I smugly lifted one eyebrow, indicating that the shop wouldn't survive if I wasn't there every day keeping it together.

A loud laugh suddenly threw him off balance. "Right, right," he managed to say through the laughter. "You're setting yourself up to be an old maid so that *my shop* won't suffer. Good one."

I rolled my eyes. "Whatever, old man."

"Pssssshhhh."

"What would you know? When's the last time you've been on a date—nineteen sixty-five?" I laughed at my own remark knowing that he wouldn't really have a comeback. I would often make snide remarks about his age, even though he wasn't really that old. But I was used to doing that sort of thing to my mom. Randy had been married for some time—at least thirty years, so I knew that he couldn't possibly understand the current dating game. "I know what I'm doing." I sounded confident, although I wasn't really. For all I knew—I would wind up an old maid. Well, there's no use in letting that thought linger too long.

He was still sort of chuckling, and I just went back to work—singing to the music that was always on in the back of the shop. I grabbed a couple of headless flower stems and used them as drumsticks. I playfully drummed along the old, homemade, wooden workbench. Annie, another flower shop slave, joined in, and before long, the whole shop was dancing around, singing "Happy Jack" by The Who and laughing.

■　■　■　■　■

The days ticked on by, and summer went by fast, considering how slow everything seemed to move. The college town was nearly deserted. Most of the students left for the summer, leaving the streets uncrowded for once and a little less work to do at the shop. I spent most of my time at the shop, joking around with Randy and the one male new employee that we managed to find. He was the delivery driver. I sometimes wondered if Randy had hired him for me. Randy was always trying to play matchmaker. After all, it seemed as if being a female was a prerequisite for working there. The new guy wasn't unattractive, but I could instantly tell that he wasn't for me. I couldn't ever explain it. I tried once or twice, but of course failed miserably. I just didn't get that "feeling." I had a weird sixth sense that I relied on. I could tell in just the few moments after I met someone, whether I'd like them or not. It had about a 99 percent success rate with females. Meaning my first impression was usually correct. It worked with the opposite sex, for the most part, but I don't think I can claim as high a success rate there.

I never really had a lot of girl friends. Even back home I never had true best friends that were girls. They were always too busy with their boyfriends and gossiping. I found it much easier to relate to boys, on a friend level at least. I was a tomboy. I knew a little too much about cars and sports. How could I not—I grew up with three older brothers, remember? My mom had remarried a few years before my dad passed away. Poor William. I'm not sure he knew what he was in for! And as if having an insta-family wasn't enough, Mom and William had a child together, Juliane. But Juliane was almost nine years younger than I am. Quite a difference. Mostly she just annoyed me when she was younger, but now we were starting to form that sister bond. She was bubbly and outgoing and made friends easily. Other than her, I only had the three other girls at the shop to relate with.

It was just a usual day at work that summer. I had stocked the front display case with several arrangements of varying prices. I had cleaned all the extra flower buckets and now reeked of bleach. I still had a few more hours till I was off and was finding it harder and harder to find something to do to pass the time. So I was in the front room of the shop, watering all the plants that we kept on hand: peace lilies, pothos ivies, azaleas, kalanchoes, and crotons. Watering the plants was a crap job, and nobody liked doing it. A lot of bending over and trips back to the one bathroom to refill the watering can. We girls would usually rock-paper-scissors to decide who had to do it that day. That day, I had lost, and I still say that Annie cheated. There's no water balloon to drench paper!

I was singing to myself again when I heard the little bell chime as the front door opened. I turned around to great the customer. Wow. Covered in grime, reeking of bleach, I just stood there staring at him like a moron. My face suddenly flooded with blood, and I could feel myself blushing from my toes to the roots of my hair. I realized I was holding my breath, and I released it before I passed out. I knew I needed to greet him, at least acknowledge him, quickly, before he decided to turn around and walk out.

CHAPTER 3

"H-hi! Can I help you?" The words came out a little breathy as I struggled to get the words out. I wasn't even sure he had even heard me because I had spoken so softly.

"I'm needing some sort of flower arrangement." His voice was heavenly, warm, and soothing. And luckily he didn't seem distracted by my odd display.

"Okay" was all I could manage to say. Obviously he was here for flowers; what else would he want? An oil change? After a moment he started walking toward me—well, toward the display of flower arrangements that were already prepared in the cooler behind me. *Pull it together!* I screamed to myself. I shook my head in an effort to gain my composure and adjusted the hair that had fallen from my usual ponytail. "Anything in particular? For a specific occasion?" I was pleased that my voice came out sounding more calm than I felt. I focused on trying to maintain some type of professional air about myself—instead of flipping my hair and giggling like a school girl.

"Well, not really," he replied.

He wasn't looking at me, but I sure was studying him. He wasn't all that tall but tall enough. It's not too hard to be taller than I am. He had very light blond hair that fell in an uneven shag that almost touched the collar of his shirt and dark brown eyes. He was beautiful. I sighed without realizing it. He turned toward me. Oops.

I quickly caught myself, turned to the cooler and looked it over.

"Well, I just made this one this morning so it's fresh. Nice and cheery." I stopped talking immediately. Maybe he wasn't looking for bright and cheery. I cursed myself—in my head again. *Nice and cheery?* Yeesh, I'm such a cheeseball.

"Ya, that will do. My—uh—sister isn't having such a good week, so I thought I'd try to cheer her up a little." He flashed a dimpled smile. I smiled back.

"Alrighty." Yes! He did want cheery. I laughed, to myself of course. Then something he said registered. "My—*uh*—sister." I've heard that before. Sister. Right. Nice-looking men came in here to get something for their "sister" all the time, but when it came to the card they wrote—well, let's just say I'd definitely be blushing if one of my brothers said something like that to me.

I grabbed the arrangement and walked to the front desk and sat down. He followed. I punched around on the calculator trying to figure the sales tax. My hands were shaking so I had to figure it a couple of times to make sure that I didn't overcharge him. What in the world is wrong with me?

"There are some cards over there if you'd like to grab one. They're free." I motioned to the rack of cards that were behind him. I continued to check my calculations. He quickly turned his head to see where I was gesturing. He got up from the chair he was in, across the desk from me. My heart did a little jig at the opportunity to appreciate his form.

"Oh, great. Thanks," he replied, a little under his breath.

He sounded a little flustered now for some reason. Or was that just wishful thinking on my part?

"Are you taking this with you, or do we need to deliver it?" I noticed, too late, that my voice had gone from professional to sing-song. Good heavens…

He was looking over the different cards to see which one would fit the occasion the best—one that would make his *sister* feel better. "I'll just take it with me."

"Okie dokie. It'll be thirty-two dollars and sixty-three cents."

His laugh caught me off guard. "Okie dokie?"

I blushed again and quickly looked down, letting out a small chuckle before looking back up.

"Hey, we *are* in Oklahoma—so I can get away with it." I joked as I defended myself and my vernacular. "*Howdy* is my official greeting too," I added.

"I didn't get a howdy," he teased. His eyes darkened, looking like melted Hershey Kisses.

Was he flirting? Could he be? Why would such a hottie even bother flirting with a mess like me? I didn't put much effort into my appearance, especially when I was at work. I got too dirty working here. I was always covered in flower gunk and bleach by the end of the day. He was out of my league. That was very easy to see. He looked like a fourth year—at least. But he was right—he didn't get a "howdy." He was lucky he even got a "hi"—without my drooling.

"Howdy!" I sang as I re-greeted him out of the blue. I pushed away my shyness as I tried my hardest to flirt a little.

I guess it caught him off guard too because all he could muster was a sheepish grin as he handed me the money to pay for his *sister's* bouquet.

We were both silent as I handed him his change. I was reluctant to do so, knowing that he'd leave now. Our business transaction was finished...

"Thanks for coming in. Please come back." I probably emphasized the "please" part a little too much. My heart took off on a sprint while my behind was glued to the chair I was still perched on. Was I just going to let him walk out? I knew Randy would help if I decided I wanted to hold him hostage. No, no, no. Kidnapping wasn't an option...yet.

"I sure will," he murmured, "if I know you will be here to help me out with my every flower need."

"Well, I'm here most of the time—until class starts again." I leaned in closer to him, even though he was standing up now, and I spoke in a stage whisper. "I'm kinda enslaved," I joked as I motioned with a head nod toward the back of the shop.

"Good." He sort of grunted the word out, and I smiled.

He picked up his flowers and blank card. Crap. I didn't even catch his name.

"I'll come back to see you—er—come back *here* next time I need some flowers."

He had caught himself but not before I noticed what he was implying. Or what I wished he was implying at least.

"Looking forward to it!" I tried to flash him the sexiest smile I could.

The beautiful stranger turned and reached for the door as he nodded. He stopped on his way out the door and winked.

My still thundering pulse echoed in my ears.

"Bye," I spit out just as the door was closing.

I sank back into the chair, exhilarated but almost exhausted from the reaction of our no more than five-minute episode. Randy poked his head from out of the back room. I knew it was coming...

"Well, well, well. I thought you had more game than that. But what do I know...I'm just an old man, right?!" I knew that smirk on his face wasn't going to disappear any time soon.

"Right," I said defiantly, "old and bald." Sometimes it didn't even cross my mind that he was my boss. This certainly wasn't the normal exchange between an employer and employee, but it seemed to be normal for us.

"He liked you," he pointed out. He pulled off his hat and scratched through his thinning hair.

"Yeah right. And you know this *how?*" I was almost hoping that he did have some legitimate answer for my question, even though the words came out of my mouth as sarcastic as possible.

He cackled. "I may be old, but I'm still a man."

"So?"

"Trust me—he's into you."

"Well, I may believe you if he ever happens to come back." The thought that I may not ever see him again was not something I wanted to explore.

"I'm sure he will. Actually, I'm positive." It sounded like he wanted me to take him up on a bet. I could hear the bait in his voice.

"Fine. I'll bite. What do you wanna wager?" I was looking down at my shirt, fumbling with the ragged bottom of it between my fingers. "I bet I'll win."

"In that case, no bet."

I snapped my head up to look at him. He was just standing there with his usual goofy grin plastered across his face. I shook my head and raised my eyebrows urging him to finish whatever thought that was tumbling around in his head. Nothing.

"No bet? Why? You know you're gonna lose—"

"No," he interrupted me, "no bet, but you *are* gonna do me a favor if he does come back."

I interrupted him with an unladylike snort. "What? Work long hours for little pay? I already do that," I snickered.

He just rolled his eyes at me. "Well, that and you're gonna do something else for me. You have to keep him around for more than a month."

"My pleasure," I grumbled. I didn't want to get myself excited, and I had already made up my mind—more like prepared myself—to never see him again.

"So it's a deal."

"Deal."

"Promise?" he pressed.

I raised an eyebrow at his one worded question. Why was he being—so—weird? I heard a car door shut outside, but my eyes were still fixated on Randy, wondering what in the world he was talking about. He was staring out the front window, and that goofy grin transformed into a devilish grin. Great. What now?

"It's pretty dead around here today," he quickly said just as I was about to look out the window to see what he was staring at, "so you're free to go if you need to go—get ready or something like that."

"For what? I don't have any plans." I was puzzled. I rarely got off work early. Even if it was dead around the shop, Randy kept me around for entertainment.

He quickly amended my statement. "Yet." He dragged the word out playfully. He turned from me to head to the back, and before I could start to quiz him on his behavior, the front door opened.

It was him. The no-name guy I was certain I'd never see again walked through the door. Was I dreaming? I caught myself quickly. I wasn't going to act like a moron around him this time.

"Forget something?" My smile stretched from ear to ear. The familiar thumping of my heart, no longer steady and calm after the few moments without his presence, gained momentum as fast as a souped-up car flying down a quarter-mile track. There was a long pause. His eyes were darting everywhere. To the floor, the ceiling, my eyes, the plants. No answer so I tried again. "Hopefully you don't have another sister whose week has suddenly taken a turn," I asked as playfully as I could.

"No, no." He chuckled with an anxious laugh. "I, uh, what's your name?"

"Evie." I waited. "And you are?"

"Oh, sorry—Josh. My name's Josh."

"What can I do for you, Josh?" I emphasized his name carefully and repeated it in my mind. *Josh. The most beautiful name in the world to me now. Okay, I'm seriously going overboard here.*

His eyes jolted away from mine and moved toward the ground. He took an obvious deep breath. "I know you don't know me from Adam, but I was wondering if—eh—maybe—uh—you'd wanna hang out with me sometime. Eat dinner or something?"

I had no idea if I was doing even a decent job of hiding the sheer thrill that was quaking through my body. It seemed to start in my heart and radiate out through every extremity, every pore. My eyes were on his even though they hadn't looked back up to find mine again. "Of course," I replied as calmly as I could. I was still so bewildered by my reaction to him. To a person I had only interacted with for a few minutes. A person whose name I had just learned. "I'd love to," I continued. I remembered that it was Friday night—a date night. *Oh please, please, please ask me to do something tonight.* I pleaded in my head hoping that he was a mind reader.

"Any plans for tonight?" he asked, his eyes finally finding mine again.

"Totally free." I tried not to frown as I regretted the words the second they tumbled off my tongue. Was the *totally* part completely necessary?

"Six?"

He was smiling at me now. His perfect features hypnotized me. Those brown eyes. His tanned skin, his blond, shaggy hair, and muscular build almost made him look like a surfer. Like he belonged out in Cali, not here in Oklahoma. I gave him directions to my new apartment, but of course he knew where it was. To me, Stillwater seemed like a sprawling metropolis compared to Cordell, but it wasn't actually a huge city. Very easy to navigate. Which was a good thing for me.

Surprisingly my heart raced even faster when he stepped out the door. We had exchanged our numbers and pleasantries and were both still smiling like a couple of idiots as he left. I peered over my right shoulder to find the clock. Just after four thirty. Then I looked down at my clothes and my filthy hands. Eeekk—I was going to have to hurry.

CHAPTER 4

I stood there in my bathroom for I don't know how long. I was taking stock of myself. I hated when I did this because I tended to focus on the negative much more than the positive. I picked up my cell phone. Five forty-five. I was all ready. I had showered and actually taken the time to straighten my long, thick blond hair. It was such a pain, but I thought it looked better that way. It always ruffled my feathers when I was in high school that my mom never allowed me to dye my hair, like the rest of the girls I knew. It wasn't until later that I realized what a favor she had done me. My hair was a beautiful, pure golden blond.

I was surprised that I had time to spare. I had rushed home from the shop to clean up my place a little bit. Mostly I just threw everything into my bedroom, knowing there was no way he'd see in there. So I just stood there looking at myself, my dark cerulean blue eyes staring back at me, looking for flaws. I don't know why I am always so hard on myself. I never quite feel good enough for anyone. Family, friends, or the opposite sex.

Maybe it's because I know all the little idiosyncratic tendencies I have, all my little personality traits. I chew on pen caps, won't touch a shopping cart before sanitizing it, forget to floss, talk to myself, and peek into other people's shopping carts at Walmart. Okay, that last one doesn't count. Everyone does that.

I also have a little compulsion to always make sure the door, any door, is locked, even though I knew I had just locked it. Only ever so slightly OCD. Then there's my almost extreme patriotism. Heaven help you if you fail to acknowledge the American flag during the national anthem in my presence. And my musical ADD. Sometimes I'll listen to the whole song. Sometimes I'll listen or sing along for a few seconds or minutes before impatiently moving to the next. And the variance in my musical style is just as alarming. Thanks to being schlepped around by my mom until I got my driver's license, I have an unhealthy appreciation for fifties and sixties music.

My brothers contributed as well. From my oldest brother, I learned to love classic rock. From my second oldest brother, an appreciation for eighties hair bands and power ballads. And from the remaining brother, an affinity for heavy metal and grunge bands. Throw in the fact that I was born and raised in Oklahoma, and you can add country music to my repertoire as well. So all these different artists and songs would be randomly mixed onto CDs. Johnny Cash, Billie Holiday, Lynyrd Skynyrd, Eminem, Shania Twain, Ludacris, Tom Petty, Queen, Dwight Yoakam, Dr. Dre, Black Rebel Motorcycle Club, Garth Brooks, the Beach Boys, and Mozart would often wind up on the same CD together. I do have to be honest with myself and point out that I have a gift for remembering the words to every song I know.

So after a quick run-through of all my weirdness, I started giving myself a pep talk. More like instructions.

"Okay, Evie. You're not going to babble, trip over your own feet, or spill anything on yourself. Just be normal. Still be *you*, just try to be a *normal* version of you."

The lame ding-dong of my own doorbell didn't register immediately.

Ah! "How long have I been standing here talking to myself?" I frowned as I realized that I was, *again*, talking to myself. I threw on some lip gloss, darted out of the bath and glanced around the living room and kitchen, looking for something embarrassing that I'd forgotten to pick up. Deep breath—here we go. Josh was even more handsome than I remembered. He was wearing white cargo shorts and a dark brown polo that played up his dark eyes. My shoddy memory hadn't done him justice.

"Hello, nice to see you again." He didn't seem as awkward as he did in the shop, maybe even a little formal.

"Howdy!" I emphasized my greeting, hoping he'd remember our conversation from the shop.

I guess he did because he let a low laugh escape his lips. Oh my. His lips. How had I not noticed those full lips before?

"Ready?"

"Yup," I instantly said, maybe a little too enthusiastically. I walked toward him, then turned around to shut and lock my front door, resisting the urge to check the lock. "So where are we headed?"

"Ladies' choice."

"Hummm…I don't know, I'm pretty easy." I froze. "I mean anywhere is fine with me," I added quickly. Good job, Evie. He's been here all of thirty seconds, and you've already managed to put your foot in your mouth. To my surprise and relief, he laughed at my obvious discomfort, and I smiled.

"All right then…" He trailed off. "How about…Joe's?"

"Sounds great."

Eskimo Joe's is kind of famous. Not only to the locals, but their legendary cheese fries and cartoon mascots (an Eskimo and his dog, Buffy) are known everywhere, in Oklahoma at least. It is a popular hangout and drinking spot for us local college kids and OSU sport nuts—since it was on campus. Luckily, it wasn't as packed in the summer, so we wouldn't have to wait forever to get a table.

The conversation was easy, effortless. We quickly learned each other's backgrounds—family, friends, plans for after graduation—the nuts and bolts of any first date. After dinner we had plans to go to the movies. Another passion of mine. I love movies, most kinds of them, too. We settled on the latest rom-com. We both just sat there in the dark watching the thespians deliver their lines but weren't really playing attention. I knew I wasn't anyway. How could I with Hunky Henderson sitting next to me? The more we talked, the more helpless I became.

This is it. This has to be it. He has to be *the one.* I instantly cringed in my seat. The one? I wasn't like that. I didn't believe in that love at first sight, fairy tales and all that happily ever after bullhonkey. I had already experienced enough real life to know that wasn't the way it worked. But how else could I justify the feelings—so strong, so soon—the instant connection.

It turned out that he grew up in Mountain View. *Mountain View!* Okay, so it's an ironic name considering there aren't any actual mountains in sight, but it was less than forty miles to the east of where I grew up, and I even had family there. On most holidays I was in the area. Our paths had to have crossed back then without us knowing. We probably ran into each other at the convenience store or had mutual friends. We were so close all along and just didn't know it. But we were brought together, here and now, in this place.

Something interrupted my train of thought, which still had absolutely nothing to do with the movie. Josh's large, warm hand had taken mine in one smooth movement. I tangled my fingers through his and squeezed gently to make sure he knew that there was no disapproval on my end. But we both kept our gazes fixated on the screen. I was afraid that if I looked at him now, we wouldn't be able to resist ourselves. That we would start kissing and wouldn't come up for air until the theater lights came back up. Fabulous. Now the thought of his lips on mine was in my head. There will be no getting that thought out of my head any time soon. I decided to try to pay attention to the movie. Just in case he wanted to strike up a conversation about it later, it may be handy to know something about it.

He still had hold of my hand as we got up to leave our seats when the credits rolled. He didn't let go of my hand till we made it to his car, only letting go in order to find his keys. He didn't open the door for me. Dang it. That would have been kind of cool. I am a sucker for old school romance. We exchanged a few details about the movie once we were in the car, laughing at the few funny parts that we both actually happened to catch. It was pretty late, but I didn't want the night to end. We were driving past Boomer Lake, and I shot him a quick grin.

"Wanna go for a little walk?" Maybe his answer would indicate whether or not he was as interested in me as I was in him.

"Sure."

Well—guess not. I don't know how to decipher that. At least he didn't say no. That was a good sign, I guess. There was a walking trail all along the little lake. If I had been with anyone else, I wouldn't have suggested it. Especially on a first date. Ever since that strange encounter I had at one of the malls in Oklahoma City last Christmas, I added a new idiosyncrasy to my arsenal: paranoia. A man came out of nowhere soon after I walked out of the mall and was frantically asking to use my cell phone. I didn't acknowledge him at first and that seemed to aggravate him more, so I started walking faster to my car. He came beside me and grabbed my left arm trying to stop me, still babbling about needing to call someone. I was able to free myself and get to my car before anything else happened. I always felt a little guilty. What if he was in trouble and really just needed to call someone? In any case, he left a few bruises on my upper arm where he grabbed me, so I didn't let myself feel too bad.

But I felt safe with Josh. If he wanted to harm me, he already would have. Right?

We found a close parking space in the deserted lot. We walked a little ways and then decided to sit down along the edge of the lake. It was a manmade lake so there was a concrete "shore." We sat as close as we could to the water so that none of the other late-night walkers would bother us from the trail. It was a beautiful Oklahoma summer night with a light breeze. Not as much humidity lingered around this late and the hard heat of the day was finally starting to dissipate. A clear, dark sky was the canvas for the millions of stars and a big yellow moon that was not quite full, but close. We lay on our backs to see if we could make out any constellations or at least some random figures. We didn't have much luck and we laughed at our lack of astronomy skills. While on our backs, his hand found mine again. This time he was on my right side. Good. Now my right hand won't be jealous of all the attention my left hand had gotten earlier.

"This has been such a…" I struggled to find the exact words to describe this night. I didn't want to scare him off, "such a wonderful night." There, not too mushy.

"I know. I can't believe we have so much in common. Why didn't our paths cross sooner?" His eyes were lit up, and his breathtaking smile softened his face.

Those were my thoughts exactly.

"I guess there's a reason for everything," he continued.

"Do you believe that sort of thing?" I was really curious. "That everything happens for a reason?"

He was silent. I wondered if my seemingly innocent question had offended him somehow. I was about to open my big mouth to try to rephrase or take it back when I noticed he was maybe just fishing for the right words. It seemed hard for him. He was looking up at the sky. A crease between his brows marred his sweet face.

"Well, I don't know. Now I do, I guess," he finally answered. He seemed unsure of his response, something in his tone.

"May I ask why, why *now*?" I asked the question so quickly I didn't even think about the fact that this may be something he really didn't want to get into, on a first date at least.

"Take us for instance," he said quickly, starting to ramble, like the thoughts were just now starting to come together in his head. "For most of our childhood, we lived in two small towns that neighbored each other, and on top of that you spent a fair share of your time in the same town as me, with your family. And from what little I've already learned about you tonight, I know we've both experienced a lot of pain."

That was true. I was able to briefly mention that my dad had passed away. That the last time I ever saw him was on my birthday. I had managed to choke back the tears earlier; somehow, largely in part I'm sure to my nerves. All he did then was nod his head compassionately.

We were both looking up at the sky now, to avoid looking at one another at the moment. Our hands were still meshed together, nice and hot now. It seemed to me that this moment would become significant somehow. Like what he was saying was going to be an "ah ha" moment, for both of us. I stayed silent hoping he'd continue.

"I know I didn't say much when you talked about your dad. I hope I wasn't rude...I just didn't know what to say. Mostly because..." He exhaled slowly. "Because I know how you feel. Well, at least I think I do. My mom ran off when I was young—never to be heard from again. My dad passed away when I was a teenager in a house fire. My grandparents raised me and my siblings."

My head snapped to the side in response. I was caught off guard. He was still looking up at the sky. I didn't know what to say. This is the first time I'd ever met anyone else around my age who had lost a parent. And he had lost *both*—for all intents and purposes.

"I'm so—so sorry," I stuttered. Then I turned my head to look up at the same sad sky he was looking at. Out of nowhere, a low rumble of thunder shook the ground. The sky seemed to acknowledge our sadness.

"It's okay." He shook his head. "I just feel like maybe we were..." He hesitated. "Well, maybe we weren't supposed to meet until now. Like we really *are* part of someone or something's master plan."

"Like God? Or destiny?" I asked, trying not to be too sarcastic. My family was extremely religious, which was great. But I had let my own self-pity and bitterness cloud the way I felt about "God." I was still young and didn't understand why I had already endured so much pain, that no one else I knew had shared—until now.

"You don't believe in God?" His eyes finally left the heavens he had been concentrating on to look at me.

"No, I do—I just…I dunno…" *That* was as honest as I could be. I really didn't know how I felt about the subject. "And fate or destiny? The thought that everything is pre-ordained? I'm kinda a control freak, so I'd like to think that I'm in charge of my life instead of everything being plotted out for me."

"Think about it. How else can you explain the fact that our paths crossed here? Now. I know God exists," his murmured. He rolled onto his left side, toward me. Leaning closer he propped himself on his elbow and with his free hand, he gently stroked the side of my cheek with gentle fingers. "And fate too, because it led me to you."

I thought I was dreaming for a moment. My heart was uncharacteristically calm. His words should have sent it into hyperdrive. I was stunned, and all I could do was stare back at him like he just told me Hitler was his uncle. My head was swimming, trying to find the right words to say. Instead of ruining the moment with words, I put my hand on top of his, which was still resting on the side of my face. He slowly leaned down. Too nervous, I closed my eyes. When his warm lips were on mine, I sighed and could feel my heart finally deciding to react to the situation. Our lips moved slowly together, in perfect union. My free hand moved to his face, and I tried to keep it steady as I let my fingertips gently trace down the side of his face and jaw. His skin was smooth and warm and stubble free. Our connection was deep and powerful, like nothing I'd ever experienced before.

We were both lost in the moment when another boister-ous clap of thunder rattled our bodies. As we felt the small specks of moisture reaching our faces, we pulled apart, smiling. Instinctively we looked up to confirm where the moisture was coming from, and we held out our hands to catch the raindrops as they increased in size and speed.

Josh jumped to his feet and pulled me off the ground. "We better get outta here!"

Lightning, thunder, and rain were instantly consuming us. There's nothing like a summer storm in Oklahoma. The fact that it seemed to come "out of nowhere" wasn't anything new. We have a saying around here: If you don't like the weather now, wait fifteen minutes.

I was squealing—in delight—as we ran hand in hand back to his car. I loved the rain, always had. Getting wet was a little inconvenient; thank heavens I vetoed that white shirt I briefly considered wearing this evening. Awkward!

In the safety of the car, we assessed our night.

"Good night, good night." I sighed as I tried to wipe some of the rain off my arms and face.

"*Great* night." He trumped my sentiment easily. Then he reached over, claimed my face with both hands, and kissed me again.

My eyes darted closed. After steaming up the windows a bit, Josh released me. I looked down at the floorboard, my brain fuzzy, as he started the car. This was definitely...*it*.

CHAPTER 5

The days, weeks, months, and even years that followed seem to fly by in harmony. Josh and I had thoroughly enjoyed that first summer we had together before classes began again. We were inseparable from that point on, bugging anyone around us with our constant PDA, little texts, and Facebook messages. We were often told to "get a room." We didn't care; we were in love! We went together like peas and carrots, as Forrest Gump would say. Our relationship was magically effortless. Josh was so even tempered and managed to put up with my emotional self easily. There was little fighting and few bumps or wrinkles to iron out.

I was still working at the shop, and Josh would regularly stop by and hang out. Randy didn't mind; he had already given his "approval" of him. He always thought he had some hand in our destiny since he seemed to somehow know from the very beginning that Josh was interested in me. And especially since he let me off work early for that first date. I guess that's all it takes to be a matchmaker these days.

Our courtship had taken the normal route. We had been dating for over two years when he proposed, on the same date as our first date and of course in the same spot where we had our first kiss, at the lake. It was perfect, and funnily enough, it was raining on that night too! That had turned into a strange obsession of ours. Sitting outside, when we could, watching the storms roll by. Josh had graduated already since he was a couple of years ahead of me, but waited to start on his master's till after I graduated, so we didn't have to be apart. Even though OSU and the University of Oklahoma were rival schools, he had decided to enroll at OU's school of meteorology. He had become a bit of a storm chaser and was so intrigued by storms that he wanted to make a career out of them.

Now it was the beginning of April. I had graduated from OSU the year before, and I was thrilled to be starting a new job as an accountant at Chesapeake Energy. The wedding was just weeks away, and I was extremely busy. Josh and I had saved all our pennies and were somehow able to buy our first home together there. Nothing special. The usual three-bed, two-bath setup. We had just closed on the home, and I was staying there alone until the wedding while Josh crashed on a friend's couch in the meantime. Neither Josh nor my mom were crazy about this, but I reassured them that I was perfectly fine. Our house was in Yukon, on the western edge of Oklahoma City. Close enough to the city to do whatever we wanted or needed, but it still had that small-town feel that we had grown accustomed to. Besides, I had a lot of work to do on the house. That awful floral wallpaper wasn't going to just come off the walls by itself, unfortunately.

It was Friday night. I was having a pizza delivered and was waiting for Josh to come by and help me. I had gotten to the point where I was finally able to paint a few of the rooms in the house. I had already started but couldn't get too far. My mom seemed to call me every five minutes about some wedding detail, so I finally put my phone on silent. Just after I did and was about to lay it down on the counter, I saw that it was ringing. I happened to glance at it, and I was more than happy to answer it this time.

"It's about time. The pizza should be here in a little bit," I said, trying to sound playfully annoyed.

"Hey, babe. You about done painting yet?" Josh asked sweetly.

"Ha! Yeah right." I rolled my eyes even though there was no way he could see me.

"Haven't you looked out the window lately?" he asked in that way of his, like I should be expecting what came next.

I took a few steps backward to peek out the back window. I happened to catch a flicker of lightning light up the darkening sky.

"Ah, I'd been too *busy* to notice I guess." Hopefully he'd catch my drift.

"Well…we're just wanting to catch some hail so we can finish up our project. There's plenty of green in the sky, so it shouldn't be a problem." He paused. "You mad?"

"No, no." I wasn't really, surprisingly. This was a common occurrence these days. "Do what you gotta do."

"If we get done too late, I'll just come over first thing in the morning. Don't finish it all without me," he teased.

"I don't think I'll have a problem there. *Please* be careful. Is Jake going with you?"

"You know I will, and yeah, we're already on our way out there."

Jake was his partner in crime. His last girlfriend couldn't handle coming in second to storms all the time, so he was single and was always eager to drag Josh around with him any time he wanted to go chasing.

"Okie dokie. I'll leave a few walls for you then. I love you." I was trying out my best pouty voice, just to make him feel a *little* bad about leaving me here along to do all the work.

"Sounds like a plan. It's supposed to be a doosey of a storm, so keep an eye on it. I love you more." He didn't seem to respond to my poutyness. His mind was elsewhere already. "See you in the mornin'."

"'Kay. Bye."

Just as I was hanging up, the doorbell rang. No harm in a little dinner first…then back to the paint fumes.

I stayed up later than I had intended. I got into a little groove painting and singing as loudly as I could along with the radio. It was nice knowing that I didn't have to worry about upsetting any neighbors. Much better than apartment dwelling.

It was about one in the morning when I noticed how late it was. I cleaned up and checked my phone. Three missed calls, all from Mom. It could wait. No calls or texts from Josh. No surprise really. The storm seemed pretty big. The lights in our house flickered a couple of times, just about scaring me to death. Even though I didn't mind the storms or staying at the house alone, I didn't like the thought of having no power. I was sure that Josh was out enjoying himself. Or maybe he didn't want to call or text so he could avoid getting put to work by me tonight. I put my phone in its normal place on the nightstand and quickly started to drift to sleep, still a little dizzy from the fumes. The gentle roll of thunder, escaping into the distance lulled me to sleep even quicker than usual due to my extreme exhaustion.

A huge crack of thunder woke me up, and I shot straight up in bed. I was confused. I blinked into the darkness while I got my bearings. I didn't have a clue what time or even what day it was. *It must be a new storm gathering momentum*, I thought thickly as my brain registered my situation. I glanced at my clock: 4:37 a.m. I got an uneasy feeling in my stomach and felt gooseflesh rise on my skin. I didn't know it then, but that minute, that thirty-seventh minute after four in the morning, I would remember forever.

My hands shook as I reached for my phone. Thirteen missed calls. I still had my phone on silent, and the light that usually illuminated the room when it rang wasn't enough to pull me out of my deep sleep. I quickly scanned through the missed calls. Most from Josh's brother, Ethan, and a couple from his grandma. My hands shook more violently now, along with the rest of my body. I tried to calm myself with long slow breaths. I tried telling myself not to get carried away until I knew what was going on. I quickly dialed Ethan's number. The sound I heard on the other end of the line confirmed my worst fears. All I could hear was sobbing and mumbling.

"Hello, hello—someone, hello—is anyone there?" I was frantic by this point. No amount of counting to ten or deep breathing would work now.

I could hear some jostling around; someone must have been juggling the phone.

"Evie?"

The voice wasn't what I had expected. I instantly determined it must be Josh's grandpa, Phil. This was bad.

My body went into shock. I couldn't speak. I managed a "mmmhumm" so that he would know that I was still on the phone.

My ears burned as he started to tell me what was going on. I was losing it. I felt the adrenaline rushing through me as I broke into a cold sweat. My heart was thundering, louder than the storm raging outside my window. Tears were streaming down my face, but I didn't feel the usual jerking motion that usually accompanied my tears when I was in hysterics. The phone started to slide out of my hand, and I didn't stop it. It fell to the floor. I could hear Phil saying my name, trying to discern if I was still on the line or not.

I woodenly walked into the living room. The room was dark in between the harsh flickers of lightning and was as empty as I felt. It was the next room on my list to paint, and I had already moved all the furniture so we could get straight to work when Josh came over in a few hours.

But he wouldn't be coming over.

The bottom dropped out of my stomach, and I curled up into a ball in the middle of the empty floor, in the middle of the room. Those horrible words began to echo in my head, and I couldn't stop the pain. I wanted the voice to leave, to stop breaking my heart over and over. I heard it once—that was enough—for a lifetime.

I couldn't stop it though. The voice was relentless and was trying to inflict more pain than necessary.

"Accident."

"Rolled four times."

"Creek embankment."

Even the soft, gentle tone of Phil's voice couldn't keep the pain from clenching my insides all over again.

"Killed instantly."

I managed a strangled scream "No!" over and over again. It was the only word that I could articulate. I felt like my body was being ripped apart. Pain was everywhere, not just in my hollow chest. I stayed there, in that same position, in the same hysterics. Time meant nothing to me anymore.

At some point the screaming stopped. My eyes were closed. My throat was raw. I was lying on the carpet incoherently mumbling to myself, my voice hoarse. I had no idea how long I had been in this alternate universe. A universe that no longer contained the love of my life. It was brutal. So brutal, in fact, that I thought it all had to be a dream, no a nightmare. Some horrible paint fume–infused nightmare. But I could see the slow movement of sunlight slithering across the floor as the minutes ticked by. Since when was there sunlight in nightmares?

I heard a strange pounding. I didn't know what it was nor did I give a rat's patootie. Perhaps it's my heart. Beating so hard that it was trying to physically break itself so that I wouldn't have to go on.

Pound. Pound. Pound.

Then a crash.

I didn't move. I was still curled into a ball. Rocking back and forth, instinctively trying to sooth myself.

All of a sudden I was weightless and no longer on the floor.

Good, I had died. This was good. Except my thought was short lived. I opened my eyes. After a few painful blinks, I was able to focus. There was a herd of blurry people around me. Mom and my brothers, Marcus, Caleb, and Jordan. Marcus's face was closer to mine than the others. He must have picked me up. Made sense. He had always been the most protective of me after Dad died. He was the oldest and seemed to bear that role.

I could tell I was in a car speeding away somewhere. I heard the engine and felt the tires move over the uneven pavement. I still had no concept of time—had it been hours or days? I had never felt so lost in my life. It felt like I was in a drugged state of numbness. I could hear voices in the car with me, but I wasn't even trying to make sense of them.

The next thing I managed to make sense of was being rushed back into some small, cold room. I was lying down now, and I started to shake uncontrollably again. My shaking made the paper beneath me crinkle. I felt another wave of pain radiate through my body. A sickening pain in my belly produced by grief that refused to ease.

More voices. I was pretty sure these weren't just inside my head though. Maybe I wasn't going crazy and maybe that was a good sign, but I couldn't muster the energy to care.

"We can't snap her out of it—what's going on?" I recognized my mom's voice, and it was shaking nearly as hard as my body.

"She's just been mumbling, not making any sense. We can't make out what she's saying, and she won't talk directly to us," my brother added. I wasn't 100 percent sure which one. What did it matter?

"She's gone into shock," another voice said calmly.

I felt cold fingertips on my eyelids as a bright light was shined into my eyes. The voice was calm, but whoever it was was moving quickly.

"What's that, Dr. Mason?" Mom asked impatiently.

"Just some smelling salts, Janet. We'll try this first," Dr. Mason said as he waved something under my nose.

It worked. I was brought back to consciousness more by the thought of other experimental attempts to bring me around than the ammonia smell itself.

My voice broke as I gasped for air.

My shaking slowed, and I felt Mom's arms around me.

"It'll be okay. It'll be okay," she chanted, trying to comfort me.

VBC Library
289 Factory RD
Clinton, AR 72031
501-745-2100 www.fcl.org
223003

CHAPTER 6

Minutes, hours. Days, nights. All frivolous to me now, but I was taken aback when it was already three days later. I was sitting in a small room in the back of the church, wearing all black. I hadn't said more than a dozen words since…since my world crashed down around me. I merely nodded when someone asked me a question pertaining to the arrangements that needed to be made. I ate little. Slept little. Breathed little.

"It's time," Mom said as quietly as possible. She reached down to grab my cold hand to pull me out of the chair. I guess they had gotten used to having to force me to move where I needed to go, like puppeteers.

I was on my feet, and they were moving toward the church's auditorium. I froze. Mom tugged on my arm to try to keep me moving.

"Wait a minute," I demanded in a weak voice.

"We've got to go out there now," Janet said.

"No!" I shouted as loud as I could. I didn't care if the whole church full of mourners heard me.

Janet dropped my hand and stepped back. Obviously startled.

"Honey, waiting isn't going to make it hurt any less. You have to say good-bye now." She spoke the words slowly—almost hesitating, fearing what my reaction would be.

I wanted to scream at the top of my lungs! How did she know? She had no idea what I was feeling—what I was going through. Had she ever had to bury the man she loved? Had to watch someone put the other half of herself into a stupid coffin and watch it be permanently separated from her? No! No, she hadn't. She was divorced from my dad and already remarried before he passed away. I was only twenty-four and had already buried more loved ones than she. Sure, her dad had died, but not when she was young, so I don't think that's quite the same. The despair I would stay in, she'd never understand.

Although I was screaming in my head, I said nothing. I let her grab my hand again, and I got in line behind Josh's family as we walked out into the auditorium and took our seats.

Sobs and sniffling were already filling up the room. Everyone loved Josh. He was quiet, slow to anger, loving, always going out of his way to help people. So why was he gone when there were so many people out there—maybe even in this room—who didn't deserve or want to live, like me?

I sat there on the blue padded pew. It felt as if there were hundred-pound weights around my neck. The invisible bulk locked me in place and kept me from bolting out the back door. A cool, comforting voice started to talk. I knew that voice. It was Benjamin Russell. He was a family friend; as a preacher, he was the go-to guy for weddings and funerals in our family. It was almost too hard to sit there, almost too ironic. The same man who was supposed to join Josh and me in marriage in just two and half weeks was now delivering Josh's eulogy. I wondered why in the world my family had allowed this. Did they not know how difficult this would be for me already, without making this connection? Then again, I guess it was a nice homage. Benjamin knew Josh and the love we had for each other. He would make this day what it needed to be: a day to remember Josh.

I listened but didn't really hear any of the words that were spoken that day. I was a robot. People would come up to me sobbing and saying how sorry they were, repeating how big a tragedy this was—as if I didn't already know. I would just stand there as they hugged me and would shrug or nod at their comments. I cringed when they said the word *lost*.

"I'm sorry you lost Josh," some teary stranger would say.

I hated that terminology. I've hated it for years. I hated it when people would say that about my dad. I didn't lose anybody. Dad and Josh weren't lost. They weren't a set of keys or that one stupid sock that disappears in the dryer. They were dead and gone. Period.

In the rare moments where I was alone, I could make out laughter. I would cock my head in the direction of the painful sound. What was there to laugh about today? I would shoot a lethal stare in the direction of the people standing in small groups, talking. They were probably just telling a funny story about Josh, remembering the good ole days. Still, it felt wrong.

Finally, we left the cemetery. I was at Mom's house. I could hear Mom in the kitchen trying to lure me in there, saying that I really needed to eat something. I didn't care. My feet moved toward the stairs. I stood there looking up at them, as though it were Everest and I would never be able to climb them. At any other point in my life, I would have bounded up those stairs, two at a time, my feet barely touching the treads as I flew through the air. But now. Not so much. My feet slowly moved. Heavy. They made noticeably loud thumps as they moved onward and upward, mimicking the sound my heart would probably make if it were still intact, if my chest weren't hollow. But it seemed as if my heart, which used to beat so lightly and happily, was gone.

I made it to my old room. It hadn't changed a bit since I left for college. Same full-sized bed with a purple floral comforter. The same lilac-colored walls. One wall was made of cork, and the pieces of my high school life were still tacked to it. Pictures. Letters. Newspaper articles featuring my basketball team winning the state tournament my senior year. Even my old batting gloves from softball were still hanging on the wall.

I managed to pull off that hideous black dress that I would now love to burn and pulled on some sweats. I climbed into bed and stayed there. For I don't know how long.

I still felt like I was in some kind of alternate universe. I could make out the silhouette of my mom coming into my room every now and then. She was forcing me to drink something, Gatorade or some protein shake—something with calories in it. I thought once about how bad it was of me to leave her with all the work of canceling a wedding, at the last minute. But she never said anything about it. And it had probably been a few days when she finally dragged me out of bed and eased me into the bath she had prepared. She stayed in the small bathroom with me as I sat there in the warm water.

I unconsciously tried to keep track of the days. How I hated the sunrises now. I cursed them.

The agony that I was experiencing was as instantaneous and strong as my first reaction to Josh. Instead of excitement and awe at the thought of his face, tears and emptiness now spread through me every minute that I thought of him. Anything about him—his warmth, his off-key singing, and the ease of our relationship—any kind of thought brought on a new wave of remorse.

My family tried to be as understanding as possible, but they could never really understand because they never really understood our instant connection. "Don't be silly" was Mom's response when I called the day after our first date and told her I was already in love.

I stayed up in my room, disconnected, for about two weeks, or so I'm told. From that point on, I was at least able to go through the motions of "living" on my own. My mom no longer babysat me while taking a bath—I was no longer on suicide watch. I would shove some food down my throat on my own every now and then. I'm sure my mom was relieved that I could now feed and bathe myself, but she was always hovering nearby. I was there, physically, just not all there. I was a zombie. I would acknowledge family and friends with a slight nod, but I still wasn't up for talking. And thankfully, everyone seemed to sense that as well and didn't bother me with the usual inane questions. "How are you doing?" "What are your plans for the summer?" "Are you enjoying being back home?" Maybe they didn't bother me with these questions because they knew my responses would be as full of grief as my face.

My life was white noise, and from then on, that's how it would stay. People, words, and life continuing on in a constant hum around me. But nothing would penetrate. No one voice or thought or touch could pull me from my despondency. The rest of my days would go on in a blur of white noise, and I made peace with that.

I had already gone through every emotion in the book. Anger. Denial. Blame. Misery. Helplessness. I would close my eyes tight to try to hear his voice again, but his final words to me brought no peace. "See you in the morning," he said. Liar. I tried being mad at him at some point, thinking maybe that would be the way out. Mad that he wasn't at our home with me, like he should have been. Mad that he let that stupid Jake talk him into going out that night. Mad that he wasn't the one driving because he could have handled that part better and avoided the accident all together. Mad that he was the one who got off easy—killed instantly. Mad that Jake lived. Unlike me. My death, which was happening second by second, minute by minute—was slow and anticlimactic and would never be over.

But being mad at him didn't help. It just brought on a feeling of guilt.

My precious Gran, the matriarch of Mom's family, was the only one who really tried talking to me because she knew she could get away with it. I couldn't ever be mean to her. She tried telling me to lean on God, to let Him ease my pain. I saw her wise eyes pleading with me to move on. She probably didn't know how mad that made me. I had tried blaming Him, too, in an attempt to make myself feel better. It didn't. And I felt guilty about that too. I knew that God didn't strike Josh down. I knew that's not how it worked. But I also felt like He hadn't intervened to save him either. So I was conflicted. I wasn't mad at God, but I was. I wanted to find some kind of peace in Him, honestly, but never could. I think I had let myself get too bitter by then. I had already asked God all the usual questions growing up, anytime I wondered why my dad had to die so young. So I knew this time around that asking rhetorical questions into thin air wasn't going to make me feel any better.

It probably wasn't a coincidence that Gran asked me to come over to her house to talk with her that day. April thirtieth. The date of my would-be wedding. I didn't even know what the date was. There were no days or dates in my white noise world. I probably wouldn't have ever figured out what day it was if I hadn't walked by her calendar hanging in her kitchen. The last square at the end of the row. Circled a few times in red ink. Red like blood. Like the vast amount of blood Josh lost that night.

"What's today?" My voice was frail as I stood staring at the red ink.

Gran just walked slowly to me, with tears in her eyes, and put her hand on my shoulder.

Her hand felt like it was a two-ton boulder. It all happened so fast that I didn't know whether it was the immense torment that immediately consumed me that knocked me to the ground or her small, frail hand. Had to be the torment.

I was on the ground, shaking again, and back in my dark place. I could see Gran hovering over me, talking to me. But I couldn't respond. The next thing I knew I was back at Mom's.

It didn't take me quite as long to recover from my relapse. Maybe a week. Then I was back to my new normal—an emotionless android. I wrapped myself in solitude and put an armor of apathy in place. As long as no one got too close and I kept myself from caring too much, then I would be fine.

I would pick a room in Mom's house and just sit there. The living room with its eclectic mix of antiques. The light pink floral wallpaper that lined the walls. The piano where I once sat and played Christmas carols as Josh sang along. The sunroom. The small addition on the south side of the house that remained painfully sunny all day. I didn't stay in that room much. The walls of my childhood home didn't seem to close in around me or even imprison me. They protected me from the world of trouble that waited outside for me. I stayed this way for months. I just figured this was the new me: new, but not improved.

And heaven forbid a storm would roll through town. On those nights, Mom would sleep on a small roll-out bed next to me so that she could stop me from screaming and waking up the whole house—or neighborhood. She finally wised up and would give me a couple of over-the-counter antihistamines to make me sleepy when the weatherman said a thunderstorm was headed our way. But even those wouldn't completely knock me out. I would still cringe with every thunder and cry with every lightning strike. I would wrap myself into a ball and rock back and forth in an effort to keep my imagination from painting me a picture of what happened to Josh on that one stormy night. Any other depressed person would revel in the misery of rain, the dark clouds, and the glum mood, but I shunned it. The dark clouds should've fit into my mood nicely, but didn't.

I could see the patience running out, on Mom's face especially. Every day she grew a little more annoyed with me and my despair. I tried a little harder to make her happy. She had done so much for me. Not only did she take care of all the—gulp—wedding cancellation details, but she also took care of my house for me. It was *my* house now. Not *ours*. I remembered, through the haze of the first few weeks, her asking if I wanted to sell it. I only remember this moment because of my reaction. I'm pretty sure I growled at her. So she took on that burden as well. I hadn't been back there, to *my* house, since, but I knew there was no way I was selling it. So it sat there just as lonely, empty, and unfinished as me.

■   ■   ■   ■   ■

I found myself standing in front of a mirror, taking stock of myself again. It had been a while since I'd done this. I put a little extra effort into my appearance today, as much as I didn't want to. It had already been six months. Six long months. Long doesn't even do it justice. I half expected to see a small, time-weathered, old woman staring back at me. But I looked the same for the most part. I poked at my thin face and realized I was more than a little gaunt.

It was New Year's Eve and the day of my first cousin's wedding. So there was no way I was going to get a "get out of jail free card" on this one. I was obligated. At least they had the common sense not to ask me to do anything for the wedding.

I sighed as I walked through the doors of the church. Yes, the same church I was to be married in and the same church where Josh's service took place. Unbearable. I focused intensely on maintaining my composure. I timed it to where I could sneak in at the last minute and sit on the back row in case I needed to bolt out of there.

I quickly realized that I probably wasn't going to make it all the way through. I stared blankly forward as the music played and the lovely bride was ushered down the aisle by her dad. Another sword was plunged into my side. I let the self-pity take over. *This girl has everything*, I thought to myself. *And she's flaunting it right in front of me.*

"What a heifer," I mumbled under my breath.

Something poked me in the ribs. "Ow!" I slapped my hand over my mouth in embarrassment. Was the sword literally there, piercing me? I turned my head slowly to the side. No sword, just one of my brothers who had managed to sit down beside me without my noticing.

Jordan brought his eyebrows together seriously and put one finger to his lips. "Sssh." But then he cracked a smile as be put his arm around me and gave my shoulder a sympathetic squeeze.

I hummed as quietly as I could to myself, trying to drown out the preacher, the groom, and the heif—bride. I'm sure the humming helped, but it did little to slow the avalanche of tears that streamed down my face.

Music had become my only ally at this point. I had found a little comfort there in the past few months. My musical ADD came in handy now. Except now I would listen to each song, each word, intently instead of haphazardly shuffling through the songs. But my collection of music still varied as much as ever. I listened to lots of sad music: "All by Myself," "How Do I Live Without You," "One Sweet Day," and some angry music too: Three 6 Mafia, Shinedown, Metallica. Songs that fried your brain and rattled your fillings. There were several Tom Petty CDs that I had worn out thoroughly as well. So at least I had a vast array of memorized lyrics to hum to myself until this dreadful event was over. I had always had a thing for music. I loved how a song could bring back a memory or shift a mood, just like a particular smell. How the lyrics seemed to effortlessly reincarnate feelings that you had once forgotten.

I went to the reception and stayed just as long as I had to. I didn't know how many more looks I could stand. I felt everyone's eyes on me…surely the bride was jealous. I got the knowing looks and the sad eyes trying to congratulate me on my small victory of being able to endure a wedding. When the happy couple started toward the cake table, I'd had enough. I couldn't cope with their smiling faces anymore. I stood up abruptly.

Jordan's hand tried to pull me back down. He hadn't left my side the entire day. He came in handy as he fought off a couple relatives who were a little too intent on trying to drudge up the past.

I carefully freed myself from his vice-like grip and managed to flash a halfhearted smile at him. He may have feared that I was about to rush the bride and groom. "Just bring me back some cake."

"Do you want me to come home with you? I don't need to be here either." He was searching my eyes, but they were dry now—somehow. I had no idea what else he saw there. Probably nothing.

"Nah, I'm okay. Just need a little alone time." I laughed without humor. *All* my time was alone time.

I got in the car and just started driving. Before I knew it, I had made it forty miles east of Cordell. To Mountain View. I hadn't been back here since the funeral. I barely remembered where the cemetery even was because I wasn't coherent the last time I was out here, six months ago.

My car seemed to drive itself there. Seemed to stop right in front of a headstone. *Hanson.* That was all I could see, and the black words looked ominous against the pale gray granite. The sky was slightly overcast and the chill in the air burned my face as I climbed out of the warm car.

My feet glided slowly forward and crunched the dry leaves that scattered the ground. I glanced around, and the cemetery was quiet. No one else was spending their New Year's Eve here except me.

I stood a foot away from his name. The name that was supposed to be mine now but never would be.

I sank to my knees involuntarily. The ground was hard, unforgiving. The surrounding grass was as dead and barren as my insides.

"Howdy," I managed to say on a half sob. The instant memory hit me hard. I looked up at the sky, trying to fight back the tears.

He's probably so mad at me right now, not understanding what I'm doing here. He used to go with me when I went out to my dad's grave, but he never understood why. He never had the same impulse to sit and talk to his dad's grave. He would stand silently next to me as I talked and cried into my dad's headstone. When he felt me getting too upset, he'd pick me up and tell me to say good-bye. I'm sure he's up in heaven yelling down at me to say good-bye. I'm sure he thinks my behavior has been pathetic and unnecessary. But I was too selfish. I wanted him here with me. It would be nice to have him here to tell me to move on, get on with my life, that this too was just part of the master plan, fate. Everything that he said to me on our first date came back to me, that fate had brought us together for some reason. He really felt that way and I did too, then.

But now? What was fate trying to tell me now? I didn't want to understand fate if this is what it brought me. So much happiness followed by so much pain. Maybe I was doing a disservice to us, to our love. I should be feeling extremely lucky that I had the chance to experience true love, however brief it may have been. I knew that a lot of folks out there would never experience what we had together. It almost seemed impossible, to me, that there would ever be two people out there who could have what we had.

The tears I hadn't realized I'd been crying slowed to a trickle, and I sighed.

"I miss you." It was all I could say but all I needed to say at the same time.

If there really is a heaven, and if Josh has been looking down on me this whole time, I wouldn't have to say anything else, ever again, because he already knew it all.

I let my fingers, nearly frozen by the falling temperature, lightly trace the letters engraved in the stone. I felt numb, but it wasn't because of the subfreezing temperature. The numbness was still radiating outward from my heart.

My ringing cell phone knocked me out of my trance. I glanced at the number; it was Mom. I had better answer so she didn't think I had gone off and killed myself. She could be a little overdramatic sometimes.

"Good-bye. I love you more," I whispered toward the stone, my warm breath visible in the cold air.

I got up and turned back toward my car as I answered the phone. "Hey, Mom. I'm fine. On my way home."

One of my favorite Seether songs was playing in the car when I climbed in and brought the engine back to life. I cranked on the heater. I hung up quickly with Mom so that I could melt into my leather seat and let the band pluck on my heartstrings. "Broken" was the name of the song, and it seemed to sum things up nicely. While the band sang about being broken and not being strong enough, I felt something shift in my chest. An ache that came alive at certain times and without much reason. I allowed myself the misery of hurting through the song and then made my way home.

CHAPTER 7

That first year was hard and, of course, a little harder for me than most. To my surprise, I made it through the holidays and the anniversary of firsts: the anniversary of his death and what would have been our first year of marriage. I had met Josh's sister and brother, grandma, and grandpa out at his grave on the anniversary of his death. I sensed that it would become a tradition.

The next couple of years continued to tick by slowly, probably because I was still living at home with Mom and my stepdad, William. I tried everything in my power to make them go by faster. I was trying to hurry up and reach the end of my life. So I became quite the little joiner. Any class or session that was offered anywhere around Cordell, I went to. I learned karate, first-aid/CPR, how to crochet, draw, and play the guitar. I think the only thing I hadn't learned was underwater basket weaving. I had even gone through the online course and gotten my real estate license. There wasn't any job I really wanted around Cordell, and going through the process of buying *my* home had gotten me curious. And it was a good job to have because I could literally work 24/7. If I wasn't showing houses, I was doing research on the Internet into the wee hours of the morning.

Keeping busy helped a little. I wasn't in zombie mode quite as bad as before. I would even let a smile creep across my face from time to time. But every minute of every day was filled with a hopeless feeling. I still felt so alone. I had our engagement picture next to my bed and every night I tried to dream about him, but I couldn't. My memory was already betraying me. I couldn't bring myself to go back to the house in Yukon yet, although I was paying the bills by myself now. Baby steps.

"I'm fixing to leave. Can you bring the pop and chips when you come? We're supposed to eat at noon." My mom was rushing around like a crazy person downstairs, trying to load all the food she'd cooked.

"Okay, I'll be there in just a few," I yelled from my room. I finished tying my shoes and stared at the picture of us.

"Here we go," I sighed.

It was the Fourth of July, and my family always had a cookout at my uncle Bo's house. Practically any holiday in the summertime we had a cookout and played some wiffle ball. I used to look forward to these days, but now it was just something else I had to force myself to get through.

Ten minutes later, I walked through the house and unloaded the pop and chips. I made the necessary rounds and gave everyone a hug.

It was a good turn out this year. All my brothers and their families had made it down this time. All my out-of-town cousins too. I almost enjoyed all the laughter that filled the house and overflowed onto the deck outside. Maybe there was hope for me after all.

I made it through the small talk and meal; filling up on hamburgers, chips, and potato salad. Afterwards, I tried to busy myself with the clean up as all the kids and young adults made their way to the makeshift ball field in the backyard. I used to be the first one done with lunch and the one gathering everyone up for the game. But not now. I couldn't bring myself to play anymore. They always asked, more like begged, but I always made an excuse.

Josh and I were awesome at wiffle ball. So much so that Uncle Bo had to put us on opposing teams, which made for an interesting game. Josh was a natural athlete. We would yell back and forth at each other, tauntingly, throughout the game. Everyone used to get a kick out of it.

After we cleaned up a little, all of us nonplaying cheerleaders would grab a chair or plop down on the ground to watch the game. I didn't feel like playing, but I still had no problem taunting and taking a few easy jabs at anyone who struck out. I was still in pain, deep down, but there were moments where I seemed a little more alive. This was one of them.

"Ah, c'mon—that was right down the middle!" I joked.

My brother Caleb just stared me down. He was the most fun to pick on since he played baseball in college.

"You're not gonna see a better meatball than that all day!"

Caleb pointed the bat at me. "You wanna give it a try then?"

I sat back with a huff. He knew how to shut me up. "Wouldn't wanna embarrass you," I said with a lightness that was new for me.

"Pssshhh..." He shook his head as he eased back into his stance.

All the other cheerleaders were enjoying my newfound enthusiasm. I had to admit that it took me by surprise a little— not sure where it was coming from.

"Your mom says you sure have been working a lot, hon." Gran was sitting next to me, probably enjoying my taunts the most. We are very much alike. We both had a dry sense of humor and enjoyed a good practical joke. She wasn't a blue-haired, frumpy grandma. No sir. She wore trendy clothes, drove a spunky little convertible, and was as beautiful in her eighties as she was in her thirties.

"Yes, ma'am. They're transferring some prisoners from California to the prison in Sayre. So they're hiring a lot of guards—fifty or something like it. So I've had my hands full trying to find them houses to buy." That was a good answer, but I'm sure that wasn't the answer she was looking for.

"Well, that's good." She paused briefly. "Taking any new classes?"

"No, ma'am." I wasn't going to make it any easier for her.

"You'd probably make more money working in the Oklahoma City area, wouldn't you?" Ah, there it was. She kept her eyes on the game still going on in front of us. She had managed to switched gears pretty quickly. I always let her push me on certain matters more than anyone else.

"Probably. A lot more Realtors there though. More competition," I responded flatly, avoiding the intention that was behind her question.

"Well, I'm sure there aren't as many as beautiful as you, honey. That ought to narrow the field a little bit."

"You're a little partial," I reminded her with one eyebrow raised. She chuckled at my expression.

"Not *that* partial," she tried to protest.

I fanned myself, trying to cool the hot, humid air around me. Oklahoma summers could almost be unbearable unless you had access to a pool—or pond. The air was hot and thick with humidity and felt like an unwelcomed coat around you.

"You can't stay here forever, you know," Gran said softly.

"I can't?" Her out-of-left-field statement bruised my healing heart. Was I finally getting the boot?

She smiled warmly, sensing my reaction. "Well, you *can*, but you shouldn't. You need to get on with your life and move back to the City—to *your* house."

Her words were like tiny razor blades, each syllable pricking me deeper than the one before. She seemed to emphasize *my* house the same why I would have. I stared at the blades of grass on the ground between my feet. The conversation, the moment, had taken a turn. It was no longer light and encouraging, but difficult and full of innuendos.

"Mmmhumm…" was all I could manage to get out.

She slowly reached for the hand that was lying in my lap and squeezed it gently. I was still staring at the ground, but I slowly looked up and met her eyes—full of love and angst.

I let out a slow sigh, hoping that she'd understand that I'd already had to contemplate that idea.

She let me have a moment before trying to change the subject. "Well, with all this money you're making, maybe you should take a little trip? Destress a little?"

"I've thought about it," I admitted. *But where would I go, alone?* I amended in my head.

"Do it then," she ordered with a smile.

"Maybe." It was all I could say for now, but at the moment, my brain wasn't buzzing with the usual excuses.

I was sitting in the kitchen the next morning minding my own business when Mom walked in, and I could instantly tell that she had an agenda. She usually skipped breakfast and went straight to work.

"Mornin'," I said cheerfully, as cheerful as I could be these days. I was hoping she'd see my decent mood and know there was no need to tick me off without good cause. "Not in a hurry to get the shop opened today?"

Mom was the owner of a local gift shop that specialized in products made in Oklahoma. Like most small town businesses, it was a constant struggle to stay afloat. And like most businesses in Cordell, the hours of operation were based on the owners' whims and around their kids' athletic schedules.

"I've already been down there—had to come back to grab something," she replied vaguely.

I sat there silently poking at the fruit plate I had made myself and stared at the local news anchor chatting away on the television.

"Gran told me about your conversation last night."

Yup—there it is. Record time. Yeesh.

"Oh yeah," I replied, feigning surprise. "I'm sure you agree with her. Fixing to kick me out?" I never had to question whether or not she caught my sarcasm. She was used to it.

"I wasn't talking about that, sweetie. The trip."

She seemed so excited for some reason. Maybe she *was* ready to get me out of the house, at least for a little bit.

"Oh, that." I sighed again at the idea. "Haven't given it much thought really."

"Why not? You've got a little extra money to spend. You've been spending way too much time working and could use the break. And you've always wanted to travel…" She let herself trail off. She was in Mom mode, full force. She didn't just have one reason ready, but several.

Mom kept her mouth closed as William walked through the kitchen to set his coffee cup beside the sink. He kissed her before turning to walk out. His eyes caught mine as he walked away, and I caught the familiar look of sympathy in them. No doubt Mom had talked this through with him the night before and he was telling me now—with that brief look—that she wouldn't be letting the subject drop without a fight.

Great.

I managed a weak smile—a thanks for trying gesture—for him before he left, then heaved an inward sigh.

"But where would I go—what would I do?"

"Well, I dunno, hon. There are a lot of places to choose from…let's see—you could go to the beach somewhere—" She cut off when she saw me wince at the word *beach*. "Or just somewhere nice and quiet," she continued.

"Humm…" I pretended to actually consider some place to go. "Don't think I'd want somewhere quiet where my thoughts could get the best of me. Need somewhere where there's plenty to do—to keep me occupied." I was hoping she'd get what I was talking about. How I didn't want to go somewhere where my "alone-ness" would be emphasized.

"New York then," she chimed in immediately.

Of course, she picked a great city that would be crawling with people and activity. And a city that I truly had always wanted to visit.

I turned my head to look at her now. She was leaning against the dark kitchen cabinets casually, staring me down with her eyebrows raised and a smirk on her face. Just waiting for my next excuse, my next move. It's like she'd known she'd already made her point well enough. I knew what she was thinking...*Checkmate*.

I just shrugged my shoulders lightly, like the idea didn't really interest me, and turned back to the news.

"You could walk around museums, eat at all those restaurants, and go to some shows..."

She continued to babble about the extensive nightlife and cultural possibilities that I could involve myself in. All the while, I was still having a hard time coming up with a good excuse for why I shouldn't go... Until she started to apparently run out of examples and started to go a little out there.

"Oh, oh! Maybe you'll see some celebrities there!"

"Not likely," I chirped in my usual pessimistic tone. Although I didn't like when people called me a pessimist. I wasn't really— even with all I've been through. I was just a realist. A very depressed, battle worn realist.

"Maybe you'll meet an actor or ball player or something and charm him right off his feet." She giggled. She probably knew that I thought that was highly unlikely so I didn't bother responding, maybe that's why she laughed. "Just make sure you meet a hunky one. There are a lot of good looking ones out there, but you need a real piece of man meat!"

Ew—yuck! Hunky? *Man* meat? What was that even supposed to mean? I was sitting there trying to blink away the random images that were now invading my brain. It was weird and totally out of character for my mom to say stuff like that. What in the world was she thinking? Where was she going with this— was she *that* desperate to get me out of the house? Man meat? I shuddered when I suddenly realized I'd never be able to look at a hamburger the same way again...

"Aww—Mom..." I managed to growl in disgust before she started making any more analogies. "I'll think about it," I added, trying to appease her.

I was staring *her* down now, and so she put up her hands, palms facing me, in defense. "Okay, okay. Just trying to help. I'm off to the shop—I'll see you tonight," she announced before I could get a word in.

She was out of the kitchen and out of the house before my head slowly found its natural place, looking forward. I stared out the bay window in front of me. The birds were chirping happily and the sun's golden rays were stretching across the yard. I tried to shake off the conversation, but all day the idea of getting away from here for a little bit lingered. I avoided Mom all day, which wasn't hard. Just skipped dinner and stayed at my office a little longer. No need for any more male/meat analogies.

I tiptoed up the squeaky stairs slowly late that night, trying not to wake anyone up. I had a flash and remembered how, at one point several years ago, my feet pounded up these stairs without my trying. My heart was so heavy that even walking was painful—and loud. Look at how far I've come...and it's only been a few *years*. I laughed at my slow development. Josh's death had definitely warped me.

I made it to my room, threw my laptop on the bed and just stood there. It was quiet and hot in my room, the fan whirling above me and the sounds of a western Oklahoma night making the only noise.

I glanced back at the engagement picture of Josh and me that was on my nightstand. I turned around and took a step toward my dresser. There, in a little white leather box with the lid open, was my engagement ring. I loved that ring: a princess cut diamond on a thin white gold band. I would still be wearing it if I could bear all the questions and comments. "Oh, it's so pretty." "When's the wedding?"

"Ahhh..." I sighed as I plopped down on the bed and turned on my laptop. "New York City it is," I mumbled under my breath as I pulled up the first online travel site.

CHAPTER 8

Somehow my mind had wandered through most of my life during what little was left of my flight from Denver to New York City.

The pilot got on the intercom and announced the local time and weather and that he was beginning the decent into JFK airport, which forced me to react to the present, not the past. I stretched out my legs and repositioned my chair into its "proper upright position."

I tried to piece together all the information I'd heard about Bradley Matthews from the past few months. He came from a famous family. His own star quality was relatively new. I think he was around my age, maybe in his early thirties. He had had several hit movies back to back. And the sequel to his first hit action adventure film just came out earlier this summer. His character Ace was sexy, smart and invincible. If Tony Stark and Indiana Jones could somehow have a baby, Ace would be it. Bradley seemed to blossom into a megastar overnight. And it was easy to see he wasn't comfortable with that. Bradley was one of those stars who shied away from the public as much as possible. He valued his privacy; can't say that I blame him. All those paparazzi parasites following you around all the time while you do the most mundane of human activities has to wear on you.

But he was classically gorgeous. Shaggy, dark chestnut-colored hair that was his trade mark. Bradley was tall, muscular, and always kept his composure while in the spotlight. He wasn't a "bad boy" and wasn't a "goody-two-shoes" either. Bradley didn't quite embody the "all American" look that most of the guys back home did. Maybe it was the clothes. He seemed just a little bit more…artsy.

He was still pretty green when it came to his stardom, but I could tell that being famous was something he was born to be. Always there running through his veins, waiting to be used. He seemed to have good manners too. I remembered that from the last press junket he did and how effortlessly he charmed the interviewers. This was no doubt instilled in him from his parents, seasoned actors themselves, who were always the epitome of class and style.

It seemed like mere moments later we were pulling up to the jet way at JFK airport. The familiar sound of shuffling filled the cabin as everyone started to gather their belongings. I quickly gathered up my purse and small carry-on. My mother always taught me to keep a change of underwear and the basic toiletries with me while traveling. That way any unexpected delays wouldn't seem nearly as bad if you could at least change and freshen yourself up. Mom probably learned that the hard way during her travels to India. My grandparents did mission work over there, and my mom often went with them. All kinds of problems seemed to pop up when making the day-and-a-half-long trip to the other side of the world. But it seemed a little odd to have these items with me now, on my way to eat dinner with Bradley Matthews.

I tried to hurry, as I was instructed. I noticed that Bradley was already off the plane by the time I exited. But these bloody shoes! They're going to be the death of me. I stumbled twice while half-running through the crowded airport. I quickly figured out where the baggage claim was and made my way (painfully) down there. I was the first one there, and I congratulated myself. Since I had changed planes in Denver, my bag was one of the first down the shoot. I grabbed it off the carousel as soon as it was within reach. I whipped out my BlackBerry and scrolled to Bradley's number.

I had already programmed it on the plane so that I wouldn't be fumbling around with numbers now.

It only rang once. "Evie?" He had a sultry phone voice, low and smooth.

"Yup. I'm headed through the doors now," I said as I turned my head left to right looking for the Range Rover he described. I saw it pull up as soon as I looked to my left again. "Ah, there you are."

There was silence on the other end of the line. Huh? I glanced down and saw that we were already disconnected. Okay... I looked up and saw the back hatch of the SUV open. I walked briskly over to it. The small street was full of cabs and disgruntled travelers. All the honking and shouting echoed loudly under the portico. I ignored the shouts from behind me as I heaved my suitcase into the back.

"Come on, blondie, get oudda da way!" Some angry cabbie was already shouting at me in a heavy, authentic Bronx accent. I smiled, enjoying my first taste of the Big Apple. I slammed the hatch shut and ran around to the side, where the back door was slightly opened for me already. I slid in quickly and was welcomed by Bradley's smile. I was a bit confused; I figured he'd be driving.

"It's official," I claimed. "I've already pissed off my first New Yorker!"

"And you've only been off the plane for what, ten minutes? Impressive..."

"I'm gifted." I shrugged.

The driver, a large, intimidating black man, was driving—rather quickly—through the crowded lanes. Weaving left and right violently. I was getting tossed around like a rag doll in the back. Bradley was better at keeping himself balanced—used to this type of driving, I guessed.

"Whoa, you got seatbelts in this thing?" I was fumbling around over my right shoulder. "Ah, here we go," I said, clicking it in place. The driver was eying me in the rearview mirror with a smug smile. It seemed I was already entertaining him too.

Bradley just rolled his eyes at me. "You'll jump in a car with a complete stranger in New York City, and yet you act like a seat-belt should be your main safety concern?"

"If he's gonna drive like a lunatic, yes. Besides, if I'm gonna be dragged off into the night to be killed, I'd much rather it be by a movie star rather than some random creep-o."

"As long as you've thought it over I guess," he said, shaking his head. "That's Melvin, by the way." He pointed to the driver. "Melvin, this is Evie. Evie, this is Melvin." Melvin waved cheer-fully as he continued his erratic driving.

"*Melvin*," I repeated quietly, eyebrows raised in surprise. The name didn't seem to fit him. "Nice to meet you." I wasn't sure if he heard me. He was already involved in a one-way screaming match with someone who had just cut him off. A slur of profani-ties filled the car.

"Hey, hey, Melvin. There's a lady present," Bradley chided.

"Sorry, boss." The smile plastered across his large mahogany face, along with the amusement in his eyes, didn't make him look too repentant.

I was staring out the window, watching as the New York City landscape passed beside me. It was different than I had imagined. At this point, it looked like any other big city I'd visited. Just a lot more cabs, angry drivers, and tall buildings.

I glanced around the interior of the Range Rover: cherry wood trim and beautiful ivory Oxford leather seats. Nice, but I could probably find a better way to utilize a hundred grand. Like paying off my mortgage! Yeesh! I felt Bradley's eyes on me and turned toward him. His lips were twitching in order to keep from smiling. Did I look so impressed? "Nice jalopy," I commented with a shrug.

"Gets me from A to B well enough." He winked at me before going on. "What about you? What do you drive?"

"A big green tractor," I deadpanned, looking back out the window again. After no reaction from Bradley, I turned. A scowl was firmly in place, but I could only laugh. "Okay, okay. I drive an SUV too. But just a plain ole Chevy."

"I would have figured you for a truck-driving gal. Some huge dually. Something a little bigger to make navigating the farms a little easier." One side of his mouth pulled into a cocky grin.

"Hardy har har. Actually, I'd love a truck. A big, black quad cab is my dream car, but it won't fit in my garage and would be hard on gas."

"I see," Bradley replied.

The city started to look a little more exciting the longer we drove. It was around nine at night, and the streets were still lined with people and every store still had its lights on. In Cordell, only a couple of the convenience stores stayed open past eight at night. We took a couple of narrow side streets, and before long we pulled up behind an old building with no sign.

"You ready?"

"Yeah…we're eating here?" I asked cautiously.

It was dark, and there was little movement around the building or even down the rest of the street, as far as I could tell. Maybe he *was* bringing me somewhere to murder me. Maybe that's how he got his kicks. The fame game was already boring him, so he decided to prey on unsuspecting Midwestern girls he met on planes. I quickly shook the ridiculous idea out of my head. Glad to know that the years of depression and small-town living hadn't rid me of my paranoia. But my face must have been a question mark because he quickly explained.

"I know the owners, and they're nice enough to let us come in the back to avoid any…unwanted attention," he said.

"Well, ain't that sweet," I drawled and made him chuckle.

"You can leave your stuff in here. We'll take you to The Plaza when we're done here. It'll be safe." He opened his door and disappeared into the darkness. I unfastened my seatbelt, grabbed my purse, and had just put my hand on the door handle when the door opened. Ah, he opened my door! That was a first!

"Right this way." He motioned toward the building with a sweep of his arm.

I hopped out of the SUV and followed him as Melvin pulled away. Bradley knocked twice, and the door opened slightly. We were let in immediately and were led down a maze of dark, undecorated hallways. I was following behind Bradley by just a step. We went through another set of double doors and I started to hear the faint thudding of music. *We must be getting close*, I thought. A fragrant aroma hit me—tomatoes, herbs—Italian maybe? I was starting to get just the slightest bit nervous. I already felt unnaturally comfortable with Bradley, but I wondered who else would be there. My mind could run wild thinking of the motley crew of celebrities that could be awaiting our arrival.

The short, round gentleman that Bradley followed waved him forward and stepped to the side, "There you go, Mr. Matthews. They're already in there."

"Thanks." Bradley shook the man's hand. It looked like maybe he slipped him a tip. Smooth.

The man went back down the hallway from where we came as Bradley held another door open for me. We were in some type of back room, simple but still elegant. There was a bar in the corner. It was dimly lit, and there were a few large, half-moon–shaped booths positioned in the middle of the room. There were four people in one of the booths. I sighed in relief; I didn't recognize any of the faces immediately. I could hear the music, a little louder now. But it seemed to be coming from the main part of the restaurant, wherever that was…

The young guy behind the bar threw his chin up, while smiling, at Bradley.

"Hey, Mark. How are you?" Bradley acknowledged.

The barkeep just smiled a little wider in response.

Bradley led me to the booth with one hand on the small of my back. I felt his warm fingers through my shirt, and my stomach knotted in an unfamiliar way. As we got closer, the people in the booth shifted to one side. Bradley motioned for me to slide in first.

"Everyone, this is Evie. Evie, this is everyone."

"Howdy!" I smiled timidly, and I instantly regretted my choice of words. But it *was* my standard greeting.

I received a chorus of "heys," "hiyas," and even a "howdy."

I just smiled. Yep. Fish out of water…

They greeted Bradley. The men shook hands with him. Then they just went back to their own conversations.

"Let's get this party started!" howled Melvin as he walked through the door, disrupting the peaceful atmosphere.

The others let out a few catcalls as he made his way toward us.

"Having fun yet?" Bradley asked softly, his lips close to my ear again, his breath swirling my hair.

"This is great," I admitted. "Thank you."

"It's my honor to buy dinner for a heroine such as you!" He finished with a mock bow, and I rolled my eyes.

"You didn't say anything about buying my dinner."

Bradley leaned back a little to appraise me. "I figured that was implied when I asked you to come with me." He was obviously curious. "Is that not how they do things down in Oklahoma?"

My lips just curled into a smile as I flushed in embarrassment. No need to tell him that I hadn't been taken out to dinner in *years*. "Well, I'm sure it is. It just makes me uncomfortable when people pay for stuff for me."

Bradley threw his head back and laughed. "Wow, I'm not sure I've heard that from a woman before. Man, you must be a hot commodity back home!"

I just shrugged since I was a little confused by his response and willed the redness in my cheeks and neck to subside. By now the other dinner guests had become interested in our discussion.

"Yeah, so what's with that? Why do you keep calling her a hero?" Melvin piped up as he threw one beefy arm on top of the bench beside him.

"There was some kid who choked on something during our flight. Evie here"—he put his arm around my shoulder and squeezed—"rushed to his aid and saved his life!" The small measure of pride in his voice didn't sound mocking.

The pretty brunette across from me (whose name I still didn't know) murmured about what a close call it was while her escort for the evening nodded in agreement.

"That's awesome," one of the other guys pointed out.

I just stared down at my lap. "It was nothing...I just happened to be the closest." My attempts to downplay my "heroics" failed. They continued to congratulate me until a tall, extremely thin and attractive server approached the table to take drink orders. Well, it was obvious that I shouldn't waste my time asking her what's good here—because it was obvious that she hasn't eaten much...ever.

"Ma'am," she said a little louder, breaking my thought. "What would you like?"

"Oh, uh—just a Coke."

Bradley looked at me. It was clear that he was unhappy with my choice. "Just a Coke? You don't want any Jack in it or anything?"

"Trying to get me liquored up?" I accused.

"Maybe. If you're this entertaining sober, you've got to be a riot with a little alcohol in you!"

I looked back up at the server. "Just a Coke is fine, thanks." I didn't want to make a fool out of myself. No need to become just some funny story that Bradley would tell all his friends about someday, and adding alcohol would only increase my chances of this.

■　■　■　■　■

I blinked, several times, still unable to focus. I was in a bed. And I was confused. I tried harder to focus. Finally, after a few moments I was able to take stock of where I was. A very nice hotel room. Very, very nice. I battled down another wave of confusion. My eyes burned, and my brain felt a little fuzzy after changing time zones and having a late night.

"Oh," I groaned.

I rolled onto my back. *I guess I'm alone.* The last thing I remembered was eating and laughing. I promptly started to piece together the previous evening. *Oh my—what have I done?!* But luckily I was able to remember more and more. But I was still fuzzy on how I ended up here and in bed. I gave myself the once over. I was still in the same clothes I wore yesterday. Humm... that's good. I stretched out in the large bed, not even coming close to the edges. My fingers grazed something unfamiliar. Something rough in comparison to the unbelievably satiny-soft sheets. I propped myself up on my elbow as I pulled it closer. It was a folded piece of paper. I had to blink a few more times in order to see the words clearly.

Evie,

I brought you back to The Plaza, as I promised. Your luggage is in the closet. I very much enjoyed your company last night. You were every bit as entertaining as I thought you'd be! I hope you don't mind the room. They wouldn't let you check in to your room this morning...in your condition. I'll talk to you soon

—Bradley

"Oh man." I groaned again as I let the letter slide through my fingers.

I'm sure that's the last I'll see of him. I sat up, slowly, careful not to make the room start to spin. I couldn't believe the room. There was a huge flat screen in front of the bed. Fresh flowers. Elegant décor. The furniture was covered in jewel-toned textiles, and it was more than twice the size of the normal suites I'd stayed in before. But I was too distracted to fully appreciate it. I swung my feet around to the side of the bed and checked the bedside table for the clock. Almost noon. I had been asleep at least ten hours. How could my body still be so out of whack? *I better hurry up and get out of here*, I thought. *I'm sure I need to check into my real room, which is probably no bigger than a broom closet.* I made my way to the bathroom and turned on the shower as I hunted through my luggage for a change of clothes and bathroom necessities.

The hot water felt good on my body, washing over my sensitive muscles. Why was I so sore? A few more faint memories made themselves known. *Stupid shoes.* My ribs were sore from laughing.

My stomach growled impatiently as I finished getting ready. I left my hair wet. I was too tired and hungry to dry and straighten it. It'd just have to be curly today. My hair wasn't really curly. It was more wavy than anything else, and I usually just called it "nonstraight." But it came in handy on days like this when I was too lazy to do anything else with it.

I was putting away all my belongings when a knock at the door startled me. *Oh no, they've come to kick me out!* I opened the door without even looking through the peephole. My paranoia must have eased up a little since last night.

I gasped when I opened the door. "Oh."

"Good morning, er, afternoon. And how are we feeling?" Bradley breezed past me and was way too chipper. He plopped down on the sofa in the front, sitting room part of the hotel room.

"Uh, good I guess…just trying to remember last night." I was rubbing my head, like that would help.

"You were hilarious." He chuckled.

"I didn't embarrass you, did I?" I asked, slightly panicked.

"No, no, no." He tried to stop his laughter but seemed to have a hard time controlling himself. "Did you know your accent gets more pronounced as the hours drag on?"

"Oh geeze." I sighed as my hand slid from my forehead to cover my eyes.

"And all your little..." He paused as he searched for the right word. "Sayings."

"Yeah, I have a few euphemisms in my repertoire. That's what happens when you grow up in a house where you can't cuss." I was well aware of all my "little sayings." Most people did find them amusing... Rotten potatoes. Holy calzone. Oh Mylanta. Son of a goat roper. I'd throw in a "blimey" or "oy vey" here and there as well, a subconscious effort to appear worldly, no doubt.

"Oh man...good times, good times..." He trailed off. "You had Melvin in stitches all night. He really likes you." He waggled his eyebrows suggestively.

I relaxed a little and chuckled to myself. I *did* remember making him laugh especially hard. "So why couldn't I check into *my* room last night?"

"'Cause you were ready to pass out. You have to at least be able to talk and sign your name to check in." He had a smug grin on his face.

"Pass out!" I spun around and landed in a club chair next to the sofa where Bradley was sitting. I'm sure my face was a bright shade of red by now.

Bradley instantly reassured me, "You had a long day and I think you were just wiped."

"Mmmhumm... Sure you didn't drug me?"

"I would never," he said in mock horror.

"Yeah, I guess you wouldn't have much need to drug a girl," I teased. "I was trying to hurry up and get ready so that I could check out of here." I glanced around the room. "I'm not sure I'll be able to pay you back for this..."

"What are you talking about?" he interrupted.

"Well, I'm sure I need to check into my own room."

"This *is* your own room. For the rest of the week," he said firmly. "I've already talked with the manager, and you won't be charged anything for the reservations you made."

"Oh—I can't—" I was trying my best to reject his generous gift, but I knew this was a futile effort.

"Stop it now. Don't insult me," he asserted as he stood up. "Just charge whatever you need to the room." He towered next to me and put his hands in his pocket. He had to be at least a couple inches over six feet, which was near giant compared to my small frame, and his stance left no room for argument.

"Th-thank you," I managed to choke out.

He nodded, backed up, and sat on the edge of the coffee table in front of me. "So, have plans for tonight?"

I looked up at him, and to my surprise he seemed serious. *What plans would I have? I've been in New York for all of fifteen hours, and I've either spent that time with him or passed out apparently.* "Nope, I hadn't really made any plans, remember? I figured it'd be pretty easy to find something to do around here."

He pulled his iPhone out of his pocket and fiddled with it for a moment. "Something touristy? How about the Empire State Building?" He paused, but I was still just staring at him like a buffoon. "I have a few things to attend to today, but I'd love to take you out tonight. Probably around nine. I'll call you. I'll just pull up in the front, and you can jump in, if you don't mind. I've been able to avoid any unwanted attention so far, and I'd like to keep it that way. I'm not really supposed to be in town till next week."

"Uh, yeah…that's fine," I mumbled as I shook my head. Why did he want to spend more time with me? It made no sense, but call me crazy—I didn't feel the need to argue with him.

"Good. I'll give you a call later then. Enjoy your afternoon!" He turned and sauntered toward the door.

83

All I could do was wave like a moron when he looked back at me as he walked through the door. "Alrighty, I will. You enjoy… being a celebrity," I called as the door shut. I thought I heard another chuckle from him before the door was completely closed.

CHAPTER 9

That first afternoon went by quickly. I had to check in with Mom. I couldn't remember doing that the night before. She was worried to death, of course, and was about to send out a search party. I had a few work e-mails to catch up on, then I ventured to the hotel lobby to buy a map and guidebook so I could plan what I wanted to do while I was in town. I didn't know exactly what I was going to be doing with Bradley, so I just made notes on where I wanted to go and what times certain tourist attractions were open.

Bradley picked me up that night and after another private dinner he took me to the Empire State Building. I was very impressed, not only by the building, but by Bradley. When I walked into the building, I noticed that the observation deck closed at two in the morning. I glanced at my watch and realized it was only a little before eleven, but the place seemed oddly deserted. Did he somehow manage to close it down for a private viewing? The idea seemed a little hard to pull off. I don't know why I was so surprised. I knew he probably had more connections than the president. Well, maybe not *more*.

While Bradley was busy during the days, I worked, slept, or did a little bit more of the touristy stuff. Visiting Ground Zero was heartbreaking. I almost talked myself out of going but thought it would be disrespectful not to. I stood there looking at the massive vacancy in the skyline. It was overwhelming. Of course I'd never seen the World Trade Centers in person, but I could physically feel their absence. I stared at the cranes and construction equipment that littered the area inside the fenced off area. Oversensitive as I am, I sniffed and tried to wipe the silent tears from my cheeks as discreetly as possible. So many lives lost. So many more changed forever. Standing there, I remembered walking through the Oklahoma City National Memorial on a field trip in the ninth grade. I almost lost my lunch while walking through the museum and spotted a baby's shoe as part of the exhibit. Nineteen children under the age of six perished that day. I still can't fathom how some people can hold such darkness inside of them—how anyone can take the lives of innocent people.

I was a senior in high school when 9/11 happened. I remember it clearly; sitting in the school library. Dozens of fellow students huddled around one small thirty-two-inch television as we watched and listened to the world change. It was odd knowing that terrorists, honest-to-goodness terrorists, were going to be a part of our everyday life now. I didn't see it then, but that moment in history, that eleventh day of September in 2001, would become the "where were you?" moment of my generation, just like the day JFK was shot to my mom's. It seems every generation has a monumental burden that it must bear. One generation had to deal with the Great Depression and both World Wars. Another had to go through the assassination of a beloved president and various foreign wars. And now, we had to deal with terrorism on a daily basis.

I wanted to ask Bradley if he was in NYC on September 11 but didn't. For some reason I didn't feel at liberty to question him about much. The entire week, we went in back ways and after hours to avoid attention. And it seemed to be working for the most part. Not once were we bothered by paparazzi or obsessed fans. Melvin was always there though, just in case. I didn't mind having him around. He cracked me up, and I figured that he'd make a nice buffer when the time came and Bradley finally got bored with me. I still didn't quite know what he thought of me. Maybe I was just a pet or something, but he never treated me that way. He was always a gentleman. He opened doors when the opportunity was there, even when there was someone else there to hold the door open for *him*. And he was always paying. That drove me nuts, but he made it clear from the beginning that he wouldn't allow me to pay for anything. This was turning out to be the cheapest, most unexpected, and magical vacation ever. I had to pinch myself several times to make sure I was awake.

I studied his movements and demeanor while we were together. I know it sounds weird and unmanly to call a man graceful, but he was. The way he moved—mercy! Everything he did seemed effortless, and he had such a confident, loose-hipped gait. I spent a lot of time memorizing his face and flawless body. On a couple of occasions, he had brushed up against me—while walking through a doorway, riding in his car or while riding in elevators. His skin seemed softer than mine. Kinda embarrassing. It was an interesting paradox though. His satin-smooth skin covering the rock hard muscles underneath. I had a "thing" with hands too. I thought that you could tell a lot about a person just by looking at their hands. His were large, of course, because of his stature. But they were warm and strong too—just like him. I kept waiting for a more "normal" reaction to him. I was obviously able to appreciate his physical appearance, but my heart never quite reacted appropriately. I kept waiting for the flush to fill my cheeks and for my tongue to tie itself awkwardly as my heart thudded wildly. But it never happened.

The week passed quickly. Too quickly. We went out at night, late, so I'd spend most of the next day catching up on my sleep and work. He took me to the Guggenheim (again, after hours) and to a couple of small restaurants. He made fun of me when I told him how I made a special trip one afternoon to ride the subway. I had always seen it in the movies and always wanted to do it. It was pretty much just as I imagined. Crowded, dirty, and full of somewhat menacing people, but no trench coat flashers or anyone relieving themselves in public. What I *didn't* tell him was that I had to psyche myself up, just a little, to go through with it. I thought, *If all else fails—what would Stephanie Plum do?* I laughed once when I realized I probably should have thought of a less accident-prone heroine and laughed again when I realized that I could probably make Stephanie Plum look like Dirty Harry.

So I got the whole New York City experience. More than that, really, since I had Bradley Matthews as a tour guide. We were always given the royal treatment wherever we went.

But still no mass of screaming fans or photographers. How was this possible? I was starting to think that he wasn't *really* Bradley Matthews. Whoever he was, he was rich and had a lot of connections. And he had a debonair quality and was well-respected, but he didn't seem like a celebrity with the lack of fanfare.

I would be heading back home in a couple of days. I wasn't sure if Bradley had run out of connections or what, but tonight we were just going to be at his apartment. Hanging out. Bradley was sort of blasé about the whole thing, and I got the feeling we wouldn't be there alone, but I had no idea who else would be there. Maybe the four people whose names I couldn't remember, if I ever knew, from the restaurant that first night.

I had gotten used to meeting Bradley under the hotel portico as he pulled up. It seemed to be the best way to keep from drawing unwanted attention. He had just picked me up, and tonight he was driving. I had no idea where Bradley lived. I just stared out the window and watched the cityscape unfold around me as he drove us through the city.

"So who all's gonna be there?" I finally asked.

"Just some friends," he answered evasively.

Friends. Great. Famous friends? Why was I so scared at the thought of other celebrities being there and yet still so calm around Bradley?

"You may recognize a few of them," he offered. "Others you probably won't. Like my friends from the other night."

"Who were they?"

"Just some high-society types. Their families own hotel chains, or they have parents who've invented some kind of computer software," he said nonchalantly.

"Right. Everyone knows a few of those…" I cracked.

We eventually pulled up to a very tall, sleek-looking building. Lots of metal and glass. The sun was going down, passing through the tall buildings, and casting lofty shadows across the crowded streets. I could see Melvin waiting in front of the building. Bradley stopped the car and got out to open my door. Melvin was hopping in the driver's seat as I got out.

Bradley pulled me briskly through the lobby and down a side hall to a small bank of elevators. I didn't even have time to process my surroundings. He slid a plastic key card in a slot, and the elevator doors opened automatically. We stepped in, and the doors closed just as quickly. He slid the plastic card into another similar slot in lieu of punching one of the numbered floors. "PH" lit up on the panel. *Duh.*

It wasn't a short ride to his floor, but it definitely didn't take as long as it did to get to the top of the Empire State Building. I stood silently in the small space. Bradley's scent filled the air quickly. Woodsy and sweet without being flowery. He seemed pretty quiet tonight, and that made me nervous. I still wasn't brave enough to ask him what he was thinking during moments like this.

When the doors opened again, I was surprised to see so many people already gathered. I noticed my fists were clenched, and I loosened them to wipe my palms on my casual khaki capris. Bradley ushered me out of the elevator with his hand on the small of my back, its usual place. It was the only form of physical contact that took place between us, and it never failed to shoot unexpected warmth through my body.

He nodded to the few people who noticed our entrance. I tried to plaster a natural-looking smile on my face, but I was instantly mortified. I did recognize more than just a few of the gorgeous faces that were studying me. I shied somewhat naturally into Bradley's side, just a little, for comfort. I heard him chuckle lightly as he tugged me forward.

"Make yourself at home," he offered.

All I could do was look up at him. *Yeah right!* I cleared my throat. "Sure, sure."

I looked around the room, trying to look past all the beautiful people. It didn't look anything like the bachelor pads I'd seen. Granted I'd only seen a couple of them, but it was more than enough to form a stereotypical opinion. Even Josh's apartment looked like all the others I'd seen: dirty, cluttered, and decorated in only a functional way.

Of course Bradley's place didn't look anything like any other bachelor pads I'd seen. It was clean, thanks to a regular cleaning crew no doubt. It was expertly decorated. Minimalist and modern. White furniture anchored in a large, open living room on top of a geometrical print rug. A dark stone fireplace and a very large plasma television were the main focus of the room. I liked the dark brown, stained concrete floors and hardwood beams that ran across the high ceiling. I gravitated a few feet forward, past a few people, toward the large wall of windows at the back of the room. A perfect view, high above the commotion of the busy city. The sky had darkened more and the scene became magical. The lights on top of all the tall buildings had to take the place of the starry heavens that weren't visible thanks to the thick air that tinted the atmosphere.

"This is amazing," I whispered to myself.

"Thanks," murmured Bradley.

I was startled by his response. I had somehow failed to sense him still next to me. He was smiling down at me, warmly. I smiled back.

I was introduced to some of the famous party guests as the night went on. I did my best to keep the same sense of calm and normalcy with them as I did with Bradley. But my face seemed to be on fire the entire time, and I had trouble spitting out more than one or two coherent sentences. *Charming.* I noticed that some of the females among the crowd weren't as interested in my presence. Exes? Surely not... Geeze, there's a mental picture that I didn't need. One of those slender, tall goddesses standing perfectly beside Bradley in their designer clothes. But that mental picture made more sense, even to me, than Bradley and me standing together. I'm sure my plainness only made his beauty more obvious. I began to feel self-conscious about the casual clothes I had thrown on without much thought earlier. Not that I had anything designer in my wardrobe at all, but capris and a blouse seemed very out of place here, in this apartment, with these people...with Bradley.

Bradley was always close by, not leaving me to fend for myself for too long. I was thankful for that. I wasn't quite sure if it was because he could sense my anxiety or if he feared some type of revolt against me from his friends. Probably just my anxiety. Most of the people I met were friendly enough—no torches or pitchforks. I answered a few of the same Oklahoma questions over and over. "Yes, I've milked a cow before." "No, I don't have a horse." "Yes, I've been cow tipping." I wasn't sure why most of their questions centered on livestock.

I excused myself from Bradley for just a moment to find the powder room. Luckily there was no line, and I locked the door once I was inside. I didn't really have to use the bathroom, but did enjoy a few minutes alone. I took several deep breaths in order to keep myself steady. I began to appraise myself in the mirror, instinctively. In this dim light, I didn't look as plain as I thought I did. My hair was soft and flowed to the middle of my back and my dark blue eyes shone with pleasure. It wasn't a reflection that I'd seen in the past several years.

I snapped out of it when I heard some talking in the hall, just outside the bathroom door. The female voices weren't whispering at all. They were in no way trying to conceal their conversation.

"What in the world is that *one* girl doing here?" one voice said.

"I don't know. What is Bradley thinking?" another one added.

I leaned toward the door and pressed my cheek and ear against it. Were they talking about me?

"Megan said he's spent the whole week with her. I don't know why. She seems boring," the first one added in a high-pitched, nasal tone.

Yep. They had to be talking about me.

"He goes from Miranda to *her*?"

Okie dokie. It took some work for me to pull my eyebrows apart and replace the scowl before I opened the door. I had heard enough. Their words stung my ears just a little bit more than I expected them to, even though I had pretty much been asking myself the same things all week.

I opened the door and had the pleasure of seeing the two goddesses' jaws drop as I walked out of the bathroom.

"I don't know about you girls, but I just can't seem to get used to these *thin* New York City doors." I laughed as I passed by them, giving them a breezy finger wave. My cheeks burned from the slight confrontation, but I smiled a little with the silence I left behind me. I was pulled to the one place I probably should have stayed away from if I wanted to avoid any more hurtful gossip. But I found Bradley quickly and planted myself next to him. He acknowledged me by curling his arm around my waist as he continued fluidly in his conversation. The unexpected familiarity of his arm around me knotted my stomach. I liked it, but it made me mildly uncomfortable in a way I couldn't explain. I smiled sheepishly at Melvin, the only one I felt as comfortable with as Bradley. I didn't know the other man who was standing there with us, but by the looks of him, he had started his partying much earlier in the day. He slurred his words together and shifted his weight often to keep steady.

I had that creepy feeling that someone had their eyes on me. I looked over my left shoulder slowly to see if I could spot the two catty women. It didn't take long. I saw them huddled with several other women, who suddenly stopped talking when they caught me looking in their direction. I giggled slightly as I glanced toward the ground.

I decided that it was probably time to find myself a drink. Maybe a little alcohol would drown out some of the sideways glances. *No, can't stoop to that; I need my wits about me.* I excused myself quietly to find something carbonated.

"I'm gonna get something to drink. You want something?" I asked Bradley as I twisted away from his side.

"No, I'll get it. What do you want?"

"No, no, no. You stay here with your guests. I can manage." I smiled as I started to walk away. "Beer?" I mouthed. He just smiled back and dipped his head once. I saw a familiar look cross his face and a flash of something in his eyes. The slight smile, one raised eyebrow, and a quick shake of the head from side to side. He did this often when I did things for myself or offered to do something for him. He wore a slightly more annoyed expression when I tried to pay for things in his presence. I guess this meant that he wasn't used to that type of behavior. As I tinkered in the kitchen, getting our drinks, I thought about the catty women again. I wondered how they acted around someone like Bradley. Obviously very differently than I did.

I grabbed a few of the empty glasses that were piling up on the counters. I rinsed them out in the sink and absentmindedly lined them on the top shelf of Bradley's top-of-the-line dishwasher. I let my fingertips graze the smooth, dark gray soapstone countertops. I'd never actually seen soapstone in person. I've shown plenty of homes with granite. Even marble, which made no sense to me as a kitchen counter, stains too easily. A couple of people walked into the kitchen and handed me their glasses before walking off, without so much as a word. Super. Now I'm the help…

I grabbed Bradley's beer and got a pop for me. I stared at the bottle of Jack Daniels lined up among the different bottles of alcohol. Then turned with a sigh. *Self-medicating won't help.* This evening was already going so great… I looked at the beer in my hand for Bradley. Should I be condoning his drinking? *What are you, his mother? He's responsible for his own actions; if he doesn't want it, he won't drink it.* I sighed yet again. But I gave myself props for being able to internalize my argument instead of conversing with myself in the kitchen of Bradley's multimillion-dollar apartment.

Bradley wound his long arm around me again after I handed him his beer. He was in the same spot, there with Melvin and the drunk guy. I took a long pull of my drink as they chattered away.

A sharp crack caught my attention, and I jumped back as the glass the drunk guy was holding smashed into the concrete floor in front of me.

"Aw, dude, I'm sorry," he slurred slowly as he bent down to pick up the pieces. "Ow!" he yelled, along with several curse words, as he cupped one of his hands.

"You okay, Cody?" Bradley asked, concerned.

Cody groaned and mumbled a curse as he headed toward the kitchen.

Only a few of us heard the commotion over the several other conversations and the music that filled the apartment. I followed Cody to the kitchen. He had his hands over the porcelain sink. The blood was already pooling into a large puddle. I reached out and turned the water on to a trickle then grabbed his injured hand. I held it under the water for just a moment so I could get an idea of how bad the cut was.

"Is it bad?"

I had no idea that Bradley was next to me until he spoke. I continued to examine the cut. My first-aid training was becoming invaluable on this trip.

"Not sure. Do you have any peroxide or a first-aid kit?" I asked quickly as I twisted Cody's hand under the water to get a better look.

"Peroxide?" Bradley repeated, dazed.

"Yeah. Hydrogen peroxide. It'll be in a brown bottle."

Bradley didn't say a word as he rushed off. Cody swayed from side to side as we stood there next to the sink. I motioned for Melvin to help hold him steady. *Please don't throw up. Please don't throw up*, I thought to myself. Blood I could handle. Someone else losing their lunch—not so much. I saw Bradley walking calmly yet quickly back through the crowd minutes later.

"This it?" he asked as he held up the correct bottle.

I nodded as I took it from him and opened the lid.

"No way! That stuff burns," Cody yelped at me as he tried to cringe away from me. It was a pointless effort. Melvin's large hands kept him from moving more than an inch.

"No. This doesn't burn, I promise. Isopropyl alcohol burns. This is peroxide; it just fizzes. If there are any little pieces of glass in there, we need to get them out." I waited for his posture to relax before I slowly poured the liquid over his bloody palm. The peroxide bubbled away as it did its work.

"There's a lot of blood," Bradley whispered in my ear, slightly concerned.

"He's been drinking, so his blood is just thin. It's not that bad a cut really," I reassured him. "Did you find a first-aid kit?"

Bradley pushed the green canvas bag toward me.

"Can you get out some gauze?"

I poured more peroxide over Cody's palm, and it fizzed very little this time. "I think you're fine. Between the alcohol and the peroxide, I'd say the cut's pretty clean. I'll just wrap it up for you," I told Cody. He nodded in agreement.

Bradley handed me the gauze, and I wrapped it securely around Cody's palm. I could feel Bradley's eyes watching me.

Melvin was still holding Cody in place as he calmly told a few of the guests that it was just a small cut—nothing to worry about.

"There ya go," I chimed as I finished taping the gauze to Cody's hand.

He mumbled a thank you as he stumbled through the crowd. I grabbed some paper towels and started to clean up the bloody mess.

"I can't decide whether you just happen to always be in the right place at the right time or if trouble seems to follow you around," Bradley debated out loud.

"A little bit of both it seems. You better watch out. Spending much more time with me could be dangerous," I answered grimly. I knew there was too much truth behind my words. My presence could be bad for him on many levels. Physically. Emotionally. And especially professionally. Or was it myself I was concerned about? I was already starting to worry about what my friendship would do to his career if too many more people saw us together. I had already heard what some people thought of me. Not that flattering.

"I'll take my chances."

"Ah, I see. A glutton for punishment, are we?"

"If you're what's being doled out as punishment, then yes. Gladly." He chuckled. "So why are you so good at taking care of people?"

"I'm not sure I am," I answered truthfully. "I just grew up in a large family. We all take care of each other."

"Well, you're not the oldest child in your family, I already know that. Older kids tend to be the more protective ones. And you definitely don't seem spoiled, so you're not the baby. So maybe it's a Southern thing," he allowed.

"Maybe," I conceded as I finished cleaning all the red blood from the white porcelain sink. "In my family, at least, all the women are pretty good caregivers. It comes naturally I guess. Not the worst trait I could have picked up."

"So that's it. You're just a 'mother hen' type?"

I laughed at yet another farm analogy. "Guess so."

Thankfully the night wore on without any other major incidents. One by one the party-goers left Bradley's apartment. With every absence it felt as if a weight had been lifted from me. I was very relaxed by the time the last person, Melvin, left.

I flung myself into one of the oversized chairs with a sigh. I reached back and twisted my long hair into a rope and brought it around my neck to rest it over my shoulder.

Bradley made himself comfortable in the couch across from me. "Well, that went well. Only one injury and only one broken object."

"You mean things are usually a little more rowdy?"

"Sometimes."

I looked around at the apartment again. It showed no signs of ever having any major damage done to it. Then again, why would it? He must have seen my wandering eyes and misjudged my thoughts.

"Don't like my place?"

"What?" I asked dumbly before I caught on to what he was thinking. "Oh, well, yes. It's very elegant."

"Elegant," he said with a frown.

I looked around again and shrugged. Not very homey. "It could use a throw pillow or two I guess."

He quirked an eyebrow and moved on. "Question time," Bradley said as he pitched forward a little.

"Question time?"

"Is your given name Evelyn?"

"No." I chuckled lightly. I had been asked that several times before. "My mom has a thing about that. She names her kids what she wants them to be called. She wanted me to be called Evie, so she named me Evie."

"What's your favorite movie?"

I laughed. "Will I be in trouble if it's not one of *your* movies?"

"No." He laughed back. "It's okay. There aren't that many to choose from... So?"

"*The Princess Bride.*"

"'As you wish,'" he quoted. "Okay, sappy romantic stuff full of dry humor. Could've probably guessed that much."

"Hey! I like other stuff too. That's a hard question. I like a lot."

"Next. Favorite food?"

"Chicken 'n dumplings," I answered quickly. I was a little off-put by the rapid gunfire-type questioning.

He pulled his eyebrows together a little. I wasn't sure if it was because he didn't know what it was for sure or because that wouldn't be what he guessed. "What?"

"I figured it'd be salad or something boring like that. That's pretty much all you've eaten around me this week."

"Well, I try to eat healthy: a lot of fruits and veggies, as organic as possible, small amounts of red meat, but I'm still a sucker for Southern food. And pop. And sweets..."

"So what gives? Why all the chick food? Afraid to eat in front of me?"

"It's not like I've been faking anything for your benefit. I told you that's what I really eat. I eat what sounds good to me. I really am a sucker for sweets. You've seen me eat cake and pop and junk like that while I've been here," I reminded him. "I don't have that much willpower."

"You obviously have quite a bit, or else I'd be wheeling you around New York City using a dolly...or a forklift or something." He chuckled.

I rolled my eyes. I thought for a moment that if I really were that big I probably wouldn't be sitting here having this conversation with him. I instantly chided myself. Nothing in the last week I had spent with Bradley should lead me to that conclusion. He hasn't acted the least bit shallow.

"Speaking of," I said as I got up and moved toward the kitchen. I opened up his Sub-Zero fridge and spotted an unopened two liter of Coke. "Have any chocolate syrup?" I asked as I poked my head around the door to look at Bradley.

"Uh...don't think so. I can get you some though."

"No, we don't need to make a special trip. Nevermind."

"What we? It'll be here in fifteen minutes," he promised as he quickly typed something on his phone.

I just shut the refrigerator door and walked back to the living room. I couldn't make my feet go all the way back to the chair I was sitting in previously. I sat on the couch with him—cross-legged near the arm. His place was eerily quiet. He stared back at me while I marveled over his good looks. It was late at night, and the dark scruff I liked so much had started to fill in around his jaw and lower cheeks.

"What's your favorite movie and food—well, I can probably guess the food. Steak?" I asked, breaking the comfortable silence.

He grinned crookedly. "Yeah, steak's probably my favorite. I guess my ordering it nearly every meal while I've been with you gave that away. Favorite movie? I have a lot too. Probably *The Shining*.

I grimaced.

"No good?" he asked in surprise.

"I don't do scary movies. I have an overactive imagination and a heightened sense of paranoia," I admitted. "I mean, I can watch vampire or alien movies, but psychopathic killer movies freak me out. I don't believe in supernatural stuff, but there are plenty of warped yahoos out there who kill people in real life. I don't need to see it for entertainment purposes. And I really don't see the point of making movies like that and giving those wackos more ideas than they already have."

Bradley tried to hide his laughter by rubbing the back of his hand across his mouth. I glared back at him.

I heard his phone buzz. He got up and went to the small intercom-looking box next to the elevator door we came through when we arrived. He pushed the red button. "Mack."

"Yes, Mr. Matthews," an unknown voice answered immediately.

"Frankie will be here in just a few with a delivery. He can come on up."

"Sure thing, Mr. Matthews."

"You sent someone out to get chocolate syrup?" I asked, shocked.

"Yeah." He chuckled again. "I have to know what you plan on doing with chocolate syrup." He winked.

"Ugh. I'm sure it's nothing as interesting as what your imagination is conjuring up."

"We'll see." Again with the sideways grin.

"So anything you want—you can just get it delivered. Any time?"

"Pretty much. This is probably the strangest thing I've ever requested though," he admitted.

I thought about this perk. Seemed a little unnecessary. "I coulda just ran down to a quick store or something," I offered.

"Yeah, right. Like I'd let you run around New York City at this time of night by yourself. And I'm too comfortable here with you to leave. Besides, what good is it to have all this money if I can't spread it around a little?"

I shrugged. I didn't know what the going rate was for a delivered bottle of chocolate syrup. I probably didn't want to know.

A few minutes later, the elevator doors opened. A young man with red hair and a freckled face walked forward, to Bradley. He slipped the earphones out of his ears and smacked his gum while he rummaged through his messenger bag. Bradley handed him a few folded bills and Frankie, I guessed, handed him the chocolate syrup. I felt my cheeks burn when he looked my direction, and he flashed a full set of teeth back at me. I could only imagine what this guy was thinking we'd be doing with syrup. Probably a version of what was roaming through Bradley's head. Yikes. Men. I was relieved when the doors shut again.

"All right," Bradley sang as he handed me the bottle. "Have at it."

I snatched the bottle out of his hand and headed toward the kitchen. I could feel him following closely behind me.

I grabbed a glass out of the whitewashed upper cabinet next to the sink. Then I filled it up with ice.

"Well, it's not chocolate milk," Bradley guessed.

I laughed as I poured the Coke into the glass.

"Spoon?" I asked.

Bradley froze for a minute then spun around. He had to open a few drawers before he found the one full of silverware. In this house it probably really was silver. Not the cheap-o metal kind that filled my drawer back home. He handed me the spoon. I squeezed a liberal amount of chocolate syrup on top of the ice and Coke and stirred it briskly.

"Ew! Chocolate Coke?"

"Hey, don't knock it till you've tried it," I snickered back. "You wanna try it?"

"Heck no."

"You're such a Nancy. Why not?"

"Look at it." He scowled as he pointed to my favorite drink. "It's...frothy."

"You drink beer; it's frothy," I accused.

"No," he said quickly. "Beer's *foamy*."

"Oh my word! Same difference."

"Uh, no. Not the same." He shook his head from side to side as he leaned against the counter, slack hipped. I took a long, exaggerated drink, and it made him quiver in disgust. I giggled.

"Told ya it wasn't that interesting," I said again.

"No, it's interesting. Just...nasty too."

His unwarranted loathing made me giggle again as I walked back into the living room. He walked back in with a beer. We were both on the couch again, and he mindlessly flipped on the television. The large screen lit up the room, which had been dimly lit during the party. We sat there, silently, simply enjoying each other's company. I yawned without being able to suppress it.

"If you're tired, we can go to bed," he offered with a suggestive wink.

Us. Bed? Oh man. "It's pretty late," I spit out promptly. "I should probably get back to the hotel."

"You can stay here, you know," he deadpanned. Something told me he was working harder than I could tell to keep his face expressionless.

Yeah, I knew. But something stopped me. I wasn't sure if it was because I didn't want to see the faces of the building employees judging me in the morning or if it was because I really wanted to stay with him. I didn't feel so alone when I was with him. Not just because of the obvious fact that I literally wasn't alone, but like the vacancy of my body, of my heart, didn't seem so apparent when I was with Bradley. I had been hollow for so long, but now I could feel parts of me filling back up again. I had grown accustomed to his presence, and that scared me. What would I do when I went back home and the aloneness was back too?

"I should probably go," I mumbled as I dropped my head. "It's just that…"

"No, it's okay. I understand," he assured me as he stood up. "I can take you back."

"No," I said firmly as I stood up next to him. "You've been drinking. I'll take a cab."

"Then I'll go with you."

"You don't have to," I mumbled again, staring at my feet. But I wanted him too. I wanted to soak up every minute I could with him. I only had one day left. I knew if I looked up right now, those thoughts would resonate on my face and in my eyes.

"I know. I want to. Come on," he said as he grabbed my hand and towed me toward the elevator.

We walked quickly through his building, and the doorman got us a cab. I noticed the cab driver looking back at us often in the rearview mirror. It made me anxious. Bradley didn't seem to notice, but he didn't make much conversation either. He was probably used to it. Bradley grabbed my hand and gave it a squeeze before I got out of the cab.

I made it back to my recleaned room and got ready for bed. In bed my thoughts turned to Bradley. I could still smell his sweet cologne on me. I couldn't sleep. I heard my phone vibrate against the wood nightstand.

It was a text, from Bradley. I smiled.

You left your disgusting drink here.

I laughed out loud, and then responded.

You drank the rest of it, didn't you? Don't lie.

It took only a few seconds for my phone to buzz again.

Definitely NOT.

I didn't respond. My phone buzzed again.

Last night in NYC tomorrow. Early dinner?

I was happy that he wanted to spend another night with me.

Sounds great. See you tomorrow.

I placed my phone back on the nightstand. I didn't hear it vibrate again, and it seemed to only take minutes before I was dreaming.

CHAPTER 10

We were having dinner tonight at "The G" as he called it. That's what he called the restaurant we went to that first night. We were meeting a little earlier than usual too, since tonight was my last night in New York. I would need to get back to a more normal sleeping schedule. He texted me the address, fake name, and what time to meet him. He had grown increasingly busy during my stay. So on a couple of occasions, like tonight, I would take a cab to meet him.

So there I was standing in front of the mirror in my fabulous hotel room that overlooked Central Park. I was all ready and just waiting a few more minutes before I headed out. I was taking stock of myself again. Kinda like I was about to go on a date, but I still didn't feel like that was really the case. Bradley hadn't really acted like that was the case. Or maybe it was me? After all, he did offer to let me stay at his place last night. I raked my fingers through my hair and sighed, not knowing how to piece everything together.

But we'd had such a great week. Laughing a lot. An unexpected friendship nonetheless, but a welcomed one. I still felt like a different person. Like there was part of me that was still holding back, but I couldn't figure out what that part was. But I was happy and that was a nice change of pace.

Eventually I went downstairs, and a cab was hailed for me. The ride wasn't long, and in minutes I handed the cabbie his fare and walked into "The G." I gave the brunette hostess the fake name: Annie Oakley. Funny, Bradley. She instantly smiled and motioned to the man standing near her. I followed him through the front part of the restaurant. It was dimly lit and already full of people. It was elegant but had a retro feel to it. Large, paper-looking orange globes hung low over each table, which tinted the room a slight tangerine.

We went through a back door, and I instantly recalled the long, bare hallway with a door on each side and another at the other end. We walked halfway—to the doors in the middle. He opened the one on our right, and there it was, the same room from several nights ago. I walked through, and he closed the door behind me.

Bradley was there at the huge booth, by himself. My stomach flip-flopped. That caught me a little off guard. I had assumed that the "crew" would be here tonight too. At least Mel…

"There you are. I was about to text you to see if you got lost." He was grinning from ear to ear.

I walked toward the booth, toward him. "Nah," I replied. Soft music was playing in the background, and this room was just as dimly lit as the front room. There was a small arrangement of red roses in the center of the table with a few tea lights surrounding it. I scooted into the booth, to the middle—where he was.

"I hope you don't mind that it's just us tonight."

"Not at all," I lied.

"I took the liberty of ordering you a Coke." He pointed to the drink in front of me.

"As long as there's no Jack in it," I joked.

He chuckled. "No. Don't want you to be hung over on your way home tomorrow."

"Me neither. I have to be alert in case there's someone else who decides to choke or go into cardiac arrest."

"True, true." He paused to take a drink. "So, have you enjoyed your trip?"

"Oh yeah. It's been…unbelievable. Thank you." I was staring at my hands, which were lying in my lap.

"You're very welcome," he said earnestly.

I could tell he was smiling. I looked up to confirm it, and my insides fired up. His eyes darkened, and my smile faltered. "It's too bad that I don't get to go home and tell everyone the true story though," I said after clearly the thickness from my throat.

"What do you mean?" he asked curiously.

"Well, it's not like I'm gonna go home and blab to everyone that I spent the whole week with *Bradley Matthews*."

His eyebrows winged up in surprise.

"Why not?"

"For one, no one would believe me. Secondly—well—I guess that's it. No one would believe me." And that was the truth. I wanted to tell my little sister pretty bad. She was a huge fan, but I had a feeling she wouldn't be able to keep her mouth shut.

He looked thoughtful for a moment then started to laugh dryly. I just took a sip of my Coke.

"So," he said seriously, "there's something I've got to ask."

"Uh oh." I chuckled. But the way he said it really did scare me a little.

"You've never mentioned it, but I didn't know if it's because you were with me or…" He trailed off without making his point.

"Never mentioned what?" I couldn't imagine where this was going.

"If you have a boyfriend or something. I haven't seen a ring on your finger, so I'm assuming you aren't married or engaged, but I never explicitly asked. Are you spoken for?"

My heart sank. *Yikes.* I thought I'd successfully avoided this embarrassing conversation. I cleared my throat. "Umm…no." My response was barely audible. I was hoping he'd pick up on my obvious lack of comfort.

He straightened up a little. I looked up at him again, and his eyebrows were furrowed together in thought. "Hummm."

He was quiet for a minute, and I thought that I had escaped an explanation. "May I ask why not?"

I was wrong. I took a deep breath. Maybe I could nip this in the bud... "I—I dunno. For the past few years I've just been working a lot and haven't had much interest in dating."

"You've said something like that a few times before. The 'for a few years' part," he pressed.

"Ummhumm."

"Why is that? I mean, what happened a few years ago?"

He obviously wasn't going to let this go. It should have been obvious that the subject was uncomfortable for me. And he either hadn't pieced it together or had and wanted more details. This was going to turn into a personal conversation. We'd somehow avoided these kinds of questions all week.

I took a deep breath. "You really wanna know?" I questioned, a little too harshly.

My tone must have taken him by surprise a little because I saw his Adam's apple move distinctly while he swallowed. "Yes," he finally admitted. "If you *want* to tell me."

I sucked in another deep breath. I really didn't know if I could tell him without breaking down. But I knew if I didn't give some sort of explanation, the rest of the evening would be awkward and ruined.

Just then the server walked in to take our order. She stood at the table waiting for us to acknowledge her, but we were both staring at each other now.

"I'll have the usual," he said without looking at her.

I broke our gaze to order. I needed just a moment to gather myself, and I couldn't do that if I kept staring into his beautiful eyes, the perfect mix of blue-green. "I'll have the grilled chicken Caesar and a bowl of the Tuscan soup." The server didn't linger.

I looked back at Bradley, who was still staring me down. I quickly ran over the tragic story in my head. But maybe to him it wouldn't be so tragic. Maybe it was only tragic to me. After all, it seemed as if everyone else was able to move on just fine. Josh's siblings, his grandpa and grandma that he was really close with. Everyone seemed to be able to go back to their normal lives. Everyone except for me. I opened my mouth to speak, but nothing came out. I cleared my throat and tried again.

"My junior year at OSU, I met a guy," I started. "I was working at a flower shop, and he came in to buy something. He ended up asking me out, and well, we were inseparable after that." *Skip to the point,* I told myself. "It was like we both knew, instantly, that we belonged together. Cheesy, I know." He smiled, but it didn't reach his eyes. Like he knew that this was hard for me but I was trying to make light of it. For his sake or mine? "So we dated for a couple of years. My family loved him, and everything was great," I continued.

He raised his hand slowly like a shy kid in school who wanted to ask a question but was scared of the teacher. I stopped talking to give him a chance to speak.

"Okay, sorry, hate to interrupt, but how did you guys know that you belonged together…so quickly?" His tone wasn't skeptical at all. It was urgent and thoughtful. Like he was doing research, and he *really* needed to know how the idea of love at first sight worked.

"I—I—I dunno," I stuttered. I blinked several times and then continued. "I really don't know. I just remember being instantly struck by him. Like I was possessed. After that first date, I knew that I wanted to be with him forever." My voice broke on the last word. He eased back into the bench, crossed his arms over his chest, and nodded his head as if my weak explanation appeased him, for now. His eyebrows pulled together as he waited for me to continue.

I sighed. "So after a couple of years, we got engaged. I had graduated the year before and had just started a new job. He was going to go down to OU—that's about two hours away—to do some more school but was waiting for me to graduate. We didn't want to be apart, especially during our…engagement." I was glancing all around me. I wasn't able to keep eye contact with Bradley, so my eyes were constantly shifting: to the bartender, the table, my Coke, the flowers. "He got a job chasing storms." I was starting to have a little trouble getting the words out now. "We both loved storms and had gotten a little obsessed with them. Josh so much so that he wanted to make a career out of it." I noticed that I said his name, but Bradley didn't flinch. He had the same blank expression on his face, but I could tell he was listening very intently to every word.

I had to stop to draw in a long breath; I needed more oxygen to the brain, or I'd pass out. "Then, uh, a few weeks before the wedding, he went out with his buddy to chase a particular storm. We had just bought a house, so I was there doing some painting." There was a long pause. He didn't push me to finish, but I pushed myself. "He never came home. He was killed in the storm," I finally muttered. I sat there, frozen, waiting for the onslaught of tears. But they didn't come, to my surprise and relief. I was strangely proud of myself for getting through the story without turning into a blubbering idiot. I had somehow managed, a few days ago, to briefly mention to Bradley how my dad died, without crying, after he asked the standard "what do your parents do" question. Maybe all the years of being numb changed me more than I thought. Or maybe it was just because I was so comfortable, strangely comfortable, with Bradley.

He still hadn't said anything. But he slowly dropped his arms and leaned forward. He braced himself, one hand on the table and one hand on the bench in the space between us. I was looking down, but I could tell that he was shaking his head. He moved the hand that was on the table, and with one long finger, he gently raised my chin to look into my eyes. Maybe he was checking for tears. At this point, for all I knew, there were tears streaming down my face.

"I'm. So. Sorry," he murmured.

"It's okay. You didn't kill him." My crude attempt at lightening the mood failed. I just shrugged and pulled my chin down again. He dropped his hand.

"How did you…deal with that?" he asked timidly.

"Not well." I barked out with a nervous laugh. "I, um, went into shock when I got the call. My mom and brothers had to come get me. The next few months are kinda a blur. I just stayed in bed, but I don't remember sleeping. I just rotted away basically."

"I'm sorry, I shouldn't have pried."

"It's okay. Honestly, I wasn't sure if I'd be able to tell you. I haven't really told anyone."

"What do you mean?" His eyebrows pulled together, his eyes curious.

"Well, everyone I knew already knew the story. I was such a hermit after that. This is the first time I've had to…explain it to someone."

"I'm sorry," he whispered again.

I was able to make eye contact with him a little easier now. "It's okay. Really. It's kinda nice to know I can talk about it now without breaking down. I should be able to. It's been over three years," I rationalized.

"I—I can't even imagine. You've already lost so much, and you're so young. But you seem…okay." His remark was in declarative form, but it came out more like a question.

"I didn't really know I was okay, really, till now. I mean it still hurts, a lot, but I don't know…" I pulled my fingers through my long hair. "I don't know how to explain it. I've just kinda been in—a world of white noise."

He cocked his head to the side.

"I've just been going through the motions. Work. Eat. Sleep. I wasn't really…living, just staying alive," I confessed. "That probably doesn't make any sense…"

"Yeah, I guess it does. I mean, everyone deals with loss differently. Me, for instance, I'd probably just be furious and mad at the world—"

"Oh, I was!" I interjected. "I moved back in with my mom then because I couldn't bear to go back to the house we'd just bought, and I think I nearly drove her nuts. I blamed everyone I could, and it didn't help. I blamed Josh. I blamed me. I blamed the guy he was with that night...I even tried to blame God." I shuddered at the thought.

"How'd that help?" he challenged.

"It didn't. Just made me feel worse. But I think it's a natural response for some people. To blame someone who can't fight back—directly. It's a way to try to find some kind of power during a helpless situation. But that was a fight that neither of us won."

"Who won then?"

"Satan. He's the only winner in that situation. Because God and my family understood the pain I was in and they forgave me for my horrible behavior, even before I asked them to, before I even deserved it. But the devil, well, he's like a lion. He's always prowling around us, waiting. Waiting for a moment when we're weak. And just like in the wild, a predator will watch and try to find the weakest of a herd. The sick or lame. And when we're at our weakest, he pounces and sinks his claws in, pulling us further into the darkness."

"Wow," he said bluntly, with eyes wide. "Never thought of it that way."

"So, yeah, for a few dark months, well, years really, I gave into the self-pity and let myself rot away. I was able to snap out of it, but that time had left its mark I guess, because I didn't really go back to 'normal.'" I did the air quotes. "But I always knew, deep down, that nobody really killed Josh. I never really thought that because I knew it was an accident. It's just the 'why,' 'why him' mode that I got stuck in. I was selfish."

"It's not selfish," he tried to reassure me. He opened his mouth like he was about to ask another question but stopped.

"What?"

"I was going to ask you something, but I thought it may be... too painful."

I was morbidly curious now. I could tell that he was interested for some reason. Research? "If it is, I'll tell you."

He cleared his throat and stared off to the side of the room, like he was searching for just the right words. "Now, I know you mentioned a couple of days ago that your dad died when you were young." He paused then tousled his hair. "Well, how was Josh's death different, if it was at all? I'm sorry," he said instantly. "That's probably rude..."

"No, um..." I looked up at the ceiling while thinking. What? Did I think the answer was written up there? Honestly, I'd never thought about what he was asking me. "I don't know. I was so young when my dad died. I don't think I really processed it properly," I said, bringing my eyes back down to meet his. He said nothing; was he hoping I'd elaborate? "I just remember thinking he was gone, on business or something, and he was just taking a long time to get back." I laughed. It sounded so ridiculous when I said it out loud. "But as I got older, I just started to focus on how he wouldn't be there for all the big moments, you know? I don't know. I guess I felt like I was growing up with a hole in my heart. I think the worst part is how hard it is to remember him now. Your body's natural response is to forget, to help you move on. I have just a handful of memories now. And sometimes I wonder if they're *really* memories at all or just some kinda subconscious manifestation of how I *want* to remember things. There's just a lot of drama too...won't bore you with that."

He managed a half smile but still didn't say anything. I had a sudden impulse to continue.

"Then, with my Gramps, it was completely different. I was pretty close to him. He was the strong male role model in my life. The constant among a thousand variables. He was a big teddy bear, but he was also the type of man you'd never want to make mad because you feared his reaction. And his laugh…" I just shook my head and smiled. "He died the summer before my senior year in high school. That night was horrible, but it was easier for me to find peace with that loss. He'd lived a full life and there was no doubt that he was in a better place and that he'd still be with us, in some small way. But it was more heart-wrenching to watch my family in pain. I'd never experienced that before. My Gran lost her husband of over fifty years. My mom, aunt, and uncle lost their dad unexpectedly. It was painful because I had already experienced that level of grief and didn't like seeing them go through it."

Bradley was still staring into my eyes, which to my surprise, were still dry. What a strange affect this man had on me. Through my entire monologue, he just nodded along. He let me just get it all out.

"Then Josh…" My tone was a little more pensive now. "Well, that was just like someone stole my spirit away. My soul was cracked. Like I thought there wasn't much point to going on after that. But it wasn't just his death. It was everything. Like…"

"At that moment everything took its toll," he interjected.

"Yes!" I exclaimed, a little relieved to have someone put it together. "Every cruel word, every loss, every speeding ticket, stubbed toe, crushed hope, burned dinner, bad date, flat tire, bounced check, bad day all added up till I was at my breaking point, and I just…just…!" I trailed off and flung my arms in the air.

"Imploded," Bradley said with a faraway look in his eyes.

"Yes," I whispered. "It's not like my family wouldn't have helped if I would have let them or if they knew how. They loved me and kept me around even though I was acting like a twenty-something toddler, and that's more than I deserved. But I've had the 'back off' look firmly plastered on my face the past few years, and suckin' it up and moving on is just how my family operates."

Bradley opened his mouth and then clamped it shut.

"Go ahead, ask," I said with a smile, guessing there was something he wanted to ask.

"I was just thinking. It seems like everyone around you seemed to move on a little easier than you after a death. I wonder if you made yourself miserable by grieving so long because you felt like it was your only connection. Your pain and loss connected you to not only Josh but to your dad."

I sat there, a little stunned. It made perfect sense. I *had* made myself miserable because I was afraid of what life might be like without them. So I carried around my grief as a way to keep me linked to those I lost. Bizarre. "Very insightful," I commented.

After a few silent moments, I nodded. "So there it is. My sob story. Betchya wish you hadn't asked me that question," I teased.

"Well, oddly, I'm not. I feel like I know you, er, understand you a little better."

"Was I *that* mysterious?" I seriously doubted that. I felt like a guppy around him. Like he could see right through me and now he saw a few of my dark spots and hadn't bolted toward the door. Yet.

"Kind of." He shrugged then took a long pull from his drink.

I just nodded again. The room was silent as the soft music in the background faded before a new song started. I heard the door open and saw the server walking in with our dinner.

It was a little too quiet now.

"So, I guess I could ask you the same question," I said with forced nonchalance.

"What do you mean?"

"Why are *you* still single?" I asked as I quirked up an eyebrow.

"Oh." He laughed. "No sad story there. Just haven't found the right one I guess."

"Bor-ring," I joked. He just laughed as he cut his steak, so I turned my attention to my dinner.

He seemed a little distant after that. Maybe it was a mistake telling him about Josh and everything else. Maybe he was offended by me asking about his love life. After all, I did know that he was a pretty private person. But surely he knew that I wouldn't go around blabbing to everyone about it. The rest of the conversation that night was light and centered on my life getting back to normal tomorrow. It sank in again that this would probably be the last time I would see, or probably even speak, with Bradley. I had kind of gotten attached to him, and the way he took care of me made me feel cherished. I wasn't sure if I was ready for the responsibility of a "relationship" (even though I knew that wasn't where this was going), but he sure was cute and fun to have around.

I guess Bradley pre-ordered a chocolate lava cake, because it was brought out just as I was finishing up dinner. He apologetically joked that they wouldn't make a chocolate Coke. Since he had found out about my untamable sweet tooth and that chocolate cake and chocolate-covered strawberries were my absolute favorite, he made sure to have something sweet for me. I was sinking my fork in when he reached for his phone.

"What is it?" he barked into the phone. His tone was more harsh than usual. "Ah, crap. Okay, we're almost done. We'll just go out the back and—" His eyes narrowed. His full lips pressed firmly into a frigid line before releasing an exasperated breath. I was trying not to stare, but I couldn't understand what was wrong. "Just have the car ready out front; we'll be there in a few."

I waited for an explanation, not that he owed me one, but he just groaned.

"Everything okay?" I finally inquired a wee bit apprehensive.

"Not exactly." He paused. "It seems we've been...followed."

"Followed?"

"Paparazzi."

"Ah." Guess he really *is* Bradley Matthews. "Do we need to leave?"

"You can finish your dessert." His face softened. The edge that was in his eyes was gone now too. "Hate for you to miss out on your daily chocolate fix," he joked.

"You and me both!" I winked.

I finished as quickly as I could because I could tell that he was anxious. His knee bounced underneath the table, and his fingers tapped the back of his iPhone. "So what's the plan?"

"Mel's out front waiting."

I started to scoot out of the booth. He put his arm around my shoulder and drew me closer to his warmth.

"I had a nice time tonight, as always," he murmured warmly. He dropped his arm and inhaled sharply. "You ready?"

"Guess so." I chuckled. I didn't really know what to expect.

He led me through the restaurant, and I could hear the commotion as we approached the front. When the front doors came into view, I gasped as a couple exited. There had to be a dozen photographers outside, just waiting.

He pulled me closer. "Just hang on to me, duck your head, and head for the car."

I nodded as we walked through the door.

Here we go.

It was utter chaos. Just as you'd expect it to be. I could hear everyone talking, no—yelling, at once.

"Bradley! Hey, Bradley! Over here!"

"Who's the girl?"

I just ducked my head, as he told me. His arm was no longer around my shoulder. He had dropped it as we walked out to grab my hand. I was being tugged along behind him as he made his way to the SUV. I could feel the photographers next to me—too close. The lights from the flashes made me squint.

"Back *off!*" Bradley snapped.

Suddenly his hand was no longer soldered to mine, and I was knocked to the ground, getting trampled. I yelped as something hard and heavy hit my head. I rolled to my back and put my feet in the air—violently kicking, trying to make room for myself. I made contact a few times with something or someone, but it didn't seem to improve my situation. All the leeches were hovering over me now, still snapping away. I was using my small purse to shield my face.

"Bradley!" I shrieked.

I continued to fight, trying to make it to my feet so that I could run. Why wasn't my karate class training kicking in now, as my CPR training did on the plane and at Bradley's house? I thought, exasperated. I tired to focus my eyes, but the pain from the blow to my temple made it difficult. Or maybe it was the blood trickling down my face. Either way, I couldn't see how to get out. I felt instant relief when I heard Melvin's voice booming over all the others.

"Outta my way!" He bellowed over and over as he pushed the attackers aside. In one motion he grabbed my arm and threw me over his shoulder like a firefighter. With his free hand, he continued to knock down whoever stood in our way as he blazed a trail through the crowd. In another quick yet smooth motion, I was being tossed into the back of Bradley's SUV. By the time I noticed where I was, the door was closed.

I could feel something wet all over my face. Blood, sweat, and tears no doubt. I was struggling to catch my breath when Bradley pulled me to his strong chest. I heard another car door slam, and we took off violently.

"She's pretty messed up, boss," Mel called from the front seat.

"I know, I know," Bradley called back angrily.

I still hadn't said anything. I was confused and shaking, but for the moment, being so close to Bradley, I didn't care how "messed up" I was. But just then, he grabbed my arms and pulled me back for examination. He gently swept the matted hair from my face and gasped slightly.

"That bad?" I was still panting, my head pounding with every rapid beat of my heart.

He ignored me to yell to Melvin, "We need to get her to a hospital...she needs stitches I think." His tone was distracting. He had always been so cool, calm, and collected. But there was anxiety and pain in his voice now.

"I'm okay," I tried to soothe him, but I reached up to my face and my fingers trembled as I grazed the gash.

I heard a ripping sound and looked back at him. He had ripped the sleeve clean off his shirt. He folded it a couple of times and pressed it gently to the side of my head.

"Ah." I tried not to wince at the pain. "That wasn't completely necessary," I quipped.

"Yeah, it is," he said severely. There was a smile on his face, but it was completely unnatural. "I don't want blood all over my car," he tried to joke.

He removed the shirtsleeve and refolded it before he placed it back on my face. He maneuvered me so that I was mostly in his lap. I didn't complain about this new position. It felt good to be held. The yearning I felt now, to be closer to him, was...puzzling.

"It can't be that bad. I'll be okay."

No one answered.

So I tried again to lighten things up. "Thanks for saving me, Mel. Leave it to the Okie to get trampled on!"

"No problem, E." He chuckled. "To tell you the truth, I was almost afraid to go in and getchya, girl." He laughed again. "You were going crazy down there, kicking everyone. I was afraid I was gonna catch a wild kick and start talking an octave higher, if you know whatta mean."

"Well, at least a few of them will have a little harder time procreating after tonight." I joined in with him, laughing.

Bradley was the only one not laughing. Mel quickly took notice and changed his tone.

"How do you want to do this? You gonna go in with her?" Mel questioned.

Bradley turned around to look behind us. His face hardened again. "I don't know. It looks like we're being followed."

I had gained control of myself now. My head was throbbing, but I wasn't shaking and I really didn't feel all that bad. "Mel, just try to lose them and then drop me off at the ER," I reasoned.

"No way," Bradley murmured.

"Why not? Things are just going to get even worse if you come with me and you know it. I'm sure I'm fine, and there's no use in you being there, distracting the doctor while he's fixing me." It sounded good to me...

Mel and Bradley exchanged a few looks.

"I just don't feel right about doing that..." he finally replied. "How would I know what's going on? How you are?"

I looked up at him, still cradled in his arms like a baby. His eyes had darkened, and he looked haunted. "I can text you the whole time I'm there, and we can meet up when I'm done...if you want."

He took several deep breaths. I just waited. I knew that he'd have to comply. He really didn't have a choice. He knew that he'd be a distraction and that whoever was following us would be just one of many. "Are you *sure* you're okay with that... Because if you—"

"I promise," I said easily. I smiled up at him, but he was reluctant to smile back. His eyes were searching mine, trying to find some emotion there...

"We're almost there," Mel informed us.

I scrambled out of Bradley's lap. I had one hand on the door handle, ready to jump out. I realized that he had hold of my other hand, not wanting to let go. We pulled into the ER, and once under the portico, I opened the door slightly. I twisted my hand free of his, grabbed my purse, and looked back at him. "I have my phone. Bug me all you want," I said as I held up my purse.

I hopped out before Bradley could change his mind, and the SUV sped off. I walked into the bustling emergency room and sighed. It looked like I was going be here for a while.

CHAPTER 11

The next morning I woke slowly but couldn't bring myself to open my eyes. I also knew I was in a bed, but I couldn't immediately remember how I got there. Oh yeah-long night plus pain pills equals fuzzy memory. I rolled onto my back and stretched. Bad idea. So very sore. It felt like I'd been punched in the ribs. Then it all came back to me. I was punched in the ribs, or kicked, last night. Sitting in the emergency waiting room, getting treated, and getting back to the hotel was a blur. I squeezed my eyes tighter as I tried to stretch out again, a little more carefully this time. My right hand grazed something warm and substantial. I snapped my head to the side, another bad idea. I slowly opened my eyes.

"Oh," I croaked as my eyes struggled to focus on the face in front of me. Bradley's face.

I sat up even more slowly and put my face in my hands. I felt the stiff sutures on my left temple. I gently brushed them with my fingertips, trying to count them. Seven, I thought.

"Good morning. How are you feeling?" Bradley's voice was full of sleep and sounded rough.

"I dunno yet," I mumbled as I swung my legs to the side of the bed. "Whoa…" I murmured, feeling a little woozy. I felt him move behind me, and I shuddered when he put his large hands on my back.

He misread my reaction and withdrew immediately.

"Are you upset that I'm here?" he whispered thickly. He had no idea that his presence warmed me. Probably because of my reaction the other night when he told me I could stay at his place.

"No, no. I'm just a little confused." I looked at the clock. Eleven a.m. Oh man. I only had a few hours till I was supposed to get on a plane.

"Now you know how it feels," he chided.

"What?"

"Last night. You didn't text me when you got back."

I just shook my head, my brain throbbing with each infinitesimal movement. I didn't remember *anything* that happened after I walked into the ER, so Bradley continued.

"You said you were about to leave the hospital and that you'd text me when you made it here. After thirty minutes, I started to panic. I called and called and texted. Nothing! So I finally just decided to come here. And here you were. Passed out. Again!" He chuckled softly.

I stood up. "Oh. Sorry. I don't know what happened." I walked across the room to the floor-length mirror. Good night! I was a mess—still in the same clothes from last night, covered in blood. Makeup smeared everywhere. I looked like I'd been run over by a bus. And that's what I felt like too.

"So...you're not mad that I showed up and stayed. Here. With you?"

"No, not at all. You didn't have to though," I replied somewhat absently. I was still appraising myself in the mirror, and I was still a mess.

"No, I always stay the night with my friends after they get trampled because of me." He got out of bed. I just glanced at him from the corner of my eye. I didn't want him to get a good look at me. He was fully dressed, but in different clothes from last night.

"Oh, good," I finally responded. "I'd hate to get unequal treatment," I teased. "I think I'm going to take a shower and clean up a little. I look like death warmed over." I grabbed a change of clothes as he laughed. He headed toward the sitting room and turned on the television.

The hot water felt good, pounding the soreness from my muscles and removing the grime. The longer I was up and around, the better I felt, and the more my head cleared. My face was a little sore, but not bad. I gave myself a once over when I got out of the shower. My ribs were decorated with several blue, purple, and black bruises. I got dressed quickly and threw on what little makeup I could. Foundation, blush, and mascara—the bare necessities. I combed through my long hair and left it wet.

"That was quick." He smiled a little crookedly as I walked out of the bathroom. I guess he was used to having to wait a little longer for a woman to get ready. I guess there's a plus to not being a model.

"I get anxious when I know people are waiting on me."

"I'd wait for you," he said, suddenly solemn, his ocean eyes piercing mine.

His serious tone caught me off guard. I kept expecting him to laugh. Instead, I was the one who had to bite my lip to keep from laughing.

"What?"

"Nothing. Well, that just sounded like a line from a Bryan Adams song or something," I giggled as I scrunched my wet hair to bring out a little more curl.

"Got a problem with Bryan Adams?"

"No, he's my favorite Canadian. I don't know…it just struck me funny." I sighed. "Leave me alone; I'm still suffering from a head injury here!" I pointed out my stitches—like they were hard to miss.

He just snickered.

He was flipping through the channels on the TV. He whipped out his phone and waved it through the air. Since it was all lit up, I figured someone was calling.

"It's Mel. He was worried about you too," he told me before answering the call. "Howdy!" He gave me a little wink when he used my greeting. "Yeah...what channel? Okay," he growled.

"Problem?"

He didn't immediately respond. He just flipped through the channels, but with a purpose this time. He finally stopped when he reached some news program.

"Mel said that they're talking about what happened to us last night," he finally said as he patted the seat next to him, beckoning me to sit by him.

They? My eyes were glued to the screen as I made my way next to him. "No way. I don't remember any video cameras." Like I would have noticed a tank barreling down the street with all the commotion...

The TV host just referred to me as an "unidentified woman." Brutal. But I guess it's good that they didn't know who I was.

"Man, what a melee. Look at you, babe! You got at least three of them in the nads!" He slapped my leg in excitement.

"Look at Mel!" I squealed in delight. Watching the episode play out on the television felt like warped déjà vu.

Mel was right about being hesitant to rush in to get me when I was thrashing around on the ground. Somehow he managed to use both of his arms to get through the crowd *and* was still be able to defend his...manland at the same time. It was hilarious, and it was all we could do to keep our laughs at a respectable level.

Bradley quickly sobered up as the image of Mel throwing me over his shoulder flickered across the screen. "That should have been me saving you."

I stared at him. What a weird thing to say. Knight in shining armor complex? "Hey now, don't beat yourself up. We can't have your pretty face getting all mangled like me!" I teased as I grabbed his face with my hands, without thinking. It was the first time I'd deliberately touched any part of him, and I immediately felt a quick jolt in the pit of my stomach because of the action.

Again, he didn't say or do anything. Something flashed in his eyes but was quickly masked. I let my hand drop. My palms prickled from the sensation of his stubble. I was instantly angry with myself for changing the casual atmosphere between us.

"I'm sorry I got you into that," he mumbled, breaking the long silence.

"Oh stop that. It wasn't your fault."

"Oh really? Would you have been maimed by paparazzi if you'd been with any other normal guy?" he barked. He worked a hand over his face as he groaned.

"Probably not." I paused, and he seemed to nod his head in agreement. "But I also wouldn't have had such an incredible week. Nothing I've done this week would have been even half as amazing if I hadn't had you there as my personal tour guide." I patted his leg, trying to comfort him. "Really, this is nothing," I promised as I pointed toward my battle wound. "When I see it in the mirror every day, I'll only think of happy thoughts…and of you."

"You must still be drugged up." He smirked. Then he gently reached up and touched my cheek, just below my gash. "Some trip, huh?"

"It was! Almost exactly how I'd pictured it, the city that is."

"What's different?"

"Besides hanging out with a celebrity?"

"Yeah." He laughed.

"Well, I always wanted to come during Christmas time. Rockefeller Center. The big tree. Ice skating. The decorated store windows…" I trailed as I got lost in the imaginary magic.

"I tell you what. My birthday's on the nineteenth of December. So how about you come back out here then, and I'll treat you to the whole New York City Christmas experience. That can be your birthday present to me."

"Isn't the birthday boy supposed to get what *he* wants for his birthday? Not me?"

"That is what I want," he said with a wink.

My lips curved as my cheeks flushed slightly.

"Geeze," he groaned. I could hear his phone vibrating.

I leaned back on the couch as he examined the name.

"My publicist. Damage control I guess. I'll call her back," he explained as he slid the phone back into his pocket.

"Ah. Sorry about that."

"Don't worry about it." He sighed. "I have a lunch meeting at twelve thirty."

"Oh." I was disappointed but managed to plaster a plastic smile on my face as camouflage. I wasn't ready to say good-bye yet.

"I wish I could take you to the airport myself, but something tells me that you'd be better off if I didn't."

He seemed hesitant to end our time together. Maybe I *was* still drugged up... "Well then," I began. I didn't quite know where to go with this. "Thanks, again. For everything."

He chuckled and shifted uneasily on the couch. "Yeah, same here." He leaned closer and gave me a hug. I breathed in his heavenly scent, trying to store it away somewhere in my memory so that I could make sense of *why* I was so intoxicated by it later. We stayed there for a moment. When he pulled away, he lingered next to my left temple and gently kissed the skin above and below the sutures. I closed my eyes and let my nerve endings enjoy the sensation of his warm lips. His mouth was still close to my face, and the hollowness in my stomach filled with liquid warmth. "Have a safe trip home," he breathed.

"Ummhumm" is all I could muster. My head was fuzzy.

He separated himself from me, got up, and walked to the door. "Let me know when you make it home, will you?"

"Of course," I promised.

"Don't forget—or pass out this time," he reminded me.

I was able to keep the smile on my face until the door closed behind him.

The trip home was uneventful, thank goodness. I spent the time catching up on my sleep. I got into my Trailblazer at Will Rogers World Airport oddly thankful to be back on Oklahoma soil. I got on I-40 and headed west. But the closer I got to Yukon, the more compelled I was to stop, even though it was late and I was tired. So I exited and wove through the streets of the addition. I pulled into the driveway in front of my house, and for a moment, I thought I wouldn't be able to go in. But I forced myself to kill the engine. I sighed, dug out my house keys, and shuffled toward the front door.

It wasn't at all as I remembered it…

My mom, no doubt, had been here and made the place livable. The house was completely put together. No painting supplies littering the ground. All the furniture was in place, all the beds made. I slowly walked from room to room. I guess it was a little easier being in *our* house considering Josh and I never spent a night here together. It was just the idea that this was supposed to be our first home that pierced my heart. These were the walls that closed in on me that night. This was the carpet that I soaked with my tears. My breathing was becoming more uneven as the déjà vu crept over me. I closed my eyes and fought off the dark memories. Luckily my phone rang. I glanced at the name, and a little wave of disappointment washed through me.

"Hey, Mom."

"Hi, honey. Where are you? Are you back?" She seemed excited to be talking to me. Most of my communication with her the past week had been via text message—through my little sister, Juliane.

"I'm in Yukon. I thought I'd just stop and check on the house. I was fixing to call. What are y'all up to?"

"Oh nothing, I just couldn't remember when your plane was supposed to land. You're at…" She paused. "Your house?"

"Yeah," I said blankly.

There was a moment of silence. I decided to break it. Perhaps she was worried how I'd react to her being there, changing things.

"Thanks, Mom. You didn't have to..." I trailed off.

"Honey—I know I didn't have to. I knew one day you'd go back, and I thought it would be a little easier if it was...finished. I hope I didn't upset you." She was anxious, I could tell. She had grown leery of trying to talk to me much about that day or the weeks, months, and years following. She, like many others, left me to my misery.

"No, no, Mom. Really. It's beautiful. Actually, since it's so late, I think I may just stay here tonight. I don't know how much longer I can keep my eyes open."

"O-okay," she managed in her surprise.

"I'll see you tomorrow," I quickly reassured her.

"All right. I love you. I'm glad you're home safe."

"I love you too. Good night."

I got ready for bed after I made a trip out to the car for a change of clothes and my bathroom stuff. I fiddled with my phone while I sat on the edge of my bed. I looked around and saw a few pictures of Josh and me, the ones I had already put up, years ago. I fell backwards across the bed and groaned. I quickly realized I wasn't ready to sleep in our bedroom, so I moved to the couch in the living room.

Just send him a quick text. Bradley *did* say to let him know when you made it home. But was he just saying that? Being polite? Our last moments together were sort of awkward. I've never had a drunken one-night stand (or any other kind for that matter), but I could imagine that same type of awkwardness there. Neither one of us seemed to know what to say or do. This was normal for me but very unlike him. Every moment I was with him, he was calm and confident, in total control. It was nice to be around someone like that. I had put a lot of effort into controlling my environment, my feelings, my everything for the past few years. It was nice to have someone else at the helm even if it was for just a week. Bradley made all the arrangements; I was just along for the ride. But there had been that barely perceptible shift in our friendship there on the couch. Right?

I stared at the blank text field. After several attempts I finally settled on something—my attempt at being "breezy." I looked at the clock. Was it too late to be bothering him? *Oh just send it already, you big sissy.* I read over it one last time to make sure there weren't any embarrassing typos.

Hey—I made it back to OK. Had a great week. Thanks!

I pushed the send button. I put the phone down, resisting the urge to watch it—to see if he responded. Without any television I didn't have much to take my mind off of it. Finally, I found an old magazine and started to thumb through it. It didn't take long before my eyelids were twitching. I reached for my phone one last time. Nothing. Back to reality.

I woke up the next morning to an empty house, of course. But it wasn't too bad overall. The night wasn't as bad as I thought it would be. My fingers quickly found my phone. Two messages, both from Bradley. I scrolled down to the first one.

Good—no other near-death experiences I hope...

After no response from me, I guess he decided to send another...

Sorry I didn't answer sooner, was doing an interview. I'll talk to U tomorrow. Nite

I exhaled slowly as I read over the words at least three times. I wouldn't respond now. I'd wait to see if he kept his word today. I quickly got up and around and headed back to Cordell. I had some packing to do.

The trip back seemed shorter than usual. I used the entire hour and fifteen minutes to relive as much as I could from the past week, analyzing every detail, trying to figure out why Bradley had taken an interest in me. I quickly gave up on that and focused on other things. Well, one thing, Bradley. I had never given much thought about what it would be like to meet a movie star, but

I probably wouldn't have thought it would be like that. Well, maybe parts of it I could have guessed. His good looks and graceful mannerisms were there of course, but he wasn't...smug. He didn't have a sense of entitlement about him. He didn't act like the world owed him anything. Bradley seemed to slip everyone a tip of some sort. Especially on our late-night, private tours. Something told me he spent a lot of money, happily, for some small sliver of anonymity. And of course, I would have expected more photographers and fans around him. Although the one night they were present was more than enough.

Bradley was born into his life of fame, money, and glamour, but even if he hadn't been, it wouldn't have been long before he was discovered. Before someone stumbled upon his face and his talent and quickly offered him a one-way pass to Celebrityville.

Bradley, or Bradley's parents, must have put special importance on education too. Although anyone could have seen that his looks could have gotten him anything he ever wanted in life, somehow it wasn't enough. I thought of the night he took me to the Guggenheim. He led me around, as giddy as a schoolboy, telling me about all the artists; their lives, their artistic styles. Not in a "hey look at me, I'm so smart" way, but in an earnest and playful way. Like he was happy to have the opportunity to share his apparent affinity for the arts with me. He couldn't have been showing off, either, because I was the only one with him. What would be the point? Did he think if I wasn't affected by his stardom that being able to explain art to me was going to make me swoon? Most of what he said flew right over my head, but I still felt overwhelmed by the beauty of the pieces there and their history.

I was suddenly more confused now than I was last week. How was I able to be so calm around him? He took me to the most spectacular places. He was spectacular himself and I was some how blasé about the whole thing. Maybe that's why he kept hanging around me, trying to answer that same question. I'm sure my reaction to him was more the exception rather than the rule, when it came to us common folk. Maybe Bradley was still waiting for me to do the whole "oh my gosh, it's Bradley Matthews," fainting thing… I was kind of wondering when it was going to hit me. In any case, I had won the best prize ever—a week with him and maybe even a friendship. Even if that friendship was long distance.

Along with being confused, now I was kind of angry with myself. I had spent an entire week with him, but still didn't really feel like I got to know him that well. We talked about the usual likes and dislikes. What kind of movies, books he liked. We both had a pseudo-obsession with music. He had lots of friends in the music biz and had an inside track to the latest music. But I was consciously careful about asking him anything too personal. I wasn't sure if he was comfortable enough with me yet to give me a straight answer.

■ ■ ■ ■ ■

I knew Mom would be at work, so I just went straight to the house to pack up my clothes. Time to move out, get on with my life now that I knew I could. I felt I owed Bradley for that but wasn't really sure I knew why. But if I learned anything from the past week it was that I could keep moving forward. That putting one foot in front of the other wasn't as hard as I had made it out to be. I was starting to feel the lead pieces of my heart move upwards, away from the soles of my feet and toward my chest. Slowly, very slowly, but surely.

"Evie?" Mom called up the stairs. "You home, honey?"

"Yeah, Mom, up here!"

She greeted me with a huge hug as she walked into my room. She held me a little tighter than usual. I didn't mind. I'd missed her.

"What's all this?" she asked with a crack in her voice. She was eyeing the half-filled boxes strewn about the room.

I looked down at my feet and cleared my throat. "I—I thought it was time for me to…move back to my house." I was careful not to use the word "home." She didn't like for any place other than her house to be called "home."

Her eyebrows rose in surprise or maybe it was relief. "Really? Well…that must have been quite a vacation. What about work?"

"I've had a couple of brokers who've expressed interest in my joining their office in the past. I'm sure it won't be hard to transfer my real estate license. Plus I have plenty in savings to cover me for a while till I adjust to the market there." I looked at her puzzled face. "What? Don't you want me to move on?" I asked, a little afraid the answer would only muddle my new state of mind.

"W-well," she stuttered. "Yes. I just didn't expect this," she admitted. A smile started to spread across her face as she hugged me again. "Looks like we're going to be empty nesters now!"

"Mom, you've got five kids. Your nest will never be empty," I teased.

Mom helped me the load the boxes into my SUV a couple hours later, and she tried to wipe away a few tears when I wasn't looking.

"Do you want me to stay for one more night?"

"No, hon, you go on. These are happy tears. You know you can call or come home anytime," she reminded me.

"I know." I had to stare down at the ground. Suddenly it was a little harder than I had thought it would be leaving. I shook my head. "Look, I'll see you soon. I'm sure you'll be up in the City shopping before too long."

"Yeah, and in any case Labor Day is only about a month away. Everyone will be down."

"Good deal," I said as I started the engine. "I'll call you when I make it back."

"Love you, honey!"

"Love you too, Mom," I yelled as I drove away.

My wheels started to hum as I made the familiar drive back to Yukon. And my thoughts found their way back to a new familiar place as well. Bradley.

CHAPTER 12

I quickly settled in—my house, new city, new office. Working in Oklahoma City (still "the City" to me) was a lot easier. There was a lot more work and plenty of ways to keep myself busy. If I didn't have enough clients to work with, there was always a ton of research I could do if the nights got too lonely. There were plenty of restaurants, and, lucky for me, I didn't mind dining alone or going to the movies by myself. I was good at being a loner.

It would be rare to go a day without talking with Bradley. I say "talk"—I mostly mean text. We had actually spoken to each other a few times in the weeks that had gone by, but for the most part we texted. I wondered if that was normal. I mean—is this how things worked now? Had I been so out of the loop that I didn't know that texting was the main way people communicated now?

I was used to texting with my clients and family as a simpler and quicker means of communication. It seemed oddly impersonal in some ways. But it was great in others. I had a chance to edit myself before I "spoke." And since Bradley had spent enough time around me, in person, he knew my sense of humor, however dry it may be, so he got most of my little quips without the aid of voice inflection. That being said, it would be nice to have a sarcastic font. But really, it was a little sad. It made me a little nostalgic. I knew the days of quill pens and ivory parchment were long gone. Handheld devices with predictive text took their place now and it seemed too…too unnatural. No two lovers, separated by time, place, or even class, could manage to sustain a meaningful relationship through texting as our ancestors could through the lost art of letter writing.

Bradley had asked for my address, that first day I moved back, and began sending me music in the mail. A lot of new stuff—new bands I'd never heard of. So I thought I'd send him stuff back—just to be silly. I sent him old stuff—a lot of Johnny Cash of course. Stuff I knew he'd probably listened to before, but I gave him specific instructions to *hear* it now. I was big on lyrics. But not everything was so serious. I sent him a lot of random stuff too—hoping just to put a smile on his face. Songs that you couldn't help but laugh at and sing along with, even if it didn't make any sense. (i.e., Beastie Boys, "Brass Monkey." How can you not smile while singing, "Brass monkey, that funky monkey"!)

Most of our conversations stayed mainly generic though. It was still hard, for me at least, to get into real deep conversations with a medium like texting. But I was slowly learning more about him. But we were still off kilter. He still knew way more about me than I did about him. He had somehow gotten me to open up about the most personal events in my life within days of meeting him, and I was still reluctant to ask him anything too personal yet. He was still really busy, traveling a lot. I didn't know if I'd ever see him again. And when I say *see* I mean *physically* see. It was weird seeing him on television or on a magazine cover now.

I squeezed my eyes tight and then tried to refocus on the computer screen in front of me. I had spent way too many hours in front of my laptop doing comp work on homes for my latest clients. Every home I'd shown them they'd want to know the entire history of the neighborhood. Average price per square foot. How many foreclosures in the neighborhood. How much turnover. Which was all fine—just a lot of work. Especially considering the few dozen homes I'd already shown them in the course of a couple of weeks.

We were pretty lucky though, here in Oklahoma. The recession hadn't hit us as hard as it did on the coasts. I was grateful for that. But it still caused us problems. A rise in inventory because of the lack of qualified buyers for instance. A few more foreclosures and short sales than usual as homeowners' mortgage payments spiked after an interest rate hike. But interest rates were low for those lucky people who were able to get qualified. Selling price to list price didn't drop. Average days on market (which was usually around three months) didn't get any worse. So, pretty stable.

My clients would often take advantage of my lack of social life and would contact me at all hours of the night and day. My fault really, because I always respond. I can't just let an e-mail or text sit there or not answer the phone when it rings. So I was a little hesitant to look at my phone when I heard it vibrate against my desk. I was sure that it was my picky clients, with whom I'd spent the entire day.

How's my fav Oklahoma realtor?

My skin felt flushed, and I smiled as I realized the text was from Bradley.

Oh, fav Oklahoma realtor? So U have other fav realtors in other states? I C how it is.

I was such a smart aleck. I waited for his equally smart-alecky response.

Ha ha. Thought I'd be coming on a lil strong if I just said fav person.

Okay. Not smart-alecky at all. Or was it? Dang texts!

Nah. I'm fine by the way. How's my fav movie star?

I laughed as I pushed send.

Good one. I'm all right I guess. A lil tired.

Me 2. Long day. What time zone are you in tonight? I asked. This was normal. I don't know why it bothered me to not know where he physically was so I always asked.

LOL. Still in NYC, will B heading to ATL soon 2 finish a re-shoot. Y U so tired?

I could almost picture him sitting on his large white sofa. Phone in hand while he aimlessly flipped through the channels on his large television. I worked even harder to picture me on the same sofa, right next to him. Had that really been a month ago? I started typing in my text, thankful that we'd started using shorthand when we texted each other.

Showed 8 houses 2day. Worn out.

Dang! Y didn't U just sell 'em the 1ˢᵗ one. B a lot easier.

LOL that would B easier. Y didn't I think of that?! But really—I'm not a pushy realtor.

And I wasn't. I treated people the way I'd like to be treated if I were buying a house. I could probably make more money if I were pushy and arrogant, but it just wasn't my style.

I can C that about U. Sounds like U need a break.

Definitely. I responded quickly and truthfully.

So the question for 2nite B4 we go 2 bed. Tell me 1 thing on UR bucket list.

I was a little thrown by his question. Our question of the day thing had become routine, but this was a little morbid. And hard. So many things rushed through my mind.

Yikes. Tuff 1. Give me a min.

I pondered the question again. Let's see…I wanted to go to Greece before I died. And Rome and Victoria Falls, Africa. I wanted to go bungee jumping, run a marathon, and take a pastry class. I finally settled on something.

I'd like 2 go 2 a fancy opera, opening nite. All dressed up & w/ a gorgeous date 2 boot.

LOL. Like Pretty Woman? Red dress & a private plane?

I laughed out loud at his film reference. That scene hadn't really popped into my head until he mentioned it.

LOL. Red dress, maybe. Private plane, not a deal breaker. That's just 1 of many things I'd like 2 do. U?

I waited anxiously for his response. He could do anything he wanted. Go anywhere he wanted to go. He wasn't as limited in his resources as I was. I didn't even want to think about all the amazing places he'd been to.

My phone buzzed in my hands. I glanced at the words and had to re-read them twice.

C U again.

Wow. I got a little dizzy then realized it was because I was holding my breath. I exhaled and shook my head a little. That wasn't what I was expecting. I decided to try to play it off.

Boring! U can C me anytime. U cheat.

LOL.

That's all I got in response.

I waited. LOL?! Was that all the explanation I was going to get? Should I have taken his response more seriously? Was he looking for a similar response from me and all I said I wanted to do is go to some stupid ole opera? My fingers twitched over the keys on my phone quickly, anxious in the lag between responses.

U asleep over there?

No just thinking.

His response was almost immediate, and this made me a little more comfortable. I relaxed into the large, black faux-leather office chair and propped my feet up on my desk.

I C. I replied.

I glanced at the clock radio after I sent the text. Just before one in the morning.

Well, I'll let U get to sleep. It's late. I'll talk 2 U soon. Sweet dreams.

I was a little disappointed. I wasn't quite ready to tell him good night yet. And if possible, he seemed a little too distant—even through text.

K. U go 2 sleep 2. U need UR beauty sleep. Nite nite.

Gee thanks. Nite.

And that was it. The last of my conversation with a movie star for that day. I decided to go bed. I had church in the morning and some more research to do. Then on Monday, it was off to Cordell.

I was rushing around my house trying to get ready to leave, blowing out candles and turning off lights. I was excited to be going back to Cordell. It was Labor Day, and we were all getting together, like usual. My family never misses an opportunity to get together—and eat! I was running late so I was a little peeved when my phone rang. I didn't really have time for a client, but I always answer. I pulled my BlackBerry from my purse, and the tension between my shoulder blades melted. Bradley.

"Hello, hello!"

"Hey there. What are you up to?"

Just the sound of Bradley's voice made my lips roll into an easy smile. "Not much. It's good to hear your voice."

"Yeah? I almost called you last night, but decided it was too late."

"I probably could have used the pick-me-up," I admitted.

"Bad day?"

"Could say that I guess. I got a flat tire on the way to church, ripped my skirt in the process of fixing it. Then—""

"Wait a minute," Bradley interrupted. "You fixed your own flat? Don't you have AAA or something?"

"By the time I waited around on someone to show up and stood by while they fixed it I would have blown half the day. I'm an Okie—I know how to change a flat. Anyhoo, later that day, my air conditioner decided to go on the fritz, had one of my contracts fall apart, then downed half a glass of milk before I noticed it was expired," I expelled all in one breath.

"Yikes. Sounds like you have the makings of a chart-topping country song on your hands there. Good thing you don't have any pets, or they would have probably gotten run over yesterday."

I laughed. He had such a natural ability to make me smile. "Yep. Just one of those days," I added after I realized I'd whined to him the moment I got him on the phone. Probably not the reason he called me...

"Well, hopefully today will be better."

"It already is." I didn't add it was simply better already because I was talking to him.

"Maybe I can help."

"Oh yeah? How so?" I asked.

My doorbell seemed to chime in response. I groaned inwardly at the disturbance. I peeked slowly out the window of my front door, hoping I could ignore whoever it was unless it was the mailman needing my signature on something... I pulled back the makeshift window covering and did an instant double take.

I fought with the locks on the door hoping he would still be standing there once I finally got the door opened. Once I flung it open, I froze. Then I poked my head out to see if there was a flock of news crews anywhere in sight. Bradley smiled broadly as he put his phone in his pocket and then placed his hands in his pockets, as breathtaking as ever. Very pleased, no doubt, with my shocked reaction.

"How, why, when..." was all I could manage to articulate.

He laughed. "Well, hello to you too! Or should I say *howww-dy, partner!*" He pretended to tip the brim of his imaginary cowboy hat as he exaggerated his best attempt at what he thought was an Oklahoma accent.

I was still frozen, unable to even chide him for his lame attempt of a Southern accent. I shook my head and blinked wildly, and all he did was chuckle as he walked by me, through the open door—into my house. I shut the door quickly behind us and realized I still had my phone glued to my ear. Nice.

"I can't believe it," I finally stuttered. "Are you really here?"

Bradley was walking around the living room, taking inventory. I was a little self-conscious. I was proud of my first little house, but it was nothing compared to his elegant apartment. My house was full of hand-me-down furniture, Walmart special "art" graced the walls and my old, thick television that hummed and whined before it reluctantly flickered to life.

"I was on my way back to Atlanta and thought I'd take a little detour," he explained, without looking back at me.

I took a few steps closer but didn't say anything. My silence must have given him the wrong impression.

"Is that okay? I guess I should have called—I just wanted to surprise you."

"Mission accomplished." I laughed.

He closed the distance between us in just a few strides, his long legs eating the distance between us. He pulled me toward him, and I melted into his chest. His arms where tight around my shoulders. Mine were even tighter and a little lower, around his waist. I fit comfortably into him, my head nestled by his strong chest. He had to lower his head to rest his chin on the top of my head. Before I had time to process how and why I so easily went into his embrace, he bent down even further for his lips to reach my ear.

"It's good to see you," he breathed into my hair.

All I could do was pull back a little so he could see me smile and nod in agreement. His eyes narrowed, and his lips tightened a bit as he lifted his hand to brush the side of my face. His warm fingertips danced lightly along the scar on my left temple. It was barely noticeable to me anymore—just a slightly pink line. I laughed to myself. I had a fun time trying to explain that to Mom. I had told her and my little sister that I had run into a movie star, but left out a lot of details. I ended up telling them I just tripped and fell and that's how I cut my face. My story wasn't challenged; my lack of coordination was no secret. But Bradley was still running over the faint line with his fingertips with a pained expression on his face, like he was trying to erase the scar from my face.

I raised my hand to his and fought his fingers out of the way so that I could casually run my fingers over the scar. "Oh yeah, looking pretty good now, huh?"

He just sighed as he looked over my shoulder. "Did I come at a bad time?"

He must have eyed my purse and keys laying on top of my purse on the couch behind us. I ran my fingers through my hair. "Uh...well, I was actually fixing to go down to Cordell for a lil family get-together—"

He cut me off. "I knew I should have called."

"It's okay—I don't have to go. I'd much rather spend time with you." I immediately blushed at my confession.

"A family thing." He shrugged. "So no celebrities allowed?"

I just stared at him. "You—you wanna come with me?" I asked in disbelief.

"Oh yeah!" He smiled so widely that I could have counted every tooth.

I ran my hand down my face as a million thoughts ran through my head. How would everyone react? Would he be bored to death? How badly would everyone embarrass me? That was the big one... I knew my family wouldn't miss a chance to get together and eat *or* to embarrass the pants off me. Oh Mylanta— this was a bad idea...

"My family's crazy," I added bluntly, trying to scare him.

"If you don't want me to go..." he trailed playfully.

I rolled my eyes. "Oy...let's go. We're already running late."

I double-checked to make sure I locked the front door, grabbed my purse, and headed to the garage. Bradley was right on my heels.

Within a few short minutes we were headed west on I-40. I managed to send off a desperate text to my little sister.

On my way—bringing someone w/ me. Tell everyone to act normal!

142

Yeah, right—like that was possible. Even if I wasn't bringing a movie star, the fact that I was bringing a male in general
would probably be enough to set their heads spinning like a top.
I ignored the several vibrations that followed my text. I knew it
was Juliane texting me back—wanting more details.

The sun burned brightly into the SUV, and I cranked up the
AC as we sped down the interstate. I turned the volume on the
radio down, a little embarrassed that the last CD he sent me was
still playing.

"So," he said, twisting comfortably in his seat.

"So..."

"So what kind of crazy are we talking about here? Straight
jacket crazy or..."

"Just your average run-of-the-mill crazy." I chuckled.
"Nothing serious. Nothing worth committing anyone over."

I thought I saw his face relax, just a little. For all he knew, all
my family members deserved to walk around a tiny, padded room
in a straight jacket.

"Whew!" He wiped the imaginary sweat from his brow.

I rolled my eyes.

"I can't guarantee that everyone will act the same way I do—
when it comes to you, I mean." He just nodded, so I continued.
"There will likely be a lot more staring and *a lot* more whispering. But that will probably have more to do with the fact that I'm
bringing someone with me at all, not just the fact that you're a
celebrity. And on the flip side, don't be offended if some people
don't even have a clue who you are..."

"Okay..." He drew out the word in confusion. "So everyone
will be whispering and staring, but not because of who I am?"

"Well, I'm sure most people will know who you are—my sister, brothers, cousins. But I'm not sure that most of the adults
keep up with the mainstream enough to really know who you are
without someone spelling it out."

"All right, I guess I can handle that." He shrugged, and I looked over just in time to catch a smile creeping across his face as he turned to stare out the window.

"When do you have to leave—I mean, when's your flight?"

"Tomorrow afternoon." He looked at me curiously. "Why? How long do you think your family will hold me hostage?"

"Depends," I said without a hint of humor. I could feel him still looking at me, so I smiled and his shoulders relaxed.

"Why don't you tell me a little about who's going be there? 'Cause I'm starting to freak out a little…"

"Oh puh-lease!" I wailed. "You schlepped me all over New York City, and I didn't ask for any kind of debriefing! You're going to meet an average Oklahoma family, and you're acting like you haven't the foggiest as to what to expect!"

"I don't want to piss anyone off," he defended himself. "As you said, we're in Oklahoma—I don't know how things are done here!"

"Same as anywhere else I reckon. Am I that different from anyone you know? You act fine around me."

"I feel comfortable around you, so I can be myself. And, yes, you are different from anyone I know. But I don't know your family. I could be going into the lion's den for all I know."

I knew he was still looking at me, but I kept my eyes glued to the road. All I could do was shake my head and grin. The little bugger didn't really give me an answer either. *Okay, so I'm different from anyone he knows. How? Because I'm average? Not famous? Hardly enough to keep up this level of interest.*

"Not a lion's den," I grudgingly reassured him; maybe he was genuinely concerned. "Unless…" I couldn't help myself.

"Oh, no! Unless? Unless what?!" he grumbled.

I giggled. "Well, you're pretty well mannered, so just keep that up. Please and thank you. Ma'am and sir. Those will earn you some brownie points."

I couldn't resist letting my eyes wander from the road to see his expression. He was staring out the windshield and nodded twice—like he was making a mental checklist. He didn't respond, so I thought I'd give him a little more food for thought.

"And whatever you do, don't, and I mean *do not*..." I paused for effect. It worked, he was staring at me know, but my attention was already back on the stretch of concrete in front of me.

"Don't—don't what?"

I had to press my lips together, hard, to keep from laughing at the anxiety in his voice. "Do not say the Lord's name in vain. Unless you want to hear crickets chirping and feel the most uncomfortable silence imaginable..."

"Oh." The anxiety in his voice left as he exhaled. "That's it?"

"What did you think I was going to say?"

"I hadn't gotten that far. Any other words or actions I should avoid—to keep from embarrassing myself?"

"Ha! I'm sure there's a million!"

"Fantastic," he mumbled. "More, more. What else?" he demanded impatiently.

"Let's see," I said as I tapped my chin. I was too busy enjoying myself to process his impatient gaze. "So if the Lord's name is a no-no, cussing is out too. Try to avoid politics, but if you can't— just remember that you're in Oklahoma—conservative. Sports are always a safe subject..."

"Okay, okay," he muttered under his breath as he added more items to his mental what to do and what not to do checklist.

"Oh, and there will be a lot of...hugging," I added timidly.

"I'm guessing you're not talking about trees..."

"No. We're just a bunch of huggers. My mom, my gran, my aunts—well, pretty much any female. Luckily, the males won't be quite so eager to hug you. Just a pat on the shoulder or a hand-shake there."

He chuckled. "I think I can handle that." He noticed that I was looking at him again, so he threw me a wink.

"Hey now—none of that."

"What?" he asked innocently.

"No need to go into charming movie star guy mode. You want everyone to swoon uncontrollably?"

He just laughed lightly again.

Okay, time to scare him a little...

"Now for the really important part," I quickly changed my tone—as serious as possible. Taking notice of the change Bradley quickly angled his body toward me, having to scoot back in the seat to shift his long legs to the side in the small space in front of him. "My brothers," I finally finished.

He waited. I said nothing.

"Brothers? A-and how many will be there?"

"All three of them." He, he, he. I had already learned through my limited dating experience that having three older brothers was somewhat ominous. "Definitely watch what you say, in regards to me at least, around them. They're pretty protective of me. Especially Marcus, he's the oldest."

"Okay, so no inappropriate joking with the brothers. Check." I just sat there and nodded in silent agreement. "Will they be wielding shotguns?" he joked.

Oh goodness, he has no clue that most everyone in my family is a card-carrying member of the NRA. Poor guy.

"Well...they probably won't be walking around with them— this isn't the Wild West out here, *but* they will have easy access to one if they need it. Plus a wide variety of sharp...and blunt objects." I met his stare and just blinked a couple of times before I drifted my gaze back to concentrate on the road.

"Ha, ha—very funny," he said as he tried to blow it off.

"All right. You can think I'm joking if you want," I said with a smile.

He mumbled something toward the window. I couldn't make it out.

"Want me to turn around?"

"Nope, I'm fine." He turned his face slowly toward me. That calm, always-in-control expression was back on his face.

"Most everyone is just a normal, blue-collar American. Nothing scary. No pitchforks. No overalls and banjos."

All I could do was smile at him. Who would have thought that *my* world would be so alarming? Of all the places in the world, you'd think western Oklahoma would be the most benign to him.

"How's Mel?"

"He's great. He was a little jealous when I told him I planned on stopping to see you."

"Oh, Mel…" I sighed. I was a little surprised that he wasn't traveling with Bradley but didn't bring it up.

He changed the subject again. "How long will we be staying?"

"We'll eat some lunch, play a little ball, hang out and talk and drive back later tonight. Is that okay?"

"Sure, that sounds good."

He paused. I noted the way he shifted in his seat. I knew him well enough already to know that there was something on his mind. I also knew sooner or later he'd come out with it.

"So…is it all right if I stay at your place, or do I need to call and make arrangements at a hotel?"

I kept my eyes locked in front of me. Sleeping arrangements hadn't occurred to me yet. I was still focusing on the mayhem that was waiting for us in Cordell. I immediately knew that I didn't want to lose any precious time with him. But I knew this question stemmed, again, from my reaction to his invitation back at his place last month.

"Uh—yeah. I have an extra room if you'd like to stay with me," I offered. I hoped that I was clear enough on that one. I wanted him with me, but there still needed to be some…boundaries. "No need to alert the Oklahoma City news crews to your whereabouts!"

"Thanks," he answered flatly.

His answer was polite, but I wondered if that was the answer he was fishing for. Maybe he *didn't* want to stay with me but felt compelled to since he showed up on my doorstep. I am no good with this stuff.

We made some idle chit chat as we continued west. I noticed that his attention was immediately held by the same thing mine was just after we drove through Weatherford. Just outside town, right past the Route 66 drive-in, was a wind farm. Tall, alien-like statues littered the landscape. The three large blades of the massive windmills glided through the Oklahoma breeze. There were dozens of them—on both sides of the interstate. They held your gaze hypnotically. Maybe it wasn't the best idea to put such interesting things next to a busy interstate…they tended to divert drivers' attention.

I had driven by them at least a hundred times since they were put up, and I still stared at them with the same awe as if it were the first time I was seeing them. I glanced at Bradley as he stared out the window, brow crinkled and eyes narrowed as he took in the landscape.

I wondered if he thought of them the same way I did. They were lovely even though they were mammoth in size. Streamlined and white. Nothing like the old metal windmills of yesteryear that squeaked and sputtered frantically with the changing speed and direction of the wind. These windmills stood strong and never moved except for the large blades. And their speed didn't correspond to the speed of the air whipping around them. No matter how furious the Oklahoma wind blew, they still churned at the same steady pace.

Another reason there were so hypnotic was the backdrop, the landscape that surrounded them, modern technology right smack in the middle of farmland. They seemed even larger compared to the cattle grazing around them. Progress—or I guess that's what we're calling it. Progress that has sprung from necessity after we've started to exhaust the earth's finite resources and are left to harvest the most rudimentary of elements: wind and solar power. Progress that is competing with the natural way of life here. The same soil that is supporting the weight of this modern progress is still sustaining the wheat and cattle that surround it. Around here, things were different and yet the same as most of the rest of the Midwest. These wind farms were a testament to how far we've come, how far we've changed and leave us wondering what the future will hold.

I didn't ask Bradley if he had any thoughts on the topic. But he turned to me with raised eyebrows.

"It's really...*flat*," he finally said.

I giggled. Once I compared the endless miles of farmland to the New York City skyline he was used to, I could only imagine how flat he really thought it was.

As I turned on the blinker to exit from I-40 at Clinton, I gave him a quick smile. "Almost there!" I headed south on Highway 183. Ten more minutes...

I let him enjoy the scenery just as he let me when we were in New York, although I couldn't imagine that this land looked as scenic to him as his city did to me. Pretty barren. Wheat fields on either side of the four-lane highway had already been harvested earlier in the summer. That was too bad. The tall stalks swaying in the breeze made the farmland look like a rippling ocean of honey. Very beautiful. Now there were just tidy rows extending as far as the eyes could see. In just a couple of weeks, the farmers would be back out to sow the wheat into the ground. And so the cycle continues. Other than that, there was one small church and cemetery in the middle of nowhere. A few farm houses. *Real* scenic.

I eased my foot off the accelerator as we took the big curve at the edge of town. We passed the Chevy dealership that was the marker to where the town began. That dealership had faired far better than the Dodge one on the other side of town that lost its franchise during the automobile crisis. It was still odd to drive by the vacant lot. No shiny Dodge Rams holding down the pavement. There would be no brand new red Viper carrying the football homecoming queen candidate around the field this fall.

"So is it what you were expecting?"

"Not exactly," he confessed.

"You weren't expecting a 'welcome home' parade for me, were you?"

He laughed. "No, just a few people on horseback waving banners."

"Yeah, they must be late."

"Do a lot of people know you here?"

I furrowed my brow in amusement. "Honey, my family's huge, the town is small, and I've spent most of my life here. You can't swing a dead cat without hitting someone who not only knows me but could probably tell you some embarrassing story about me."

I met his eyes as an unfamiliar expression flickered in his eyes. Discomfort? He didn't respond, so I asked, "Was it the 'honey' or the dead cat thing?"

"I'm not entirely sure," he replied honestly.

My cheeks burned because the "honey" totally just slipped, but I was compelled to explain. "Well, as for the endearment, you'd better get used to it because in a few minutes you're gonna be honeyed, deared, and darlinged to death. And the dead cat thing—well, it's just an expression. I don't make a habit out of handling dead animals."

I couldn't be sure which part relieved him more.

CHAPTER 13

Two minutes later I was pulling up in front of Uncle Bo's house. Cars and trucks littered both side of the street. We were the last ones here. Great. An entrance. I killed the engine and waited for Bradley to stop rubbing his hands incessantly along the jeans on his thighs.

"You ready?" I grinned from ear to ear. There wasn't anyone in sight. Everyone was already inside the house or on the back deck.

He just stared back at me.

"Oh come on," I said as I opened my door.

I caught a whiff of the air. The smell of freshly cut grass, honeysuckle, and burgers and hot dogs on the grill hung heavy in the humid air.

Bradley walked behind me as we went through the front door. Everyone was scattered. A few already eating at the dining room table; several in the living room chatting away. I could see all the kiddos on the back deck running around.

"Evie!" announced my uncle just as we stepped in the door. He made his way across the living room toward us. He was tall and athletically built with a full head of black hair that was flecked with silver.

I glanced at Bradley. I smiled warmly in an effort to erase some of the tension from his face. "Relax," I said in a stage whisper. He smiled back, more easily this time.

Uncle Bo wrapped me in a bear hug. "Good to see you, girl."

"You too," I said as he released me. His eyes instantly moved past me, to Bradley. "Uncle Bo, this is Bradley. Bradley, this is my uncle."

"You can call me John," Uncle Bo said as he extended his hand toward Bradley.

"Hi, John. It's nice to meet you," Bradley replied flawlessly as he took Uncle Bo's hand. I knew I'd have to explain later that I had no idea why I called him Uncle Bo when his name was really John.

"Hope your belly button's saying howdy to your backbone 'cause we have a ton of food! Come on in and make a plate. We didn't wait for you." He laughed as he patted Bradley on the shoulder, leading us toward the kitchen.

I introduced Bradley to a few more adults—aunts and uncles—as we made our way to the kitchen.

"There you are, honey!" Mom was almost running toward me with her arms extended. I don't think she noticed Bradley till she had me in her arms and caught a glimpse of him over my shoulder. "Oh…"

"Mom, this is Bradley. Bradley, this is my mom, Janet."

"It's nice to meet you, Janet. Evie talks about you all the time," Bradley said with a smile. Smooth operator.

"Well, hi…yes, it's nice to meet you too," my stunned mom answered back. She looked back to me and then back to Bradley a couple of times. I just shook my head. She cleared her throat. "Everything's here—go ahead and make yourselves a plate."

I grabbed Bradley and towed him toward the buffet line. Hamburgers, hot dogs, baked beans, cole slaw, chips and dip, deviled eggs, fruit and veggies lined an entire counter. Another was dedicated to desserts and homemade ice cream, and I eyed those as I quickly made my hamburger. I made sure that he had everything he needed and giggled at the sight of his plate piled high—two hamburgers, a hot dog, and a sampling of every side.

I could feel the eyes of my nosey family members boring into the back of my neck.

We walked through the back doors, to the deck where all my brothers, sisters, and cousins were. You could hear the figurative pin drop as they all looked up at the same time when we sat down at the patio table.

"Holy crap!" someone gasped softly.

I whipped my head around to see my brother Jordan with his hand covering his mouth, eyes wide. I glared at him.

"Everyone," I announced, "this is Bradley." I pointed to Bradley, who was sitting next to me. Like I really needed to point out the movie star sitting among us...

Bradley already had a mouth full of food, so he just waved.

I eyed everyone. They were all staring, impolitely. "Come on, guys," I mumbled, "act cool."

"Uh, hi."

"Hey."

"What's up?"

I just shook my head at their lame responses and dug into my food. Finally, some normal conversations picked back up. Marcus and Caleb were arguing over which John Wayne movie was the best. My sisters-in-law were trying to convince my nieces and nephews to eat a little bit more before they continued playing.

"You okay?" I whispered to Bradley as the chattering around us continued.

He just nodded once, and I smiled.

"There she is!" sang my Gran from behind me.

I scooted my chair sideways to turn to greet her. I stood up so I could hug her.

"Your momma told me you finally got here," she continued. "And that you brought a very handsome man with you."

Oh, geeze! I swallowed down my last bite of hamburger. "Gran," I grumbled.

She laid a hand on Bradley's shoulder, and he scooted his chair in much the same way as I had. "Hi, honey. I'm Bess, Evie's gran," she proudly declared.

"Hi, Bess. I'm Bradley Matthews. It's nice to meet you." He smiled warmly at her, and I felt my heart melt a little as well.

"Bradley Matthews?" She paused to look at me. "The movie star?"

Great. The one person who I figured wouldn't have a clue as to who he was, was the one who stood there with her tongue hanging out of her mouth! And she was the one person I couldn't get mad at for embarrassing me.

"You done good, honey!"

Bradley dipped his head and chuckled softly. I elbowed him.

"Yes, Bradley Matthews the movie star," I finally conceded in an annoyed tone, looking around the table again. Everyone else had ended their conversations when they heard Gran make the observation.

I don't know why, but I started laughing, and others joined in.

All in all, it was going better than I thought. I left Bradley alone at the table to go get dessert. When I came back, he was laughing and talking with my family just like anyone else would have. He didn't seem bothered by their interrogating. He seemed to have won everyone over rather easily. No big surprise really.

"Ball time!" we heard Uncle Bo call from the yard below us.

Everyone got up and headed down to where he was.

"Ball time?" Bradley asked as we maneuvered down the hill, toward the clearing.

"Yeah—wiffle ball. You wanna play?"

"Wiffle what?" He laughed.

"Come on; you'll see."

We stood there in a line waiting for Uncle Bo to split us into teams. I motioned secretly to Uncle Bo to put us on the same team. Usually, most of the couples were split up to make it more interesting. It was the beginning of September, and it was still almost a hundred degrees today. I could feel the sweat starting to gather at the nape of my neck. I slid off the thin hair band that I kept on my wrist most days. I gathered up my hair and knotted it behind my head. I felt Bradley's eyes on me, and I glanced his way. He gave me a slow, wolfy smile, and I felt my knees turn to the consistency of jelly.

"Okay," Bo hollered to get everyone's attention. "I'll go over the ground rules since we have some newcomers."

"That would be you," I whispered as I nudged Bradley, and Uncle Bo continued.

"Three strikes and you're out. No balls. The ball has to go past the bases here, or it's an out. If it's over the street, automatic homerun. If you get hit with the ball while you're running bases, you're out. Got it? Okay, Evie, your team—take the field first."

I grabbed Bradley and lugged him toward the right side of the outfield with me as the rest of our team took their positions. "Think you got the gist of it?"

"You can throw balls at people while they're running?" he asked, concerned.

"Don't worry your pretty little head," I mused. "It's just a ping pong ball."

"Ping pong ball? How are you supposed to hit that?"

"You'll see. Heads up—just catch the ball if it comes at you out there then get it to Bo—'kay?" I giggled as I put a little space between us, evening out the outfield.

He stood there, knees slightly bent. Waiting. I wondered if he'd ever played any kind of sport. His stance was natural, and his eyes were trained on the batter.

My family played as they normally would, cat calling and flinging out zingers to one another. The adults who weren't playing lined up as usual on the "sidelines" to cheer us on. We got three quick outs, and it was our turn to bat now.

155

"I still don't see how you guys hit that little ball. Why do you use something so small?" Bradley quickly mentioned as we made our way to the side of the homemade field.

"We have to use the smaller ball to make things harder. Traditional wiffle balls are too easy and the game turns into a homerun derby. It's pretty easy. Just keep your eye on the ball. Uncle Bo will probably be nice to you and throw 'em right down the middle for you."

"I'll go first," Bobby, my cousin, said as he stepped behind the plate.

Uncle Bo was the designated pitcher for both sides. This time my brother Marcus had opted to play catcher for the other team.

"Here ya go, Bob-o." Uncle Bo laughed as he flicked the ball toward Bobby.

Bobby let it go right down the middle.

"Woooo-eee," cried Uncle Bo as he removed his hat to wipe the sweat from his brow. "Don't get much better than that, son!"

"Psshhh…" Bobby rejected as he took a practice swing.

Bobby launched the next pitch past center field and made it to second.

We stood there briefly, deciding who the next batter would be. I motioned for Bradley to go next. "It's easy cheesey. Eyes on the ball."

He walked slowly to the makeshift home plate, and Marcus handed him the thin plastic bat. Bradley shifted his weight from side to side and took a deep breath as he settled into positioned.

"Right down the middle," promised Uncle Bo. He was known for throwing nasties to the older boys, but took it easy on us girls—and newcomers.

Bradley just nodded as he slightly bounced the bat up and down, just above his right shoulder.

Whoosh. Bradley swung at the first pitch, and the small, white ping pong ball bounced lightly behind the plate and was quickly picked up by Marcus who tossed it back to Uncle Bo.

"Pretty close. Here we go!" I cheered for him.

Whoosh. Strike two. This time Bradley let out a frustrated growl, and I slapped my hand over my mouth to contain my laughter. It was fun to see him frazzled. He hit the ground with the bat before he got back into position.

"Just a little behind," Uncle Bo offered.

"Come on, Bradley—you can do it!" My cousin Steve had taken to the cheering with me.

Uncle Bo flicked the ball out of his fingers, and it fluttered quickly through the air.

The next sound we heard was definitely not a whoosh. *Thwack!* Bradley had connected with an object, but that sound couldn't have come from a plastic bat hitting a feather-light ping pong ball.

I stood there—frozen. My cheeks full of air, eyes bugged out trying to contain the hysteria. Everyone else was frozen too, not sure what reaction would be the best. Only a couple of seconds had passed since the unexpected sound.

"Ow!" Marcus groaned as he rubbed the side of his head.

I burst out laughing. I doubled over to brace my hands on my knees only to straighten to wipe the tears from my eyes. It must have been contagious because everyone else was howling with laughter too. Marcus and Bradley were the only two not laughing!

"Dah nuh nah—dah nuh nah!" I heard someone sing above the laughter, mimicking the ESPN sound bite—like this moment would've ended up on their highlight reel.

"Oh my gosh—oh man—I'm so sorry," Bradley quickly apologized as he stepped cautiously toward Marcus.

Marcus just threw his hands up in defense and gave Bradley a wild look as he stepped backwards.

I quickly jogged over to them. I grabbed Bradley's hand as I walked by him on my way to inspect my brother. "Oh come on. It's a little plastic bat—no permanent damage done," I insisted between chuckles.

"Good thing you don't part your hair on that side of your head there, Marcus!" I choked on a laugh at Caleb's comment.

Marcus plucked the bat out of Bradley's petrified grip and reared back like he was about to hit me—to show me just how much it didn't hurt.

"Oh please." I giggled as I pried the bat from his hands.

Just then Uncle Bo walked up to us and grabbed Bradley's shoulder as he tried to quiet his laughter. "Well, son, at least we know you can make contact with a slightly larger object!" He continued to chuckle as he walked back out to the field.

"I'm real sorry, Marcus..." Bradley continued.

Marcus shook his head and finally let him off the hook. "It's okay. I mostly use the other side of my brain anyways..." he grumbled.

"Alrighty then. We're all good here. Except—sorry, Bradley— that was strike three!" I pulled Bradley back to where the rest of the team was still standing. He rubbed his head as if he was the one who had gotten hit with a bat. I squeezed his hand. "It's just a plastic bat. Don't worry about it. It was funny!"

He just glared at me. "Still. I whacked your *brother* upside the head with a bat. Geeze..." he sighed as his perfect lips pursed into a frown.

I bit my lip, stifling the laughter that was building in my chest again.

The game continued without incident. I couldn't help but notice that Marcus was cautiously standing a few feet farther behind home plate than where he had been earlier. My team won, of course, and Bradley even managed to make contact—with the ball—a couple of times. Luckily, no one picked on Bradley too much. Most everyone razzed Marcus—telling him if he wasn't going bald, he would've had more hair to act as a cushion.

We said our good-byes not long after that, then headed to Mom's house. Once inside the confines of my vehicle, Bradley lost it.

"I'm such an idiot! Ah man! Holy—"

"Hey now," I cut him off before he could finish his profanity. I laughed again. "Holy smokes—it's not that bad, I promise," I said as I leaned closer to him in order to get him to make eye contact with me.

He turned his head, and I was startled that our faces were so close. For whatever reason, the air inside the small space changed. Anger wasn't present, but electricity was. It was too much, and I had to look away. I shifted back into my seat as I started the engine, a little dazed.

"We'll go to my mom's for just a little bit; then we can go back to the city."

"Do whatever you want—I don't want to mess up your trip home just because I somehow managed to hit your brother—your oldest, most protective of brothers…"

"I promise, Bradley," I interrupted. "Everything's fine. Funny stuff like that happens all the time. I'm sure getting hit in the head with a wiffle ball bat by a movie star will end up being a highlight for him."

I finally managed to make him smile, just a little bit.

Another two minutes later, and we were at my old house. My family was all there already. It took a little longer than usual to say good-bye to everyone at Bo's. Mostly it took longer because everyone made a point to say bye to Bradley.

I parked in front of Mom's two-story house. I always thought it looked like a gingerbread house. Perfectly square and with classic shutters framing the windows, perched on top of a hill. I'm sure it looked nothing like Bradley's parents' house…

We walked into the sunroom where we naturally gathered to watch something on television or to play the Wii.

"Hey, Evie—I saw some butter lying out in the kitchen. Why don't you go take care of that," my brother Caleb ordered.

"Ugh," I moaned. "I just got here!"

He didn't answer, just blinked then turned back to the TV. I sighed again. The only empty seat was on the couch, next to Marcus. I figured Bradley would rather follow me than stay in there.

"Come on," I mumbled as I turned from the room.

"Butter? What are you going to do with butter? Not another game I hope..." Bradley questioned, slightly alarmed.

"What?" I laughed. "What would we do with butter? This isn't New York City..."

He laughed.

"Cookies."

"Ah."

He watched me carefully as I started to pull the ingredients together. I punched in the temperature on the oven. He leaned up against the wall as I continued. I quickly and easily pulled items from the cabinets around me, almost without looking. Mom's kitchen was laid out so well that I never had to take more than two steps to get what I needed.

"You don't need a recipe?" Bradley asked curiously as I counted out the six tablespoons of brown sugar.

I spun around. "If you only knew how many times I've made chocolate chip cookies..."

He moved closer to me so that he could see what I was doing more clearly, more intently.

"Never seen anyone make cookies before?" I asked, creaming the sugar, butter, and vanilla together.

"Well, not like this."

What was that supposed to mean? Was it because I wasn't a four-star chef? Because we weren't in some fancy restaurant or ballroom? "What, none of your model girlfriends made cookies?" Maybe just a little below the belt...

"No." He chuckled, unoffended. "Why would they make something they couldn't eat?"

"Good call—don't know."

"It looks like it may be a little too difficult for some of them…" he added regretfully.

"Holy mackerel! *Please* promise me that you'll end up with someone who can at least read the back of a bag of chocolate chips," I commanded.

"Deal," he simply said as he looked into my eyes. His eyes had darkened, and I swallowed hard.

I just went back to work. Luckily Mom came in and broke the awkward silence.

"Should've known you'd be in here making cookies," she noted.

"More like ordered."

She laughed easily, used to the dynamic between her children.

"You made quite an impression, Bradley." Mom smiled as she patted Bradley on the back.

"On something other than the side of Marcus's head?" Bradley joked.

I was relieved that he was able to joke about it now. Mom laughed again.

"Yes—everyone was quite taken with you. I'm sure you're used to that though," she added.

Bradley stared down at me. "Well, most of the time," he said. I guess he had been aware of my unusual reaction to him. I just finished mixing in the chocolate chips and started to put them on the cookie sheet.

"Will you be hitting the road soon?" Mom directed this question to me this time.

"Yes. Once the cookies are done, we'll probably be on our way."

"That's probably best," Mom said quietly and then paused. "There's a storm gaining momentum around Elk City."

"Oh," I said as I slid the cookie sheet into the oven. "We'll stay ahead of it then."

After all this time, storms still made me very uneasy. Especially the thought of driving in them, near them or even in the vicinity of them. I must have been too distracted by the recent events to see the ominous clouds gathering to the west.

"Maybe you should at least take Bradley on one drag before you leave town." Kudos to Mom. She always knew how to change the subject.

"A drag?" Bradley mused. "Oh yes. Lets."

"Do you even know what that is?" I charged.

"Nope. Don't care. Gonna drag. Whatever that is."

I rolled my eyes. I was pretty sure he was the first person that I ever met who didn't know what a "drag" was, and I was pretty sure I didn't want to know what he *thought* it was.

I was a little anxious now as I waited for the cookies to finish baking. I almost wished that Mom hadn't said anything about that stupid storm. Thank goodness it only takes ten minutes for cookies to bake. We started our second round of good-byes. Everyone was very friendly, including Marcus. "No hard feelings," he told Bradley with a smile.

I was munching on a cookie while I pulled out of Mom's driveway. Bradley sighed as he stretched out his feet in front of him. "Drag time!"

"Sheesh. It's not that exciting. I promise."

He waved his hand forward, motioning for me to get on with it.

I pulled onto Glenn English and headed south, toward the one stop light. At the red light I reached down and flipped to the local country station and turned the volume up. I rolled the windows all the way down. I slid my hand down the side of my seat, found the lever, and eased my seat back just a little. Watching me, Bradley did the same. Only he misjudged the movement of the lever, and his seat suddenly thudded all the way back, several loud clicks revealing his error. I bit my lower lip, hard, to keep from laughing when I glanced over at him. He was fiddling with the lever again trying to get his seat back into position quickly. He met my eyes, and we both started to laugh, drowning out Garth Brooks on the radio.

On green I turned left. I sang along to the music as I drove through the ordinary town. A few dilapidated houses. A couple of storage places. I pointed those out to Bradley. "Those are newer. There was a tornado that tore through this part of town back in October of 2001." There was one newer gas station. But other than that, the town was mostly the same. Things were slow to change around here. It was more obvious in the way we gave people directions. Instead of telling someone to turn at the corner of Elm and Sixth, we'd say to turn at Mrs. Hall's house even if Mrs. Hall hadn't lived there for ten years.

I put on my blinker and turned left into the funeral home parking lot. The two entrances at the back of the parking lot made it easy to go in one way, make a half-moon turn to the left and go out the other. I was heading down Main Street now, going the opposite direction than before.

"So this is dragging?"

"Yup. Well, almost. We've done about half a drag. Also known as riding around. Only thing to do around here on the weekends," I explained.

"You just...ride around in your cars?"

"Well, we used to. I don't know what the kids do these days. Gas wasn't three bucks a gallon when I was in school..."

Bradley was curiously gazing out the windshield as I turned right at the stop light. It looked like he was eyeing the courthouse that was in front of us. I probably should have taken him around the square, pointed out the family-run drug store where I had my first chocolate Coke, my mom's little shop, and the refurbished one-screen movie theatre, but my attention was diverted by the dark clouds that hung in the distance.

After a minute or so we passed the Sonic Drive-In, but instead of turning in to finish the drag I kept going north. "We'd pull in there and go around and finish the loop. And that's it. The whole drag." I laughed. "Whatta drag!"

"Interesting."

"We'd drive around with friends and then would flash an on-coming car if it was someone we wanted to pull over to talk to. I know. It's stupid. Probably especially stupid considering the things that you probably did when you were in school."

"Actually, it would've been nice to just get to hang out and not be bothered by anyone. You don't know how good you had it. It all sounds so…innocent."

I wondered what exactly he meant by "innocent," but I didn't ask for an explanation. He sounded melancholy, and I didn't want to dredge up some bad memories.

CHAPTER 14

"Your family's really great," Bradley said, his face beaming.

"I know. I've been blessed."

I was still distracted by the black and dark blue clouds that were following us as we drove east on I-40. It wasn't long before I started to see flickers of lightning too. It was too bad that Bradley was going to miss out on an Oklahoma sunset. I'd always thought this had to be one of the most boring states, but it did have a few things going for it: long, hot summer days that enable you to lounge by the pool or pond all afternoon, jumping in once the heat got to you; peaceful sounds of crickets, wind rustling the leaves on trees, and the coo of the mourning doves lulling you to sleep; and of course the sunsets with pastel pinks, purples, and blues feathering across the western sky. Blending the horizon and merging the earth and heavens together. The heavy sun sinking into the distance as the last of its orange light crawled over the miles of red dirt and farmland.

We don't have to deal with the same problems as people in larger cities. There's no smog, no Corleone wannabes, or multiple serial killers to deal with. Things are still simple here. We learn to dodge potholes and road kill doing eighty on the highway and still think of tornadoes as a warped form of entertainment. And we can even produce our fair share of celebrities. Gene Autry, Vince Gill, Carrie Underwood, Toby Keith, Reba McEntire, Garth Brooks, the Hansons, James Garner, Chuck Norris, and finally Brad Pitt. I know most Oklahomans claim Brad Pitt as an

Oklahoman even though I'm pretty sure he was only born here and has probably never stepped on red dirt since leaving. Okay, I'm mentally babbling...

"And that had to be the *best* hamburger I've ever had," he added, redirecting my attention toward him. This is where my attention should be.

"Yeah, I'm pretty sure that was Steak."

"A steak hamburger?"

"My brother's cow *named* Steak," I clarified with a cheeky grin.

"We ate your brother's cow?" he asked, horrified.

"Okay, city boy. You do know where hamburgers come from, don't ya?" I teased.

"Yeah." He shook his head, glowering at me. "No, I mean, we ate your brother's...pet?"

"I don't know if 'pet' is the right word. He'll buy a calf every year. Feed him, take care of him, and yes, even name him, but once he's big enough—he'll have him slaughtered."

Bradley just blinked.

"It's not so uncommon. Around here at least," I reassured him. "It's pretty smart actually. Marcus can control the cow's environment, make sure he gets only the best feed, and then only takes enough of the meat for him and his family. He sells the rest so he actually breaks even at the end—or maybe even comes out a little ahead. Plus you have the luxury of knowing exactly where your meat comes from and what it ate before it wound up on your plate."

"Oh," he simply said. "Okay. Makes sense I guess..."

I could only imagine the images flitting through his head. My smile widened at the thought.

"So," he changed the subject, "after meeting your family, I'm even more confused."

"How so?"

"Well, a few of them, after a while, didn't seem so afraid to ask questions."

"Oh mercy—sorry." I shook my head. I thought I had kept pretty good tabs on everyone, making sure they weren't hounding him.

"No, it's okay. But I've always wondered why you weren't as… inquisitive as most other people I meet, thinking maybe it was just how you were raised. Guess not!"

"Well," I hesitated, "I didn't know if you trusted me enough."

He just waited for me continue.

"I mean, you didn't know me, and I didn't want to ask you anything too personal and make you think I'd go running off to the *New York Post* the next day." I let my head drift to the side to see if I could decipher any emotion from his composed face. Nope.

"Oh," he said flatly.

"It wasn't because I wasn't interested. I was just being…cautious." *Just as I am now. Afraid that if I say one wrong word—it will be the end.* I'd never see his gorgeous face or hear his sultry voice again.

"So you're still reluctant to ask me anything, even now?" he asked curiously with a smile.

"Well, not so much now…since you've broken the ice by attacking my big brother with a plastic bat," I taunted.

"Yeah, that should help lighten things up a bit." He chuckled.

We both just sat there for a moment. I had to bite my lip rather hard to keep another round of hysterical laughter from taking me over when the recent memory from this afternoon entered my brain again. I thought maybe this would be the best opportunity I'd have for *really* talking to him. In my experience, you could have a pretty deep conversation while riding in the car, something about being able to answer more honestly when you could respectfully decline eye contact. So I figured I'd give it a shot. I tried to steady myself by taking an unnoticed deep breath. My brain shuffled through the list of questions I had stored away. Mostly centering on his love life and upbringing.

"So I'm free to interrogate now?" I questioned lightly, knowing what obvious answer I'd get, now.

"Fire away."

"I'm guessing you want me to break it down a little more than the broad 'what's it like being an international superstar?' question—or would you like to start there?" I asked, still testing just how I wanted to start.

"Yeah, that's a little generic," he said, disappointed.

"Okay. Hum…well, you were pretty much raised in the spotlight, so to say, weren't you? So who raised you, took care of you on a daily basis, your parents?"

"Uhhh," he said, seemingly taken a little by surprise by the first formal question. "I remember my parents being there a lot, when I was little, but I did have a few full-time nannies that helped with the day-to-day things for me and my little sister while my parents worked. Knowing as many families as I do in the entertainment industry, I can say that my parents were more involved than a lot of other people I know. Some people don't really have a lot to do with their kids once their born. They're like an accessory or political statement. They only have them around when they feel like it or if it benefits them in some way. I'm glad mine weren't like that. Once I got older, they were very involved with me and made sure to keep me out of trouble and focused."

"Focused? How?" I pressed.

"They didn't want me to turn into some spoiled, overprivileged partier who just mooched off them. They made sure that I was dedicated to my schoolwork and didn't let me get too involved in the industry until I was older. I think they wanted to make sure I knew there were other possibilities out there for me, that I didn't have to follow in their footsteps. Or maybe they didn't even want me to. I never really asked them—what their intentions were.

"They always made sure I was disciplined too—not because they were afraid that it would reflect badly on them, but because that's how they were raised by their parents. My grandparents struggled through World War Two and the Great Depression, just like everyone else and firmly instilled their values into my parents. Just like yours, it seems."

He eyed me again, like he was trying to bridge the gap between our two worlds with a few words and one careful look. "Except my parents didn't go on to become Oscar-winning actors," I reminded him.

He nodded, accepting the comparison.

"Did you go to college?"

He smiled and laughed, just once under his breath.

"See, this is why I didn't want to ask you anything. I feel like you think that I should know some of this stuff already—and I don't!" I was oddly self-conscious about the fact that I didn't keep up with the tabloids.

"No," he said quickly. "It's just weird describing this everyday stuff with someone who doesn't really know it already. But it's nice…" He shook his head like he was trying to remember my question. "There are a few celebrities who choose to go to college here in the States, like Harvard or Columbia, but I wanted to go somewhere where I wouldn't be as…noticeable. I figured I wouldn't be as well known overseas, so I went to Oxford to study classics and modern languages."

"Yikes," I interjected. Like it wasn't enough that he was breathtakingly handsome, he was a nerd too. His extensive knowledge had already led me to believe that he had some type of formal training, especially after my Guggenheim tutorial. But I didn't need another indicator that we were worlds apart. My little degree from Oklahoma State University paled in comparison to his accomplishments. Obviously.

He chuckled at my reaction. "I just kind of plowed my way through it. I had been undecided, up till then, whether or not I was going to go in to entertainment. After my first year, I figured I wanted to take a shot at it at least but wanted to finish my studies first. So I finished there and came back here and lucked out by getting a few back-to-back movie roles."

Yeah, like luck had anything to do with that. Not that he got the roles just because of his name either. He was talented. But when does that happen? When does a new star have multiple successful films, back to back. It was more than luck. I don't know what it is or was, but it wasn't just luck.

Either his own words upset him or somehow he was reading my thoughts because his mood suddenly shifted and his eyes narrowed uneasily.

"I sometimes think that it's happening too fast," he continued, without any prompting from me. "That my success, or whatever you want to call it, is happening too fast, too soon. Shouldn't it be spread out over a few decades rather than just a few years...?" he trailed.

Was that a rhetorical question? Surely he didn't expect me to have the answer to a question like that. I just kept my eyes on the road ahead of me and tried to forget about the storm creeping up behind us.

"I don't know," he suddenly said. "Maybe I'm doomed. Nowhere to go but down from here. They can't all be blockbusters and—" He stopped abruptly.

"And what?" I asked instantly. I liked that he seemed to be on a rant but couldn't figure out why he'd stopped.

He drew in a long breath. "It won't be long, I'm sure, till I make some mistake, give a crappy performance, or just wind up making a flop. I guess I'm kind of worried that I'll be instantly written off as a fluke," he confessed. His words came out a little slower, a little sadder.

"Doubtful," I replied automatically. But on second thought, what did I know? He probably had more of an inkling of what his future would hold better than me in those circumstances. "You seem to be handling it all very well though, considering it's all happened so fast."

He didn't answer at first, and I wondered if he was so lost in thought that he didn't hear me.

"My parents," he said quietly, staring forward blankly. "They've helped a lot. It's nice having someone to tell me what to expect and what they did, to have someone to prepare me a little."

That must be nice. I wish I'd had someone to prepare me more for all the craziness in my life. But I didn't. I didn't know a single person who had gone through the same things as I had. When my dad died, both of my mom's parents were alive, and I always felt like she had no clue how it felt, and I felt guilty when I realized that I was unconsciously holding that against her. And when Josh died, I definitely didn't know anyone who'd experienced that same level of loss, so I had no shoulder to cry on there either—proverbial or literal.I was irritated that our conversation had taken on such a gloomy vibe. Another reason I was avoiding this—I knew I'd say the wrong thing. I was desperately trying to find a way to lighten the mood. He must have been too.

"It does have its perks though—being famous." He laughed.

Either he was a really good actor, or he wasn't as affected by the previous conversation as I thought… "I'm sure," I said with an eye roll. "What's your favorite part about that then?" Surely this would be a lighter topic.

He slowly leaned his head back and rested it on the headrest as he thought. "I guess it's just nice to have the means to do what I want. Sounds shallow, I'm sure, but it's nice to be able to get on a plane and come see you—for instance—without having to think about it. And I have several charities and organizations that I have the opportunity to work with, and it's nice to be able to do that."

"Yeah, that part would be nice I guess." I never worried about money much. I guessed it was since I had enough to pay the bills. I worked and made money, just never spent much of it. Except for the necessities: mortgage payment, car payment, food, etc. I never spent much on myself, and when I tried (by taking a trip to

NYC) somehow I spent close to nothing. "I bet I can guess what your least favorite part of being a celebrity is," I wagered.

"Probably. What?"

"The paparazzi—people always following you around."

"Yes. That would probably be it," he answered glumly. "Well, not just that really. The whole being in the spotlight thing. I don't get the fascination with me or other celebrities. The most fascinating thing we do is make movies, and everyone can see those. The constant obsession with what we're doing and who we're doing it with is infuriating. I can't go out to dinner with a female without it turning into a marriage proposal. I can't hug a man without a headline about me being gay. I have to watch what I say in public for fear my words will be contorted into something completely different."

I nodded my head. I'd had only a glimpse into his world, but I could see how that part would be miserable.

"What about you? What would be your favorite and least favorite part?" he asked, cutting the silence.

"Hummm…" I exaggerated. "Let me see…well, the paparazzi thing would probably be my least favorite too. Or maybe a tie with that and the whole fashion thing."

"You don't like clothes?" he asked, surprised. Probably another shocker for him considering all his conquests had been models or actresses who were probably more into their looks than I am. But it shouldn't be *that* much of a shocker considering my wardrobe.

"It's not that—I just don't get the point. The whole 'fashion police,'" I air quoted, "just seems so pointless. Who cares what people wear to the grocery store or to the gym or while they're playing with their kid or something? I've never been into labels I guess. Who cares who made it if it still looks hideous? What a waste of money…" I trailed until a fresh thought made me giggle. I lifted a hand from the steering wheel and waved it across my body. "I bet they'd have a field day with me. Jeans and a T-shirt— pretty boring."

Bradley just smirked. "I guess I don't worry about that part as much. Kind of hard to get into too much trouble with your wardrobe as a man. But I do have a stylist. And the best part?" he encouraged.

"Well, I always joke that there would be one thing I'd love to do if I won the lottery or came into a lot of money somehow."

"And that would be…"

"I'd want to start some kind of program for veterans. 'A man who is good enough to shed his blood for his country is good enough to be given a square deal afterwards. More than that no man is entitled to, and less than that no man shall have.'" The quote burned my throat.

"Theodore Roosevelt."

I should have known that Bradley would know the man behind the quote. I nodded.

"My dad." I cleared my throat so I could continue. "He served in Vietnam, in the navy. He died of CLL—a type of leukemia that is caused by exposure to herbicides. And since my dad never spent a day on a farm in his life…"

"Agent Orange?" he concluded flatly.

I just bobbed my head again. He didn't ask me to elaborate… yet. I now had my right arm resting on the center console. My hand was dangling in the space between us. Bradley reached for it slowly and squeezed it.

I must not have been paying attention to my speed because we were already coming up on the Yukon exits. I must have let my lead foot take over because the eighty-five miles passed in a blink.

"Almost home." I smiled. I didn't want the bleakness hanging around any longer.

He just answered back with a wide smile that lit up the inside of the car.

Within a few minutes, we were settled inside my house. I was rustling up something for us to nibble on in the kitchen. After

Bradley was finished assessing the living room, he walked toward my direction. He hesitated by the bakers rack against the dining room wall. His long fingers traced the cherry wood case that held the flag that was once draped over my father's casket.

His eyes flickered with sympathy as they met mine.

He walked slowly to the breakfast bar and plopped down on the stool.

"Chicken taco salads? I think that's all I have here."

"Trying to get me to eat healthy?" He laughed. "Sounds fine—if it's not too much trouble."

"Well, you could probably stand to cut back on the red meat a little," I pointed out as I pulled the ingredients from the refrigerator. I threw some marinade on the chicken while I grabbed the necessary cooking equipment. "And the alcohol too."

"What? I don't drink that much."

"Uh huh. If you keep it up, you'll have to get a dog and name him '*Liver* Spot'," I laughed.

Bradley rolled his eyes and then smiled that crooked little smile. He was quiet as I continued to assemble dinner.

"Can I help?" he finally asked.

"Sure. Can you shred some cheese?" I said as I tossed the block of Colby-Jack his direction.

"You can buy cheese that's already shredded. You know that, right?" he asked as he moved to the other side of the counter. "It's not that hard." I groaned as I got out the metal cheese grater. "Just don't shred any knuckles in there," I ordered.

As he turned his back to get to work, it finally hit me. *Bradley friggin' Matthews* was in my kitchen shredding a two-dollar block of store-brand cheese. Any right-minded female between puberty and menopause would kill a Boy Scout for the chance to have him in their house, and here I was ordering him around like Martha Stewart! I bit down on my knuckle to stifle a squeak and got back to my own duties before he caught me gawking.

"Okay, sorry, but I have to ask," he said suddenly, causing me knock over the salt and pepper shakers I was setting down.

"Okay, ask away."

"So your dad was a blue water navy veteran?"

"Yes. When my dad was diagnosed with CLL, his doctors knew it was because of exposure to Agent Orange. That was the only explanation considering his age and service background. When I was in college, the VA openly admitted that CLL was directly caused by exposure to Agent Orange. So, because of that, my brothers and I were supposed to be entitled to some survivors' benefits." I sucked in a long breath, slowly and unsteadily.

"Long story short, we keep getting denied benefits simply because my dad was in the *navy*. A loophole. They keep saying since my dad was on a ship, there was no way he could've been exposed. Which is a crock—and even they know it. It's so disheartening. And it's not because of the money—we wouldn't have gotten a ton of money or anything. I mean, that would have helped in college. To not have to work two jobs and be a full-time student, but it's like they're discrediting my dad's service to the country. His death was caused by his service. Period. It's not like we want his name added to the Vietnam Wall or anything," I rambled. "Although I guess it could belong there. He didn't take a bullet to the chest, but he died all the same."

I sighed. "Anyhoo. It just ticks me off. It's like the government is going out of its way to dishonor him. And many other veterans and their families. Sticks in my crawl that so many people are treated so horribly after all they do for us, for our country." My little rant had gotten me worked up, as usual, and I was cutting up a tomato with a little more fervor than necessary and moved on to the chicken that I was taking off the George Foreman grill.

"That's horrible," he agreed.

I shrugged as I turned around to meet his gaze. I recognized the look in his eyes, and it wasn't pity. It was pure sympathetic warmth, and I realized now that it was the same look he was giv-ing me after I spilled the beans about Josh.

But a moment later, his eyebrows pulled together angrily, and he seemed to shake off some thought. I didn't ask what it was. I just smiled at him. My change of mood confused him, and he cocked his head to one side—inviting me to explain.

"Josh used to make fun of me 'cause I also had this other little thing I always wanted to do but never had the...funds." I laughed a little as I took the shredded cheese from Bradley. "Whenever I'm out eating and I see military personnel, like in fatigues or something, I always want to buy their meal. If I were rich, I would just go around to all the restaurants and anony-mously pay for the meals of anyone who looked like they were in the military. Weird, huh?"

"Nah." He laughed back as he made his way back to his chair behind the bar. "Sounds like you."

"So anyway, to answer your *original* question—about what I'd do if I was rich and famous. I'd like to set up some kind of fund for veterans and their families—for those who aren't getting the fair shake they deserve. Or if they just need a little extra help. If the government isn't going to take care of its veterans, I'd be proud to!" I exclaimed, my chin pointed primly in the air.

Bradley nodded in agreement.

"Your dad would be proud," he said sincerely.

My eyes darted to the floor quickly. "Yeah," I mumbled. Then I took a bite of the chicken I had finished dicing up. That would give me some time to find my voice again while I fought back tears. I pulled the golden brown taco shells out of the oven and quickly assembled the salads.

"Somehow you were supposed to be interrogating me, and we wound up talking about you again," Bradley said as he watched me work.

"Funny how that keeps happening." I eyed him suspiciously. Like he was somehow able to steer the conversation as he pleased.

I just stood there, across from him. I placed his salad in front of him, and he dug in. I was just eating at the counter. I didn't dare sit next to him while I was still somewhat emotionally unstable. I needed distractions. Somewhere to escape to if I needed wipe my eyes or compose myself. "Well, the only other topic left is your love life, and you didn't elaborate on that too much when I asked you the first time."

"That's the only topic left?" he asked grudgingly.

"Stalling?" I challenged.

"No," Bradley said abruptly. "There's just nothing more to it than that. If I had met someone interesting enough, I guess I'd be taken by now."

"So that's how it works. You find someone 'interesting' and you marry them? Sounds easy."

"Hardly. Is that how it works here?"

"No, no, no." I waved my finger in his face. "It's your turn, remember?"

"What do you want me to say? I just haven't dated anyone that's done it for me. Everyone I've been with, in that way, has been…" He made a motion with one of his hands, creating circles in the air like he was trying to generate the words to finish his sentiment. "So one dimensional," he continued. "There wasn't much under the surface. The surface was nice," he winked, "but that can only hold your attention for so long."

"Geeze. You're such a male."

He laughed.

"I guess it's hard though—considering your occupation."

"How so?"

I frowned. We were back to me talking more than him.

"Who was it…?" I trailed, trying to remember. "Oh yeah—Rita Hayworth that said, 'They go to bed with Gilda, they wake up with me.' Are you ever worried that the person that you're with is more enamored with your most popular or recent character—instead of you?"

"Kind of. Mostly I worry *why* they want to be with me. I question their motives. Paranoid I guess, but I feel like the people I've dated in the past had more to gain by being with me than just companionship."

I felt guilty for some reason. There was no telling what he thought I was doing with him. What he thought I had to gain by being with him. What did he think my motives were? I was tempted to ask, but he interrupted my train of thought.

"There's plenty of time I guess."

"Maybe." I regretted my response immediately. Now he'd want me to elaborate. So I gave him a short explanation before this turned into another sidetrack conversation. "If my experiences teach you anything, it's that we aren't guaranteed tomorrow." As if God Himself were acknowledging my statement, a loud crack of thunder sent shockwaves through my body.

"True," Bradley said calmly. He eyed me curiously, seeming to notice my reaction to the thunder and choosing not to comment on it.

"I don't know how anyone in show biz stays together. I guess your parents," I remembered, taking another bite of salad. "They seem to have it figured out."

"They were married before they got famous. Maybe that has something to do with it," he suggested.

"Maybe. But still. Marriage is hard enough without all the extra pressures of stardom, the crazy schedules, the expectations, the temptations."

"What do you mean?"

"My word." I laughed, playfully annoyed.

"I'm sorry; I can't help it apparently."

"Evidently. It's like spending the evening with the D.A. 'No, Mr. Matthews—I don't know how my fingerprints ended up on the bloody knife,'" I quipped, hands raised in the air. "I think you missed your calling as an interrogator."

"I'm not usually so inquisitive," he said, seeming just as confused as I.

I cocked a brow in response.

"I'm used to people spilling their guts without my prompting." He shrugged one shoulder.

"Okay, so you missed your calling as a bartender."

He smiled around a bite of food as I continued. "Anyway, back
to the subject. Mind you, I don't know exactly what I'm talking
about since I've never actually been married, but I went through
all the pre-marital counseling. Being married is the hardest job
in the world, and anyone who doesn't realize that going in is in a
heap of trouble."

He gestured for me to continue.

"Okay, I was raised in the Bible belt and in a very religious family, so our backgrounds are probably different on this.
Marriage is more than just a commitment between two people.
It's a bond that is honored before God. Most marriage vows and
ceremonies acknowledge this, right?"

He nodded. Man, I'd never given so many monologues in my
life.

"But we're human, and we succumb to everyday pressures, so
that makes it hard to remember that marriage should be bigger
than just the merging of our physical and emotional selves. It
seems, from where I'm standing, that most show biz unions are
just a contract rather than a covenant. Like when things get hard,
which they inevitably will, or when they meet someone else—
they just get divorced and move on. And with your job, you're
continually put in the position where you're intimate with people
on set. So if you're involved with someone while making a movie
where you're kissing someone else all day on set… Well, it's not
hard to see how that would cause a problem. Kind of the grass-
is-greener-on-the-other-side syndrome. Isn't it kind of common
to fall for your costars?" I asked rhetorically.

"It's bound to happen when you spend that much time with someone and get all wrapped up in the moment. I don't see how actors can stay married to other actors. It's just asking for trouble. It looks like that *to me*. Marriage is the deepest level of commitment. I'm not so bold as to say that just because you're committed to someone that you can't or won't fall for somebody else. You can obviously fall in love with someone else, so it's important to be so deeply committed that you never put yourself in a position where that can happen. Where I come from, there are only a few reasons to get divorced; irreconcilable differences isn't one of them."

"So I'm doomed?" he asked pointedly.

I turned my back quickly to him, placing the dirty utensils in the sink. I was constantly saying the wrong thing to him. Pointing out all the dirty details of his job. Sheesh. Why did he continue to do this to himself? Masochist?

"Nah," I responded lightly as I turned around. "I guess that's the beauty of it. You have a choice in the matter. This is just how *I* think of it now. Not everyone does, obviously, and not everyone would want that type of commitment. The horribly high divorce rate in this country proves that. And that's fine. To each their own." I threw him a smirk. "But you've always really wanted to be a producer or director or something anyways, right? Someone who isn't required to make out with everyone on set? So you should be fine."

He smiled halfheartedly. But I could tell by the cloud in his eyes that he was lost in thought, like he'd never given what I'd said any thought—till now.

I walked over to him, and he spun around on the stool to face me. I playfully hit him on the shoulder with the back of my hand. "I'm just rambling. Crazy Oklahoma girl and her crazy thoughts."

We moved into the living room. I flipped on the television out of habit and waited for it to come to life. I never watched a lot of it, but always had it on in the background. Instead of plopping on the couch, I sat on the floor and leaned up against the chocolate-colored faux suede ottoman. He joined me.

"So while I was dragging in Cordell during high school, what were you doing?" I asked, less cautious than before.

He laughed without much humor and didn't answer immediately. "Well, more than just riding around with friends. My parents kept me out of trouble for the most part, but that didn't keep me from…experimenting."

"Oh."

"Didn't do any of that? Experimenting?"

"Depends on what you mean by 'experiment' I guess. Alcohol and drugs are just as much of a problem here," I pointed out, not knowing if that was what he was talking about. "I drank a little," I admitted sheepishly.

"A little?" He laughed.

"Well, it was nice to give my brain a rest, ya know? It was easier to block out the bad memories and pain on those nights. But I got caught and haven't really touched it since." By high school I had lived through enough to turn most people into alcoholics. Some of the pain my family knew about, but there was more of it that no one knew about.

"Yeah. I know how that goes," he agreed.

"So…you…?"

"Um…" He cleared his throat. "Yeah, I pretty much tried it all."

Wow. My imagination could get carried away with such a vague statement. I looked down between us. My fingers found his arm, and I softly trailed the crease of his inner elbow. The static electricity in the air caused a little shock. I wondered what, if anything, had been sent surging through his veins.

"Yeah," he acknowledged as he started to cringe away from my touch.

I grabbed his arm more forcefully to keep him from getting too far away: physically or emotionally.

He stared at me as my fingertips fluttered against the inside of his elbow one more time.

"I know. Poor little rich boy. What could be so wrong with his life that he'd have to resort to recreational drugs..."

"I wasn't judging," I mumbled, interrupting his rant. Did he think I was so small minded?

"You think differently of me?" His words drew up into a question, but it felt more like an accusation.

I had to swallow the lump out of my throat before I could respond.

"No," I murmured honestly. "I just wish I knew you then. I wish that I could have taken some of your pain away...and carried it in *my* veins so that you wouldn't have had to put anything in yours."

I blushed at my stalker-sounding admission.

"Always the mother hen." He laughed, a little darkly.

Before I had a chance to respond there was a flash of lightning followed, very closely, by pulsating thunder. The lights flickered off.

CHAPTER 15

My body froze, and I felt Bradley stiffen next to me. Whether it was because of my reaction, my last words, or the storm—I didn't know. We both stood up. His strong hands found my waist. I trembled at his touch.

"Holy moly!" I exclaimed. Hopefully he would think I was talking about the storm.

"That sounds close."

I twisted out of his grasp so that I could think clearly. I grabbed his hand so he could follow me to the large kitchen window. It was like watching a fireworks show. Each streak of lightning lit up the sky. Even when I closed my eyes, I could still see it. The rain pelted the window in sheets. And I continued to shudder with each thunder. I finally had to back away from the window. I glanced at the one battery-operated clock in the dining room. Ten fifteen. It wasn't really late, but I needed to be in the confines of my room. I didn't know how I had held out for so long, probably because I didn't want to lose it in front of Bradley. But I wasn't confident that my strength would hold.

It was then that I noticed that his hand was still in mine. Confused, I just tugged on it to lead him to his room for the night.

"Well, it's no suite at The Plaza," I teased, a little unsteadily, as we found our way blindly through the living room between lightning strikes.

"I'm sure it'll be fine," he said thickly. I'm sure the thought of being blown away by the storm that seemed to be enveloping my small house was starting to creep into his consciousness, a fear, if it was one at all, which he would never dream of telling me. One, well, because he was a man. Since when did a man admit to being afraid of anything? Second, I'm sure he didn't want to bring up the subject of deadly storms around me. I knew they were deadly. Since meeting me, now he did too.

We stood there in the doorway to the small guest room. Just one queen-sized bed and one bedside table with a lamp that wouldn't work now.

"I'll be just down the hall here if you need anything." I tried to free my hand from his grip but couldn't. He moved closer to me, placing his free hand on the left side of my face. I quivered again, and I was suddenly aware of my pulse. For the first time in ages, I felt it convulsing out of control. My breathing was staggered. I was desperate to get away, but my feet were locked into place. His hand slid down my face. My neck. Through my hair. And settled on my lower back. I closed my eyes and could see another flash of lighting burning through my eyelids.

"Good night," he murmured.

My legs effectively turned into jelly. He turned away from me, and I felt my shoulders lurch forward in protest. Or was it disappointment?

"Night," I managed to croak.

I tried to make sense of my nonsensical physical reactions and quickly wrote them off as anxiety over the storm.

I washed my face in the dark and threw on a black tank top and some pink and black striped shorts. No Victoria's Secret here. I settled into bed and curled up in the familiar fetal position as the storm continued around me. My head was still spinning even though my breathing and pulse had found a more natural rhythm.

I was busy trying to stay calm as the storm raged on outside. I was startled some time later when I noticed a large figure in my doorway. Out of instinct I bolted upright in bed. But the figure ignored my reaction and came closer. Of course it was Bradley. It took a half second after I was startled to put the pieces together, to remember that he hadn't only just been in my thoughts, but just down the hall. He gauged my expression as he approached the side of my bed. I had no idea what my face was telling him or what he could see in the darkness. I lay back down; in a more natural position, on my side, facing him. He slowly climbed onto the bed—on top of the covers. I was cuddled underneath the sheet and thin blanket even though the room was plenty warm from the lack of air conditioning.

He settled into position beside me, on his side as well, facing me. My eyes readjusted to the darkness so I could see him. His eyes were soft and warm, inviting. I felt as if he had some super-power, at least over me. I was instantly at ease. I let my eyes roam over his manly physique. He wasn't wearing a shirt. Only baggy pajama bottoms that looked as if they'd seen better days. My eyes followed the curve of his bicep and noticed the muscles moving while I felt his fingers intertwining with mine. His strong, hard chest was lightly covered with dark hair. His long neck gave way to a strong jaw. His matchless face: the slope of his nose, the dark perfectly arched eyebrows. He had a wide mouth and the top lip had a perfect bow. His dark untamed hair fell gently across his forehead. Bradley's eyes were curiously examining my own, no doubt noticing that I was giving him a full appraisal.

The flickers of light from the lightning made it easier to appreciate his beauty stretched out before me. It wasn't long before I no longer shuddered at the storm weakening outside but longed for the light that it cast on him, reflecting off his golden, tanned skin. Being able to jet-set across the world did wonders to keep a nice, tanned complexion. I concentrated on keeping my breathing even and slow, matching the rise and fall of his chest to mine. The electricity from the storm seemed to seep into the small room and wrap us in its fever. Heat that I'd never felt in my life flared through my body. I shivered as he gently traced each of my fingers, my palm, and then up the inside of my forearm, an innocent brushing of fingertips that was like a punch to my solar plexus.

We never said a word. We just lay there. His fingers only left my skin once—to brush my hair behind my ear. I grabbed his hand as it fell back to the bed. I ran my fingertips across the palm of his hand, down each long finger—mimicking what he'd done to me—before meshing my hand with his. My eyes gained weight after each blink. I fought their heaviness but eventually lost. The sound of thunder rumbling in the distance now didn't hold the same fear as it had just hours before.

■　■　■　■　■

The slight humming of electricity and the air conditioner kicking on woke me as the warm sun burned across my bedroom. All remnants of the storm were long gone, except for maybe one. I opened my eyes, and it was if neither of us had moved a muscle the entire night. Bradley was still stretched out in front of me, his fingers still wrapped in mine. Dark stubble covered the lower part of his face. His eyelids fluttered, his long, dark lashes tickling the thin skin under his eyes as he continued to dream.

He looked as beautiful now as he ever had. Of all the movies I'd seen him in, he never looked as perfect as he did now. It wasn't at all like going to see your favorite band perform live and then being disappointed when they didn't sound as good as they did on the radio. Maybe it was because he was here in person that he seemed so flawless, so real—so much so that if possible, the movies had never done him proper justice. But he belonged in movies. Not here in my small, plain bedroom with such a small, plain girl.

I stared at our loosely locked fingers. They seemed to sum it up: two very different halves trying to make a whole.

My self-consciousness got the better of me. It was hard to leave him there, but I was afraid that my natural morning look might scare him off. I slowly slid my fingers out from under his, slipped off the bed, and crept quietly to the bathroom.

It was pleasant not seeing the red puffy eyes that usually stared back at me the morning after a storm. I changed, brushed my teeth, and got myself together quickly. As I cracked the door open I saw Bradley stretching out his long arms and legs across the bed, filling up the king-sized bed. I watched muscle and sinew flex and ripple as he moved. I rested my head on the side of the door, and a smile broke across my face.

"Good morning," I sang, shocking myself a little with my giddiness.

"Oh man, don't tell me you're a morning person," he groaned.

Who wouldn't be a morning person if they had him to awaken to? "Sometimes. After I get a good night's sleep. When's your flight?"

He sat up in bed, ruffling his fingers through his dark hair. I saw him glance at the clock. It was almost noon.

"Two twenty." He sighed.

"Oh wow! We better hurry! Hungry?"

I didn't wait for him to answer. I ran off to the kitchen to whip up something. I saw him cross the living room and grab a black bag from his room. He yawned and threw me a groggy smile before he headed into the hall bath.

I grabbed eggs, milk, and bread and started to assemble the French toast. I cracked two eggs into a bowl, turned to put them back in the fridge, and froze. I looked across the living room and remembered that Bradley wasn't too far away, taking a shower. I was very set in my ways, not used to cooking for anyone other than myself. I sighed and cracked three more eggs into the bowl. I whipped the eggs with a little milk and cinnamon and drenched the bread in it before laying it in the buttered frying pan.

I had a stack of warm French toast and some fresh fruit lying out by the time Bradley joined me, hair still wet from the shower. Gloriously beautiful. I noticed him sniffing the air as he walked across the living room. He came up behind me and curled his arms around me. "Hummm." He sighed. "Good morning," he finally whispered as his clean-shaved cheek grazed mine.

I smiled briefly before my cheeks broke out in a guilty flush. I couldn't pinpoint why that happened, but I cleared my throat and moved away. "So we're finally up now, are we?"

"I could have slept all day. I was very comfortable until I noticed I was alone. You made all this?" he asked, eyeing breakfast.

"Well, we don't have home delivery here like you do. And when I twitch my nose to get things to magically appear like Samantha on *Bewitched*, all that happens is I sneeze."

He pursed his lips thoughtfully. "So you made this."

"So I made it."

"Smart aleck."

"I know," I said with a smile.

He was going after the toast with unabashed hunger, and something made him freeze. Suddenly he looked up at me with horror and pointed one finger in the air. My brows pulled together in confusion, and he reacted instinctively. He grabbed my arm and pulled me, roughly through the kitchen toward—I don't know where.

"What is going on?" I demanded.

He stopped abruptly, and I finally heard the noise that was causing his distress and pulled back on his arm, trying to stop him.

"It's *not* a tornado siren, Bradley," I blurted out quickly, trying not to laugh.

He just stared back at me, baffled.

"Well, it is I guess." I batted my eyes as I thought. "But it's just the noon whistle. No tornado," I reassured him again. Every Saturday the tornado sirens squealed at noon. Of course I didn't think anything of it. Most days I didn't even hear it, which is why I guess I didn't notice it even though it was Tuesday, not Saturday. I guess they were doing some kind of test. If I ever read the local newspaper I probably would have known about it.

He dropped my arm and rested his hands on his knees while he caught his breath. I continued to stand there—trying my very best to keep from laughing, but just like the day before on the makeshift ball field—I failed.

Bradley looked up at me disapprovingly. "Give a guy some credit here," he chided. "I was trying to rescue you."

"And what exactly did you plan on doing?"

He hesitated. "I hadn't gotten that far yet…"

"Some knight in shining armor!" I teased.

"I was trying to get you into a doorway or something."

"That's for earthquakes, you jackwagon." I chuckled.

"Agghh," he grumbled as he walked back to the kitchen.

I walked after him and turned him around so that he was facing me again. Time to soothe the damaged male ego. "Thank you," I said solemnly but with a smile, "for saving me."

"Very funny." He rolled his eyes and went back to picking at the fruit. "I'm tempted not to ask you now."

"Ask me what?"

"Nope. You made fun of me. No dice."

"Ah, come on!" I felt as giddy as a toddler on Christmas morning. I guess my excitement overwhelmed his need to tease me.

"Well, there's this…benefit event thing that I'm going to. Not this Saturday, but the next, and I was wondering…" He looked at me and fought with the twitching corners of his mouth.

I leaned my head forward, toward him, about to topple over if he didn't finish the sentence quickly.

"I was wondering if you'd like to come with me," he finally finished.

"Oh." I didn't know what I was expecting, but it wasn't that. Like a date?

"It's in L.A. Of course I'd fly you out that morning and put you up in a hotel. Whole nine yards," he added flatly.

I mentally rejected every item in my wardrobe. *Blame it all on my roots, I showed up in boots and ruined your black tie affair.* I shook Garth Brooks' voice and lyrics out of my head, suppressing a giggle. I could probably manage something other than boots, but... He saw my hesitation and started to quickly amend his offer.

"Designers are forever sending me stuff, so I'm sure I could rustle something up for you to wear. I promise I'll take care of everything. But will you? Will you please come with me?" He almost begged, holding my gaze with deepening eyes.

I could easily come up with a few dozen other reasons why I should say no. My tendency to put my foot in my mouth. A red carpet just begging me to trip over it. More photographers willing to capture how mismatched we looked together. Whispers. Curious glances. But something inside of me suppressed my eternal pessimism. "S-sure," I stuttered.

"Good."

I stood there. Still wondering what I had just agreed to. Me. L.A. Some fancy benefit. If anything spelled a disaster, it was that. Oh boy.

I unwillingly took Bradley to the airport a short time later. We had another friendly good-bye. His hands were a little tighter on my face as he held me in position. His lips lingered a little longer than usual on my pale pink scar. I let my hand fall from its standard position on his shoulder, down his bare arm, my fingers memorizing the feel of him.

I didn't understand the mixture of feelings that consumed me as he got out of my car and turned his back to me. I stared after him until he was long gone, until horn blasts suddenly jolted me back to reality.

The days and nights couldn't have gone by any slower. Although Bradley and I kept in constant contact, it wasn't enough, not after having him so close to me and knowing that in a number of measurable hours I'd be with him again.

I was still unsure whether or not this invitation of his had any ulterior motive other than companionship. Whether it was a friendly gesture or more. But after all this time he still hadn't made any real "move." And I was sure that I wouldn't be the one to breach that careful yet fuzzy line.

He made all the arrangements, just as he promised. First class all the way. I was a little embarrassed when a long black limo picked me up at my house and even more embarrassed when there was one waiting for me at LAX. I had to contain my enthusiasm when I climbed in the back and saw Bradley there waiting for me. My heart thudded wildly as he hugged me tightly hello and continued with his standard (for him anyways) greeting: a warm kiss on my completely healed wound.

We made small talk, and he apologized for not being able to spend the day with me, due to uber important celebrity business I'm sure. My heart sank a little bit at this news but continued to pound wistfully as he promised we'd have all night together.

My jaw dropped as we pulled up to the famous W Hotel, and he laughed at my small-town reaction. He handed me my room key and gave me a few instructions.

"They'll direct you to where your suite is, and after that, well, all I can do is apologize." He chuckled, making it sound like he was sorry he wouldn't be able to witness whatever I was about to get myself into.

I felt my brow wrinkle as confusion and panic washed through me.

"I let my assistant hire some…help for you today. Hopefully they're not too intense."

"Help?" I squeaked.

"You'll see."

Uh huh.

Before I got out, he grabbed my hand. He flipped it over and pressed a kiss into my palm then protected it by bending each finger into a loose fist. I was a little dizzy as I stepped out of the limo.

My bag was already waiting for me once I stepped away from the car. I was greeted by several well-dressed employees who somehow knew my name as they directed me toward my room, er…suite. The contemporary décor inside (and out) of the hotel was amazing. Definitely different from The Plaza and yet the same, like something out of a dream. I also recognized the familiarity of style—contemporary, just like Bradley's apartment.

I cautiously opened the door to my room and was startled by the flurry of activity. I double-checked the room number on the door before stepping inside.

"Ah! There she is. *Finally,*" a light masculine voice called.

By then someone had my hand and was dragging me into the large, open suite.

There were two men in front of me now. They looked a lot alike: short in stature with dark, spiky hairdos and olive complexions.

"I'm Nicko," one of them declared as he eyed me up and down.

"I'm Geev," the other said, doing the same type of assessment.

I didn't move a muscle. I just stood there as they made whispered comments to themselves. *Uncomfortable much?* I sighed.

One of them, I think Nicko, motioned for me to turn around for them. I obliged, awkwardly.

"We'll have to make some adjustments for sure," one offered.

"Hem, yes. But a good frame. Not a complete overhaul," the other agreed.

My face was screwed into a scowl as I finished my turn and saw them standing there, one with hands on hips, the other with fingers steepled under his chin, black-framed glasses nestled in their messy hair. I was trying to process their comments. With just a few words I was likened to a rusty ole muscle car, and I was pretty sure I was handed a sideways compliment, kinda like I was being told I had a face that was made for radio.

"You have one hour until your first appointment, so we need to pick a dress quickly," Geev insisted as he started unzipping the large white garment bags that were hanging nearby.

"Oh-kay," I answered hesitantly. First appointment? I wasn't aware of any appointment.

I tried not to notice the designer names as I tried on the dresses, afraid that it would make me more nervous than I already was. Okay, so I'm not a girly-girl, but I'd have to be dead ten years not to appreciate these gowns. The fabrics were soft and light, the colors vibrant and unlike anything I would have picked for myself. After trying on at least a dozen dresses, we (and when I say "we," I mean the fashionista twins) finally decided on a conservative red strapless gown that had a slight floral print on it. It was tight in the bodice then flowed gracefully from my hip to the floor. It was absolutely gorgeous, and I wouldn't do it justice. They pulled out several pairs of designer shoes. After rummaging around, they settled on moderately high heels with delicate silver straps. They looked great, but I was sure they weren't gonna feel so great after a few hours.

The guys were nice enough. Once they noticed my jitters, they did their best to reassure me as they went on with their work. I finally found out that my first appointment was one of many to help me get "red carpet ready," which just freaked me out even more as I threw on a pair of jeans and a t-shirt, of course, hoping that it would be appropriate enough for walking through the hotel to get to the salon/spa. I waited in the living area for a hotel liaison to come escort me to the appropriate place. Heaven forbid I walk myself down there!

I looked around the room, now that I had a minute to myself. Angular lines. Soft color pallet. Luxurious textiles. If I hadn't had the luxury of being in Bradley's apartment, I'd think that this was the most heavenly place on earth. My spirits were instantly lifted when I spotted a silver tray that rested on the small, rectangular, dark wood dining table. Chocolate-covered strawberries. *That sweet man*, I thought as I got up and reached out for one with excited fingers. I thought I was alone in the room, so I was surprised when my hand was unexpectedly slapped.

"Hey!" I whined, recoiling my hand.

It was Nicko. He waved his stubby little index finger in the air from side to side, telling me no.

His eyes widened in shock when I just glared at him as I reached back out for one. I exaggerated my first bite. "Ummm…" I moaned with pleasure.

I laughed as he walked away in a huff, rolling his eyes. Poor souls; they obviously hadn't had much interaction with a strong-willed Southern woman.

The rest of the afternoon flew by as I was rubbed, waxed, plucked, scrubbed, and exfoliated nearly to death. I did enjoy the massage and getting my nails done. I tried to focus on Bradley, which wasn't too hard. He texted me throughout the day to make sure that everyone was treating me nicely and that I was having a good time.

I was instantly anxious again when there were even more people waiting for me when I entered the suite again. They started fussing with me immediately. Hair, then makeup, then into the dress, which now wasn't a foot too long for my stumpy stature. The crew stood there looking at me, making sure everything was in its proper place. I stood in front of the full-length mirror, hardly recognizing myself. I had to fight for my hair to be kept down instead of in some up-do that would give me a headache. My golden hair fell softly down my exposed back. My face seemed flawless except for the *very* slight hump on the bridge of my nose that I now had thanks to a rogue volleyball when I was seventeen. It was nice to see something that made me feel like *me*. The fashionista twins high-fived themselves, evidently pleased with the final product.

"Okay, now walk," Nicko ordered.

"Walk?" I echoed blankly.

"Walk."

I shook my head a little to clear my thoughts. I remembered to stand up straight, shoulders back as I walked across the length of the room. *Graceful, graceful, graceful*, I chanted to myself as I walked slowly.

"Relax a little," Nicko suggested. "You're not going off to war with the Third Reich."

"That's better," Geev applauded as I let my shoulders relax.

I was all too happy when they finally filed out of the room after a few more pointers and I was alone. They had gotten me prepared physically, but I had no idea what I was in for. Was there really going to be a red carpet? Who all would be there? How would Bradley be introducing me to people? I sat down, very carefully—careful not to rumple the dress—and took deep breaths to keep the hysteria away.

Three soft raps at the door took my breath away again. The door opened, and I stood up quickly to greet whoever it might be walking through the door. At this point, I didn't know who or what to expect.

I relaxed a little when I noticed it was Bradley. He blinked a few times, eyebrows raised high.

"Wowza."

Blood flooded to my face, matching my cheeks to my dress as I stared down at the carpet. I looked back up as he walked toward me. He was wearing a black tuxedo with a wide silver tie. The black material clung to his broad shoulders. He plunged his hands into his pockets, sweeping the coat aside, and I noticed how his lean torso tapered to narrow hips. His pants fit perfectly around his muscled thighs and long legs. He looked classy and very Bradley. His hair was still tousled but with some measure of control. His sideways grin kept my breath uneven. He reached out for me, and I offered him my hand without realizing it. He

195

took it happily as he came closer. Thanks to the heels the twins put me in, I could no longer nestle into his chest. My chin still wouldn't graze the top of his shoulder if he were to pull me any closer to him though. He bent and softly kissed my forehead.

"You're beautiful," he breathed.

"You exaggerate," I shot back instinctively. My need to self-deprecate to keep from getting hurt was obviously still intact.

He clicked his tongue and pulled my chin up.

"You look amazing," I said after I cleared my throat. I was trying to keep from talking as much as possible so that he wouldn't catch on to my nerves.

"Ready?"

I nodded. We left the room, and I didn't so much as take a purse with me. I could feel every pair of eyes on us as we walked through the lobby. Bradley walked proudly, tall and poised. I tried to focus on my posture too so that I wouldn't look so unnatural next to this godlike creature.

Once inside the limo, I drew in another long breath to steady myself.

He chuckled, and the sound vibrated over my skin. "Nervous?"

I wrung my hands together in my lap. "Anxious I guess. I don't like not knowing what to expect. I mean, what am I supposed to do? Are you going to be with me the whole time? Do I need to step away if people take pictures of you?" I rambled.

He chuckled again as he took one of my hands with his. He twisted our entwined hands up to his perfect mouth and kissed the back of my hand. The sensation brought on a new rush of anxiety. Why now, of all times, did my body start reacting so differently to his presence, his touch? My stomach knotted.

"I'll never leave your side," he promised. "Don't worry—it'll be fine. Try to have fun."

I nodded as I tried to clear my head.

"My parents are excited to meet you," he suddenly chirped after some time.

"Whaaa-aat?" I croaked.

He laughed low in his throat. I'm glad he found this so friggin' amusing. My heart started acting up again, pounding so hard that it rang in my ears.

"You didn't tell me I'd be meeting your parents," I accused.

"Look who's got their hackles up," he teased.

I felt the limo coming to a stop, and I panicked as I looked at the window and saw flash bulbs lighting the darkening sky. There was a crowd. A red carpet. TV cameras. People holding microphones. Every nightmarish thing you could think of. I could feel myself starting to hyperventilate.

"I at least gave you a heads-up," I reminded him in between my short, shallow breaths. I looked up at him, and his face and his eyes were suddenly intense, smoldering.

The intensity burned through me as he slowly leaned his face closer to mine. My stomach knotted even tighter, and my breath caught in my throat. He looked down to my mouth, and I licked my lips in response. He moved his free hand to stroke my cheekbone then rested it along my jaw with a few fingers moving through the hair at the base of my neck. I could feel confusion trying to take over as other emotions, most of them unrecognizable and foreign, warred within me. He moved his mouth slowly toward mine, and something close to panic shot through me.

The limo door suddenly popped open just when his flawless lips were about to press to mine. With a groan he dropped his head to my bare shoulder, and his silky hair pressed against my check and neck. Nothing like a first *almost* kiss! I remembered to breathe again as he pulled back. That smirk of his was plastered on his face as he started to get out of the limo. He didn't let go of my hand, so I had to slide along the seat as he stood upright once outside.

I heard the flashes from the photographers' cameras pick up speed as he looked back toward me—still halfway in the limo. With shaky knees (for more than one reason) I stood up, next to him. He squeezed my hand gingerly and started moving forward. My feet were a little more reluctant, and as I would have predicted, I stumbled slightly. Since Bradley had a hold of me, he kept me from face planting but saw no problem with laughing at my expense. I nervously checked to make sure I wasn't in trouble in terms of having a wardrobe malfunction and tried to hide my shaking hands.

It was chaotic but not in the same way it was when we were in New York. The photographers were kept at bay by red velvet ropes. If it were me, there'd be barbed wire, an electric fence, or a good old-fashioned cattle guard between us and those leeches. That would be much more entertaining as well. We weren't alone either, which made things a little better. The red carpet was full of other people. I tried not to stare at any one face too long. Every time I looked up at Bradley, his eyes were already on me, his lips offering me a tender smile.

We stopped a few times along the carpet and posed for pictures. Bradley pressed my body tightly next to his. His hand freed mine on these occasions to wind around my waist. I tried not to blink wildly at the barrage of flickering lights. It would be my luck to be immortalized in picture, with Bradley, with my eyes closed.

Thankfully things were calmer on the inside. People were huddled together in small groups among the round tables that scattered the elegant room. Flowers and twinkling lights filled the banquet hall. The flowers—red roses, dark pink peonies, and white hydrangea—so close to the warm lights filled the room with their fragrant perfume. My eyes were busy taking it all in while Bradley tugged me along.

"Evie," he murmured as he stopped.

My eyes caught up with where we were now standing, and I had to catch my jaw from dropping. Two of the most gorgeous people were standing in front of me. The woman was a tall, lean brunette with sparkling blue eyes. The man was a spitting image of Bradley, only about two decades older. His parents, I concluded quickly. I forced my lips to curve, hoping the smile seemed genuine instead of petrified.

"These are my parents, Brad and Susan. Mom. Dad. This is Evie," he continued warmly.

"It's nice to meet you, Evie," his mom said, in a musical voice.

"We've heard a lot about you," added his father.

"Thank you," I said quietly. "It's very nice to meet you too." I tried to act as calm and cool as I had when I first met Bradley, but I wasn't completely sure it was coming off the same.

We chatted briefly, and just the same as with Bradley, I could easily forget his parents' star quality. Salt of the earth, so they say. They were very down to earth and easy to be around. They didn't seem so interested in Oklahoma. None of the livestock questions I had grown accustomed to from the New Yorkers I met. No talk of cow pies or calf fries. We all sat at the same round table as people gathered on stage. A few more couples took their place at our table. I tried to calm my nerves as I placed their faces—more celebrities. Duh.

I let my eyes wander around the room. Everyone was interested in what was going on, but no one was that interested in me. No one gawked at me as I walked in with Bradley or stood there talking to two of the most well-revered actors in the industry. There were no small groups of women huddled together and throwing displeased looks in my direction. To them I was just another cocktail waitress, aspiring actress, or—well, I was going to say model, but I'm about half a foot too short, and you can't count my ribs when I wear a bathing suit. It was the first time I didn't feel uncomfortable being with Bradley in a crowd of people. Chalk one up to the fashionista twins.

The presentation on stage continued as a multicourse dinner was served to us. The man speaking urged the importance of clean drinking water in underdeveloped countries and the welfare of millions of uncared-for children. I tried to pay attention to the cause that was being supported but was hard-pressed to keep my eyes off Bradley. He welcomed my attention and reciprocated.

With a round of applause, the men and women left the small stage. The room darkened as multicolored lights lit up a small wooden dance floor in the middle of the room. I tried not to notice as a few couples wandered that way and went back to enjoying my fancy chocolate desert.

The rest of the table was busy talking among themselves. I finally finished my desert and my second glass of champagne. I wasn't aware at first that I had accepted the drinks but was very aware that I didn't want to drink too much.

I thoughtlessly mouthed the words to the eighties song playing in the background while Bradley and I stared at each other.

"Dance with me," he ordered.

"Oh…" I mumbled, twisting my face.

"What? Two left feet?" he guessed, smothering a chuckle.

"Bah. That would be an improvement. I'm a horrible dancer."

"Oh, it can't be that bad." He tugged at my hand as he stood, but I resisted. "Is that a no?" he asked, enjoying my humiliation.

I sat there, still reluctant, shaking my head, pleading with my eyes for him to stop. He kept pulling on my arm, and I gave in with a sigh. "Just consider it a disclaimer." He laughed out loud as he led me to the dance floor and took hold of my other hand.

"It's eighties music," he pointed out. "Just move around."

He jiggled my arms back and forth to get me moving. I shifted my weight uneasily to the beat.

Bradley let loose. He started doing every eighties move he could think of, one right after the other. "The Chinese typewriter." "The Hammer dance." "The churnin' butter." "The African anteater ritual." "The fishing pole." He was a one-man homage to the tackiest American dance era.

"Come on!" he yelled, trying to get me to join.

I just laughed at him and glanced around, wondering why no one else was staring and laughing at him as well. Everyone else seemed to be enjoying themselves too, uncaring about what was going on around them. I slowly let go, letting myself enjoy the moment. I hadn't seen him so open before. His eyes were smiling at me and held that same note of affection.

Bradley kept on with his eclectic dancing until the song slowly morphed into something completely different. My heart sank a little bit when I picked up on what it was. A slow song. A love song. One of Beyonce's latest hits: "Halo."

A few more couples crowded the dance floor as Bradley quickly pulled me to his chest. No escaping now.

He wrapped his long, strong arms around my waist. I let one hand come up to rest at the nap of his neck and rested the other one on his opposite shoulder. My chin didn't quite end up resting on his shoulder, and I tried to make an effort for my face not to touch his jacket for fear that my Hollywood makeup would rub off on him. He twirled me effortlessly around in small circles. It seemed with every passing second he was pressing closer. I could feel his torso moving in and out as he breathed. I could feel his fingers trailing down my bare back after he freed them from my hair.

Everything around me started to blur. I was only aware of Bradley and my heart, careening out of control, trying to escape my chest. That's what it felt like at least. And somehow it managed to pick up speed with every passing moment. With every touch of his fingers, skin against my now blazing skin. With each breath that whirled in my hair.

I was dizzy, and it wasn't because of the spinning—or the minute traces of alcohol in my system. The butterflies moved from my stomach to my head, confusing me further. My throat closed up, and I licked my suddenly dry lips. My skin was on fire along the trail from where he moved his hand, from my back to its new position. His gentle hand had glided up my neck and stopped on my jaw again. Just as it had in the limo. I swallowed hard. He lifted my face so that he could stare into my eyes.

Bradley's eyes were smoldering, darker than I ever remembered seeing them, with passion burning behind them now. I was no longer in control of my breath. Long past slow and steady and more like panting now as his thumb gently moved back and forth along my jaw line.

I saw Bradley's eyebrows pull together slowly as he stared into my eyes. It was like he was in pain. I parted my lips slightly to ask if something was wrong, but in that same instant he crushed his lips to mine. A lightning bolt shot through me.

I trembled as my lips worked feverishly along with his. Slow at first and then building deeper. I kissed him back with a hunger I didn't know I had. I let my hand slide from the top of his shoulder. My fingers slid under the lapel of his tux as they continued down. My hand found its way under the jacket and rested on top of his heart. Both of his hands tightened: one still fixed on my face, the other clutching my waist. I twisted his shirt in my palm as I felt his pulse racing as quickly as mine. My mind was empty and still racing through a million thoughts. All those thoughts broke off as something snapped me back to reality. The song lyrics. The words suddenly stung me, and I worked to listen a little harder but still moved my mouth desperately against Bradley's.

Beyonce's voice echoed in my head as she sang about falling without even realizing it, being awakened and finding her saving grace.

The chorus continued as my brain struggled to process the earlier lines. That was it! I finally made sense of the emotions coming alive inside of me. I fell, but I didn't remember the falling part. I had jumped from a great cliff and was suddenly at the bottom, looking upward—wondering how I made it all the way to the bottom alive.

I pulled my lips from Bradley's with a soft gasp as I made the realization.

I was in love with him. I loved Bradley.

Oh, my mutinous heart. What have you done?

I felt a spear of fear and guilt stab through my chest. We both stood there panting. Bradley had let his head droop and leaned his forehead against mine as we worked to steady ourselves, the electric current still sparking between us. I ran my tongue over my swollen lips where the taste of him still lingered.

My mind raced, trying to piece together all the information and every moment that led up to this as we stood swaying to the music. Our bodies were welded together, and we moved as if an invisible current was tugging us back and forth. I was at a loss. I was so sure that my heart had been so firmly broken that the capacity to love, in any way other than a familial way, had been beaten out long ago. I wasn't ready for this. My chest burned, and my palms started to sweat when I considered who I was in love with: another man who was so far out of my league that even our names looked strange together in the same sentence. I was suddenly and irrationally afraid for his life. I had been in love once with someone who was out of my league, and the universe seemed to react violently—ripping him from my grasp, permanently. Would lightning strike twice?

I felt Bradley twist his head to the side, and I felt his lips at my ear.

"I love you, Evie," he purred in his low, silky voice.

Stunned, I gasped involuntarily, breaking our tight hold on each other.

I was astonished and couldn't do anything but stare back at him. Almost mad. I never in a million years thought that he'd reciprocate my feelings for him. I blinked owlishly in confusion as I crossed my arm and gripped my knotted stomach. The soft, sincere look in his eyes was long gone by the time I looked back up to meet his gaze. Confusion and anger seemed to have taken place there, obviously trying to process my reaction and lack of articulation.

The dance floor suddenly felt very crowded. I felt the couples bumping into me as they twirled around and as I stood there staring at Bradley. But still, no one noticed.

He quickly tugged me off the dance floor and across the room as a different, peppier song started to play in the background. Before I could make sense of anything, we went through a pair of double doors and were standing in a bare, harshly lit hallway. Alone.

Bradley stood in front of me with a careful foot of space between us but held one of my hands in his.

"I—I—I," I stuttered, not knowing where to go with this.

I longed to say those three seemingly harmless words back to him, but something held me back. The thought of *someone* held me back. I tried to reason with myself, saying that Bradley didn't really love me. How could he? I was just a shell of a person. Just now put together, with his help, but still not whole.

I swallowed back my previous words as this new train of thought took over.

"How—how could you..." I trailed in disbelief, but his fingers moved to my lips to keep me from finishing.

His brow was wrinkled, but his lips drew upwards into an uneasy smile. "Because you're beautiful, inside and out. You're strong—I know you think you're not," he said quickly, sensing my rebuff. "But with all you've been through, you're still here. You make me laugh. You're warm and generous. You make me think about the world in a wonderful new way. You showed me that there's more to me than I ever could have been without you. You've flooded my life with more meaning than I ever thought could exist. Evie..." He hesitated as he moved his fingers from my lips and took my face in his hand. He took advantage of this new position and pulled my face upward so that I had to look into his burning eyes.

"Evie. How could I be anything *but* in love with you?" he stated matter-of-factly.

Boy, could that guy deliver a line.

"I love how you want to learn how to do the 'Thriller' dance for no particular reason other than being able to dance in your living room. I love how you buy shampoo based solely on how it smells. I love how not only do you know how to change a flat tire, but don't think twice about doing it yourself, even if you're wearing a skirt. I love how you constantly weave your fingers through your hair without knowing how it boils my blood. I love how you're just as beautiful to me standing here in this amazing gown as you are in just jeans and a T-shirt. And most of all, I love how your once broken heart is still large enough to care for complete strangers."

He tried to pull my face closer to his for a kiss, and I resisted. His words rang in my ears and reverberated against my soul, but not even this eloquently delivered speech could ease my rising fear and doubt. He took a step back as he tried to make sense of the emotion that washed over my face. Rejection. Something I'm quite sure he'd never seen in a face of a woman that he stood across from—especially after a speech like that.

He dropped his hands and took a few more steps back. My feet were still glued to the floor. My heart, my heart that I was suddenly so aware of, hung heavy in my chest and caused my shoulders to lurch forward.

Bradley shook his head quickly from side to side.

"I don't believe it," he angrily whispered as his eyes burned straight through me.

And he was right. I couldn't believe it either. After years of life without any love in it, I thought I was barren. He was willing to love me, undeservingly, but I wasn't ready to let him. He'd found the chink in my carefully placed armor. I thought I was safe from anyone's love. Keeping to myself for years, I'd thought I'd ensured it. I had carefully reconstructed my life and just recently had started to feel happy again. I had no way to deal with the curve ball Bradley just threw at me.

I was on the edge of another cliff, and it would only be minutes before I started to spiral out of control. There wasn't a thing
I could say to make him understand, mostly because I didn't
understand myself. I had no rational reason for not being able
to tell him about the war I was unleashing on myself, trying to
make sense of the past while trying to get a grip on the future.
So I didn't say anything. I watched his face twist further into
anguish as I took a few step backwards. I felt the tears welling
up in my eyes, so without a word I turned my back on him and
ran the wrong way, headlong toward the past, letting my once
possible future stand there, bewildered as I raced down the long
empty hall.

I made it back to the hotel, and through the tears I could
only manage to scribble two words down on the elegant hotel
stationery—not knowing whether or not he'd ever read them.
"I'm sorry." I left the sorry excuse for an explanation on top of
the scarlet gown in which I'd rejected him and headed back to
misery.

CHAPTER 16

The return flight to Oklahoma was like a flight back into zombie mode. The only difference was I consciously turned my world into white noise this time. My mind shifted through the events that happened just hours ago. But unlike my previous zombie life, there was something I was hyper aware of—my heart. Instead of feeling like my soul and heart had been ripped from my body— like after Josh died—I now felt every mutinous beat. How had I fallen in love with Bradley Matthews without my own consent? My body and heart reacted instinctively while my brain was still foggy from the pain and loss.

I had made no attempts to guard my heart from this type of pain because I thought I had no reason to. Not only did I think that my proverbial heart was obliterated, but why would I ever think that Bradley Matthews would ever feel this way about *me*?

And now, not only was I sickened by my own feelings but by my actions as well. I was horrified that I left Bradley—without one single word—there in that hallway. The look on his face would surely haunt my dreams. His perfect, stunned, saddened face.

Stupid, stupid girl.

I tried to make myself feel better by rationalizing. Surely he didn't feel as deeply about me as I did for him. I went over the sweet words he'd spoken to me again and again. I told myself that he was a skilled professional. Making words sound sincere was easy for him. But I also remembered the broken rhythm that his lines were delivered in. Like the thoughts were just then coming into his head. He'd had no idea that he'd need to explain his feelings for me until he saw the indecision on my face. It didn't feel like a scripted monologue.

I also tried to tell myself that he couldn't possibly know me well enough to be in love with me. We'd barely spent any time together. But what did that have to do with it, really? I knew I loved Josh after one evening. When you know—you know. Maybe that's why he was so curious that night at "The G" when he asked me how I "just knew" with Josh. Maybe he was experiencing the same thing—with me! I also remembered how he seemed to recall the most inane snippets of our conversations. About how I rambled on one night (via text) about wanting to learn the "Thriller" dance. That's probably another reason why he was surprised when I was reluctant to dance at the benefit. He probably thought that I at least had some smidgen of talent.

Bradley also noticed little personality quarks that I didn't ever think anyone would notice. Did I really run my hands through my hair that much? And how did he know about my smelly good shampoo habit? I didn't even remember bringing that up. A part of me realized that I was afraid to believe what he said to me, afraid to believe he felt the way he did. Because if he loved me and I loved him, how could it ever work?

I dropped my bag with a thud when I made it to the safety of my own home. I collapsed to the floor as the tears I'd been holding back finally washed over my face.

When I looked at myself in the mirror the next morning, the reflection was intimately recognizable. As flushed, swollen, and haunted as I remember seeing in the days, weeks, and months following Josh's death.

I waited till the appropriate time that Sunday to call Mom to tell her that I was back in Oklahoma. I had no intention, coward that I was, of telling her what happened. I was able to fend off her questions by simply saying I was tired and that I'd fill in the details later. My mom was almost as excited as I was about my trip to L.A. and had begged me to take pictures. I told her that probably wouldn't be appropriate. I was glad now that there was no photographic evidence of that night. Until I remembered that there would be—thanks to all the media coverage.

I still couldn't figure out why my stomach churned the way it did. I was used to the crushing loss but couldn't figure out why it felt so distinctly different. I also couldn't believe that guilt and shock managed to overwhelm my loving feelings for Bradley that night. Or was it self-preservation? After all, what kind of future could we have together? There were no two people who didn't belong together more than Bradley and I. No two worlds that were so far apart. Even if he did seem to somehow fit into my crazy family/world, there was no way that I belonged in his.

Of course there were no calls or texts from Bradley. My harsh dismissal severed our tie absolutely. Maybe *that* was the reason for my pain, knowing that I'd never see the shimmer in his blue-green eyes, feel the strength of his arms around me and the sensation of his lips on mine. That last thought was almost too terrible to bear. But I could remember with proper detail the electricity and passion that coursed through me during those brief minutes of unity.

Maybe it was because my memories had grown so faint, but I didn't remember that same intensity matched at any other time in my life. And that was almost unbelievable because I knew that I didn't ever think that I could ever match the love or fire that I felt with Josh. A fresh wave of guilt pounded over me.

I knew that particular reaction would be harbored in me, but the force of it took me by surprise. I knew that Josh was probably yelling at me, from wherever he was, telling me how stupid I was. I knew that I wasn't cheating on him, but that's how it felt. My heart, now beating as furiously as ever, was torn in two. I could remember standing in front of Bradley, hearing what he said, and doubt still washed over me. I was afraid to love again. Period.

What if I take another leap of faith and end up alone again? How could we possibly have a life together? Given who he is and what he does it's a million to one shot that we'd make it. When push came to shove and Bradley was standing in front of me, pouring out his heart, all I could do was stand there like a fool. My fear had eclipsed my feelings for him, and I ran away.

After several days of brooding, I finally left the house to get some groceries. One can only live off peanut better and jelly sandwiches for so long. I was thinking about how miserable it was that I was such a loner before. I'd kept to myself for so long that now I had no girlfriends to confide in or analyze my situation with. I sighed as I stood in line at the self-checkout waiting for the teenager in front of me struggle with the impatient checkout machine. I let my attention drift to the magazine rack. The small basket of items I held crashed to the floor. The teenager stared at me and tried to fight back some laughter while I scrambled to wrangle the items back into the basket.

My fingers trembled as I reached out for the item that had startled me—an entertainment news magazine. And who graced the cover? Not only my now unrequited love, but me. A picture of us standing happily, side by side, dressed to the nines and gazing into each other's eyes. I quickly grabbed the magazine and threw it into my basket as the teenager left with his bagged groceries.

I quickly checked out and made it to the confines of my car before whipping the magazine back out for further scrutiny. Tears started to tickle my face as my fingertips traced the beautiful lines of Bradley's figure. The headline was like a fresh dagger piercing my heart: "Matthews smitten by mystery date." I managed to make it home before I flipped to the full article about the benefit. Several other images of us together filled the two-page spread. There was a lot of speculation as to who I was. They had correctly assumed that I was the same girl from the New York City "incident." But they still hadn't learned my name or even my origin. Something told me that Bradley had gone to great lengths to keep them from learning anything about me. Another loving act on his part that now seemed to be wasted. Or maybe he was protecting himself? In case things ended this way...as I would have told him they inevitably would.

I was secretly pleased that I wouldn't be instantly recognized back here, in Oklahoma, even with these pictures littering the newsstands and news programs. I knew it was me because I remembered those precious moments. But the lovely woman standing next to Bradley looked so unlike the real me that no one else would be able to put two and two together. Except for one...

Those stupid magazines must have just been put on the rack. Mom called me later that afternoon exploding with vicarious enthusiasm.

"Oh honey, you looked just beautiful. As you always do, but even more lovely."

"Umm...yeah," I mumbled back. "Thanks."

"Everyone is wondering when you'll bring Bradley back down. For Halloween maybe? Will you be down then?"

"I'm sure." I hesitated. I wasn't sure whether or not I should tell her what happened. I'd water it down... "I don't think he'll come back down with me though." It hurt me just as badly to say the words as I thought. Each syllable more difficult to enunciate than the last.

"We didn't scare him off, did we? I thought everyone behaved rather well myself..."

"No. I think I scared him off. Actually, I know I did."

"Evie..." she rebuked me.

"Never mind, Mom. Just drop it. Please," I begged.

"Okay, okay. Well, I was really calling you to let you know that we're on our way to the City now. Juliane needs some new back-to-school clothes. Would you like us to drop by so you can join us?"

"All right." I made a conscious effort to not sound quite so melancholy. I didn't want her to worry about me, as she inevitably would if I let her hear or see the pain I was in.

"Sounds good. See you soon."

I quickly tried to straighten up my house. Cleaning was the last thing on my mind this past week. It would be kind of nice to be around someone. I had reveled in my little miserable bubble long enough, but I was worried that Mom would instantly be able to place the emptiness behind my eyes.

Mom greeted me with her usual hug and kiss, and I lingered a little longer than usual. Of course she noticed.

"Gotta use the bathroom!" Juliane called as she ran past us.

"L-O-L," I spelled absentmindedly.

Juliane stopped abruptly and turned quickly on her heels to face me.

"Did you seriously just say 'L-O-L' instead of *actually* laughing out loud?" she asked, obviously humored.

I had to think for a moment. Did I? "Uh, I guess so…"

"You need help." She laughed as she turned, her long brown hair fanning around her as she disappeared into the bathroom.

"You have no idea," I mumbled under my breath.

I laughed inside my head, but even with some amount of effort, it didn't escape through my mouth. Not even the slightest upward movement from my lips. See what technology has done to us? Well, me at least…and maybe it wasn't all technology's fault.

I turned around to find Mom holding the magazine, rumpled from my constant handling. Whoops. Forgot to put that away…

"So…" she said, right on cue. "What happened?"

"Mom!" My tone was petulant, but she didn't seem to notice—or care.

She just raised one eyebrow and planted one foot out to the side. That was her patented "you have ten seconds to tell me the truth, young lady" look. I'd definitely seen this before.

"I screwed things up," I blurted. "I don't want to talk about it."

Mom looked over the cover, at the two of us. "He loves you." Her observation took me by surprise. I guess I shouldn't have been surprised. She always seemed to know things like that—she could read people. Maybe it was a mom thing. I'd be willing to bet that she knew I was in love with him before I did. Well, of course before I did because it wasn't till a week ago that *I* finally figured it out. Finally put all the pieces together.

I sucked in a painful breath and stared at my feet, the same feet that had carried me away from the place I most badly wanted to be.

"Evie!" Her harsh reprimand startled me. "What did *you* do?!"

I was abruptly flustered and without defense. I hadn't thought that I'd need to prepare one. I wondered why she was being so harsh now. She'd always understood when it came to my previous heartache. "Kinda brutal, Mom."

"You think you don't belong in his world. Don't you?"

"Isn't it obvious?" I pointed to the picture of us that she was still holding.

"It's obvious that you *could.*"

"Yeah, with a whole day of preparation and unlimited resources, the hunchback of Notre Dame would look good standing next to *him*. I think he loved the ease of my lifestyle more than me."

She shook her head violently side to side, causing her charcoal and gray hair to swirl around her oval face. Then she slowly walked toward me.

"First, my daughter is no hunchback," she murmured humorously. "Second, I seriously doubt that he loves you just because of your lifestyle. I'm sure your life seems more peaceful than his at times, but I can't imagine that would be the basis of his feelings for you. Maybe he sees that peace and wants a little for himself—and maybe he knew that you would keep him grounded, keep him sane, keep him, *him*," she said seriously. "I hope you didn't hurt him."

"Mom," I said on a sigh.

"You never really belonged here either, you know. You were never just a small-town girl. I never saw you settling down young, like all your classmates, content with such an unchallenged life. I saw you going out into the world and changing it, making it better."

"And you? You think you're where you belong?" I challenged.

"Yes. I chose my life, and I'm happy with it. I still have regrets. I still have wants, just like anyone else. But I'm where I want to be."

"So?"

"I'm just saying you were never one to do something just because that's the way it was supposed to be. You challenge; you question. You've always felt the need to rebel against convention."

"Oh yeah. I'm a regular Johnny Yuma," I said dryly.

She laughed once. "Well, here's your chance again. Show the world and show Bradley that you belong with him. Don't let the world tell you that you don't. Don't let *you* tell you that you don't."

Why was she pressing this? "I'm in enough pain. You're not helping any. Why are you doing this to me this time around?" I demanded.

"Because! This is different. I could never imagine what it must have been like for you to lose Josh. I lay awake at nights, even now, wondering—trying to fathom the pain you went through and how you managed to survive it. But you didn't *choose* it. Nothing you did or didn't do could have changed what happened to him that night. But you're *choosing* to be miserable now, and I'm not going to just stand by and watch you deprive yourself, to watch you make a horrible decision," she ranted.

I said nothing. My eyes were closed now. Weak dams trying to contain a monstrous lake of tears.

"It's okay to love someone again. That's what Josh would want for you now. It doesn't tarnish the love you had for him or make it any less real. If anything, it's a testament to the strength of the human spirit. Of love."

I broke into sobs as she pulled me into her arms. She saw what I was doing to myself so easily.

"I could see it happening," she added as she stroked my hair to calm me down. "I could see that you loved him. I should have said something sooner," she apologized.

I just shook my head against her shoulder. "Oh Mom!" I blubbered.

"Shhh, shhh, shhh," she murmured.

Finally my shoulders quit convulsing as I gathered my composure. Juliane was in the room now, and her eyes were moist when I glanced at her. She must have overheard the conversation. She was rather emotional—just like me.

"Don't just let him go, honey. Not without a fight and definitely not without letting Bradley know how you feel. He deserves that much."

All I could do was nod again. I didn't want to disagree with her now and start a new argument. I didn't want to tell her I wasn't strong enough to face him again.

They went on to the mall without me. I stayed to wallow.

The weeks dragged on without any contact from Bradley. That left a widening hole in my heart. My heart was completely mangled now: torn in two and with holes shot through it. But somehow it managed to keep on beating. I found a new, yet familiar robotic way of life. Work. Eat. Sleep. Generally in that order: heavy on the work and light on the sleep. Lying in an empty bed didn't help being lonely, a bed that once held Bradley and me together.

I began ritualistically going to the grocery store every week. Not necessarily for groceries, but to buy one of those sleazy entertainment magazines. I felt it could be my only connection to him now, which was ironic because I was supporting something that I knew Bradley hated: an invasion of his (and every other celebrity's) privacy. But I didn't care. I scoured each page for something, anything. A picture, a line, a blurb—anything that proved that he was still alive and that he hadn't just been a figment of my warped imagination.

It was the night before Halloween. I was going to head to Cordell the next day so I could see my little nieces all dressed up as princesses. I was lying awake in bed, as usual, when I heard a familiar sound. I sat up in bed, resting my chin on my knees listening harder to make sure I wasn't imagining things. I wouldn't put anything past me these days. But the low rumble that lightly shook the walls of my house was distinctive. I waited for the panic to set in. For the fear to churn in my stomach. But nothing.

Hmm… Odd.

I walked across the dark house to the kitchen window and pulled up the blinds. Rain was pounding into the grass and gathering on the uneven patio. The sky was illuminated erratically with large, angry bolts of lightning. I stood there in awe. My heart started to take on a quicker rhythm, but it wasn't because the fear had finally set in. It was because, for the first time in years the sounds and images of a storm brought with it a new deluge of memories.

I wasn't trying to block out the horrible recreation of my beloved Josh's last night on this earth, as I usually would. My body quivered as the memory of my one full night with Bradley flashed inside my mind as quickly as the lightning dancing outside. I braced myself against the window and could feel the drops of rain against my palms through the thin, cool pane of glass.

And then—an epiphany. Maybe I was going crazy because it seemed to me that the storm was trying to show me something, that it was time to let go of something and start over. Some people thought that storms were symbolic in that way. That the rain washed everything clean—a new start, a fresh beginning.

Cleansing. Energizing. And for me, yet another square one. I had had to find the will to start all over a couple of times before, so I could manage it again. And I would do it this time with resolve, with full recognition of what I wanted. My feelings wouldn't be a surprise to me now.

For the first time in weeks, I was able to sleep peacefully. The thunder clapping through the sky, and the steady beating of rain lulled me to sleep quickly.

The next day I stopped by the Mountain View cemetery before I headed to Cordell for the evening's festivities. The scene seemed the same from when I was there so many months ago. But what would change? Except for maybe a few more fresh graves of the new tenants.

I sat cross-legged in front of Josh's headstone. I smiled, looking up and letting the sun's rays warm my face as the cool autumn air blew around me.

"Oh, Josh," I murmured quietly. No need to speak up, he could hear. "What a mess I've made, huh?" I tugged at the brown grass near my feet. "I've been such a fool all this time. I tried so desperately to keep you with me but missed everything that could have given me peace. All I had to do was stand still and feel the warm breeze against my skin to feel your arms around me again. Instead of shying away from rain, I should have lifted my face toward it and let the falling moisture touch my lips. With that, I would've felt your kiss again. I could have kept you in my heart without growing bitter." I sighed and wiped the back of my hand across my cheeks. "I guess I just wanted to tell you thank you. Thank you for showing me how to love you so unconditionally that I didn't think I could ever let go of you. But I think I've learned how I can still love your memory while becoming a part of someone else's life—if that someone will still have me."

I wondered if Josh had asked God Himself to send the October thunderstorm last night to awaken me. It didn't seem too unrealistic. I knew that he was up there—with the rest of my family—doing all he could to help me see the doors that were being opened for me.

"Thank you for blazing into my life and for not letting even a little death keep you from leaving me. You'll be here," I promised, as I patted my heart, "forever."

I wiped the tears from my checks again before standing up. "See you on the other side."

I enjoyed the rest of the day with my family, and of course they seemed to notice my more optimistic outlook. No one asked me directly about Bradley—thanks to Mom, I'm sure. I spent the trip back to Yukon wondering what I was going to do now. I needed to make some kind of contact with Bradley, to make peace with it at least. So I would know that I at least tried. But what would I do? I didn't even know where he was or what he was doing. I got an idea as I stumbled upon one of the many CDs that Bradley had sent me.

The next morning I continued my embarrassing ritual and bought one last magazine. I flipped through it haphazardly not expecting to find what I was looking for. I gasped as my eyes caught something as I scanned the pages. I had to go back a couple of pages. I blinked several times and tried to swallow around the lump in my throat. There he was. And who was *she*? A very beautiful, very skinny brunette. They got caught by the paps coming out of some trendy nightclub in New York City.

I moaned like an animal in pain as I clutched my chest.

I scrutinized the picture further. Bradley was standing beside the goddess while Mel tried to get the photographers out of the way so they could get to the black Range Rover. I let myself relax a little as I noticed no real physical contact between the new couple. No hand holding. No arm around the waist. I let myself irrationally hope that they were "just friends." Besides, didn't Bradley himself say that everyone was way too willing to turn any woman he was with into his girlfriend?

I wouldn't let this latest development make me waver. I was going to make contact with him. I had already burned a CD with just one song on it. I would mail it to him. According to the recent magazine article, he was in New York—at least he was a week ago. I decided to be brave and send him one text—to let him know I was sending something. With my luck, my package would get lost in the mail and my lame attempt to win him back would go completely unnoticed. So at least now—he'd know. And if the package didn't show up for some reason, he'd know and if he wanted it—he could let me know. And if it got returned to me, *I'd* know.

Okay. Now what to text?

Hey, it's me—

Wait. No good. My name and number had probably long been erased from his phone. I deleted the last few characters.

Hey, it's Evie.

Alrighty…and?

Hey, it's Evie. Don't want 2 bother u but wanted u to know I'm sending u something in the mail.

I stared at the words for several minutes but quickly pressed send before I chickened out. My fingers trembled and my heart raced as I continued to stare at my phone. I didn't really expect a response, but it still stung a little as the minutes passed and my phone showed no signs of life. Not even an "undeliverable" or "error" message. So I sealed up the CD and note explaining the song that was on it and drove it directly to the post office. I watched it slide down the blue metal mouth of the mailbox in front of the post office. I wasn't aware that I was still sitting there blocking the drive-through till I heard the honking behind me.

I quickly pulled away and sighed. That was that.

I let Mom in on my plan. She seemed pleased at my effort but tried to prepare me in case I didn't get the response I wanted. And that subtle hint turned into a cold hard fact. Days passed without any reply from my text to Bradley. Weeks passed, and I hesitated as I opened the mailbox every day, afraid that I would see my package with "return to sender" brutally marked all over it. But nothing.

The nothingness consumed me and almost hurt more than a cruel rejection. But I figured my punishment fit my crime. He owed me nothing.

I slipped back into my robotic routine out of comfort. But there was more life to me than there had been previously. Sometimes when I smiled it would even reach my eyes. My clients seemed to appreciate that my dry sense of humor had returned. It helped fill the nothing. I started to go to church more frequently. I started to make friends.

But there wasn't a day, not even an hour, that went by that I didn't think of Bradley. At night, I drifted to sleep by letting my mind replay every moment (except for that last horrible exchange) we'd had together. I tried to remember the feel of his lips on my skin. I tried to recount the number of times they had pressed against my now almost nonexistent scar. I would fall asleep with my arms wrapped around a pillow, but it was nothing compared to the way it felt having his arms securing him to me.

I ended up cutting out the magazine pictures of Bradley and me before they fell apart from all my handling. I found an old photo album that was about half full of pictures of Josh and me during college and a random assortment of family shots. I carefully placed the pictures of Bradley and me between the plastic dividers. Everyone I'd loved was in that album now. Another reminder of how life came full circle. Finally, the two halves of my heart could coexist without harming each other—or me. My heart that was once torn in two had slowly fused together. And with that fusion it was capable of more love than I ever thought possible. As I continued to think of Bradley, my feelings for him only grew stronger. They didn't fade away in a human response to try to ease the pain of losing him. There was something within me now that made the loss manageable. Something that was never present after losing Josh. Hope. When I lost Josh, I knew I'd never see him again. It was concrete. Final. Undoable. But with Bradley, it wasn't quite so finite. The possibility of seeing him again, feeling him, loving him kept me alive—kept me, me.

CHAPTER 17

I stood there shivering against the brisk north wind in front of my office. I was trying my hardest to shake Margaret, one of my previous clients, off.

"Oh, I don't know, Margaret—I'm pretty busy these days."

"Come on, dear, it's just dinner," Margaret pleaded, her dark eyes smiling at me.

Margaret was one of my first clients when I moved to Oklahoma City and started doing real estate here. I always tried to keep in touch with my clients. Not just in hopes they would refer their friends and family to me, but I was genuinely attached to some of them. Margaret on the other hand, kept in touch with *me*.

She'd call at least once a week to check up on me. I had an adopted third grandmother. She was small, frail, and an actual blue-haired grandma with a sweet disposition. She sold the home she had shared with her husband for almost forty years. She wanted to downsize after he passed away, so I helped her buy a small one-bedroom home in Yukon. She was one of those older ladies people couldn't help but love. She was warm, friendly, and always had plenty of homemade candy on hand. Her small frame, stooped shoulders, and awkward old-lady gait tugged at my heart.

Margaret had no clue about my self-complicated love life. All she knew was that I was single and therefore must be in desperate need of a husband. Ever since finding that out, she'd tried to fix me up with everyone from her grandson to her auto mechanic.

I stood there trying to come up with a decent excuse, not wanting to be rude. I thought about Bradley. About the days and weeks of not hearing from him. About the small spark of hope that I was trying to keep aflame in my chest that we would be together again. Margaret caught me in a moment of weakness.

"Okay," I agreed, grudgingly. "Who do you want to fix me up with this time?"

"His name is Chris. He's a charming young man. He works with my son up at the high school—he's a coach," she replied happily. "I'll give him your card and tell him to give you a call."

I felt a wave of nausea curl in my stomach as I watched Margaret finally drive away. I climbed into my SUV and quickly turned on the heater. I wrung my numb fingers together in my lap trying to generate some heat while my Trailblazer warmed up. What had I just agreed to? With any luck, he wouldn't call.

Wrong.

I got a call from Chris the very next afternoon. He seemed nice enough. A math teacher and boys basketball coach at Mustang, another small suburb of Oklahoma City just south of Yukon. We made plans to meet the following night for dinner.

I requested that he meet me at the office. I didn't want him coming to my home, the shrine of loves lost. I tapped my foot impatiently as I stared out the front window waiting for him to arrive. Three minutes late.

I saw the vehicle he described pull up into the office parking lot. A red pickup truck. Shiny. New. I stepped back and sat in one of the leather arm chairs in the lobby of the office and waited for him to come in.

No ritualistic habits for tonight. No appraising myself in the mirror. No pep talk. No special outfit. I figured the clothes I'd had on all day while showing houses was just fine. A step up from my usual jeans and T-shirt, I was wearing black dress pants and a lavender sweater. I wasn't sure why I was even going. I knew this guy didn't stand a chance but also knew that I had no real reason for saying no.

I had fiddled with my phone the night before as I contemplated canceling the date. I scrolled through my text messages again hoping to see something that I had missed before—like a message from Bradley. Yeah right. Still nothing.

The front door opened and the alarm beeped three times, as it always did, to alert that the door was open. I hadn't asked for a description from Margaret, so I had no idea what I was expecting. A small part of me was still hoping and wishing that it would be Bradley Matthews walking through that door. Of course it wasn't. It was a skinnier man. Not unattractive. His hair was reddish blond, along with the goatee that framed his mouth. That same mouth smiled at me as he walked toward me.

"Evie?"

"Yes. Chris—nice to meet you," I said as I stood up.

We shook hands awkwardly.

"Thanks for picking me up here," I added as I grabbed my phone, coat, and purse.

"No problem. Ready?"

I nodded and headed for the door. He followed. I felt hollow, just like before my heart was awakened by Bradley. No quick change in tempo that sent blood surging through my veins. No shortness of breath at the touch of another's hand.

I locked the office door behind us. When I turned around, Chris was already opening the door. The driver's side door. I walked gloomily to the passenger side. I had grown accustomed to Bradley's manners. I was a little surprised that Chris didn't escort me to his vehicle. Come to think of it he didn't seem all that excited about this "date" either. Maybe he could already tell that I wasn't all that into it. I decided to try a little harder to be pleasant.

I opened the door, climbed into the truck, and was assailed by the reek of tobacco. I tried not to wrinkle my nose as I took short, shallow breaths. A smoker…fantastic.

"Chili's okay?" Chris asked as he brought the truck to life.

"Uh, yeah. That's fine."

The short ride to the chain restaurant was quiet. The loud engine kept me from trying to make small talk. I was a Midwestern girl and appreciated the sound of a throaty V8 just like anyone else. But this was just racket. After every rev of the engine, a loud popping sound would reverberate through the cab of the truck. Glass packs. Wow. Somebody was stuck in the nineties.

Thankfully we were seated promptly once we arrived, but I was the one who had to force some small talk after we ordered.

"So, how do you like coaching high school basketball?"

"It's good. A lot better than junior high. That's what I did last year and hated it. The girls were so weak and uncoordinated. But the high school boys should have a pretty good year," Chris answered as he took a couple of sugar packets and stirred them into his glass of tea.

I nodded, trying not to grimace, and then sipped my water. If I was a drinker, I would have ordered some alcohol—something strong to make me a little chattier. I must have been a little lost in thought because I barely noticed him leaning across the table and reaching out his hand. However, I did notice, with a jolt, when he unexpectedly yanked a hair out from the top of my head.

Break my legs and buy me a bicycle, he's crazy! I was so shocked all I could do was reach up and smooth the top of my hair instinctively. Or maybe it was defensively. I didn't want to spend the evening being slowly morphed into Mr. Clean. That is without a doubt the strangest thing that has ever happened to me. I couldn't have been more surprised if he showed up wearing red Stilettos instead of sneakers.

"Sorry, that was bugging me. Stickin' straight up." That was the only explanation I got.

"You like sports?" he asked, unaware of my flabbergasted expression.

"Yeah. I like watching football a little bit better than basketball," I managed as I worked to calm myself. The paranoid woman inside of me wondered what he did with the hair he plucked from my head. Is it on the floor? Did he stick it in his pocket to take home to add to his shrine of hair? Is he saving it as DNA evidence?

Chris twisted the paper wrappers from his straw between his fingers. His hands were large, and I noticed that his fair skin was covered with freckles. I wasn't sure if my response pleased him or not. At this point, I didn't care.

"Do you like to hunt?" he asked

"No."

"Like boxing?"

"Nope." I twisted a little uncomfortably in the booth. This was starting to feel like an interview. I sucked down some more water. "So do you live in Mustang?"

"Yeah. I live in the apartments on the golf course with a friend."

We just sat there. Neither of us seemed to have anything interesting to say. Now I know why people talk so badly about blind dates. Are they all like this? I mean, I thought the fear of a blind date was getting set up with a horribly unattractive person. But I'd gladly take an interesting troll over a handsome man who is about as entertaining as a bump on a log and equally rude.

The server, Mike, interrupted our silence. He was slightly gawky with his large glasses hanging unevenly on his face. He picked up my glass to top it off. Another restaurant patron was passing behind him and unintentionally bumped his arm. He pitched forward and dumped my newly filled glass of water all over Chris as he freed a hand to brace himself from falling.

Chris cried out shrilly as the cold water splashed all over him.

I gasped as the cold water from the pitcher, still in Mike's hand, poured down my back.

Not only could I feel the water pooling in the seat around me, but I could feel a dozen pairs of eyes turn in my direction as Chris started to berate the teenager.

"What is wrong with you, man? Dude, I'm drenched!"

"O-oh—I'm s-sorry," the poor server stuttered as reached for some napkins to offer to us.

"Oh, like that's gonna help. I'm soaked! You're helpless. How hard is it to wait tables?" Chris yelled as he stood up, shaking a few ice cubes out of his lap.

I sat there. Stunned. My cheeks were inflamed despite the chills covering my body from the ice-cold water. I was totally embarrassed to be associated with the angry lunatic who sulked off in the direction of the restrooms.

Mike used the back of his hand to slide his glasses back into position on top of nose. I couldn't be sure, but I thought I heard him sniff. He started to scoop the ice cubes back into the pitcher and laid down a wad of napkins on the table to start soaking up some of the water. The restaurant chatter seemed to pick back up now that the show was over.

"I—I'm sorry," Mike stuttered again as he worked to clean up the mess.

I was helping, trying to soak up the water that was on the bench next to me. I felt so sorry for him. Obviously embarrassed, his hands shook as he took the soaked napkins from me.

"It's okay. It's just water," I replied with a smile. "Luckily, I'm not a wicked witch, so I don't think I'll melt."

Mike smiled weakly. A bus boy had made his way to our table and quickly cleared the table of napkins and water. Mike quickly reset the table with fresh drinks, napkins, and forks. He left just before Chris made his way back.

I was mortified that I still had to sit at the same table with this person and sorry that I hadn't driven myself so that I could leave his sorry butt.

Chris plopped down on the bench with a harrumph. I rolled my eyes in disgust and had to bite my lip. I so badly wanted to tell him off and demand that he take me home, but I feared his reaction.

Our food made its way to our table in record time, and it was delivered by the manager of the restaurant himself with many apologies. Chris said nothing, so I was left to deal with the uncomfortable situation myself. I thanked him and repeated that it was no big deal.

We sat in silence. I picked at my food mindlessly. A few pairs of eyes would wander in our direction, and I would duck my head to avoid their gaze.

After what seemed like an eternity, the manager came back to make sure we knew our meals were on the house.

"I'd hope so!" was Chris's smug reply.

I groaned. "Thank you, sir. Don't worry—no harm, no foul."

"Have a good evening," the manager said to *me*.

Yeah. Right. A good evening. It would take Doc Brown and a time traveling DeLorean to turn this evening into a good one.

Chris got up quickly without as much as a thank you. And it was clear that he wasn't going to be leaving poor Mike a tip. So I dug through my purse, found a twenty, and tossed it into the middle of the table before I left. Hopefully that would make Mike feel a little better and understand there weren't any hard feelings, on my part at least.

I walked briskly through the restaurant and through the parking lot. Chris was already in his truck, waiting.

More silence, from Chris at least, on the way back to my office. Chris reached over to turn the radio up as soon as I climbed into the truck. Charming. Luckily the ride back to my office only took a few minutes.

"Well...okay then," I said, clearly irked as I opened the door.

"Bye," he called, equally irritated.

I shut the door with more force than necessary, and he retaliated by peeling out in the parking lot.

"Jerk," I mumbled.

The cold night air blew against my back, still damp from the water. I punched the button on my keyless remote and climbed inside the sanctuary of my Trailblazer.

I started up my frozen SUV and sat there. I wrapped my hands firmly around the steering wheel. Feeling my frustration mount, I started to thrash violently in the driver's seat. Banging my hands against the innocent steering wheel and screaming into the void.

"Ahhhh! For the love of Pete! Come *on!*"

My Chevy continued to rock side to side a couple of times even after I finished my tantrum.

Okay. Just a little breakdown.

I turned up the radio, hoping that by some miracle the song playing on the radio would help calm me down. I clicked the "seek" button a few times till I found a station that wasn't playing a commercial.

I laughed, out of pure exasperation. Of course it would be something that made me think of Bradley. I sank into the bucket seat. I wished that the cold on my back would radiate through my body to numb my aching heart. A voice almost as seductive as Bradley's filled the emptiness of my small vehicle.

I had to shut off Gary Allan's song before it was even over. I didn't want to hear him singing about the best he ever had while I sat there thinking about the love I lost. I fumbled for the power button through my tear-blurred eyes. If anything articulated what I was feeling right now, it was those words. It was definitely taking some time to patch me up. Haunted? Yeah, I'm haunted all right, but I also had to own up to the fact that I was largely responsible for the pain I was in. And that realization didn't make things easier either.

I drove home in self-imposed silence. I flipped on the lights and illuminated the lonely rooms of my house, one by one. After all this time, I still hadn't gotten used to coming home to a dark, empty house. I kept waiting for the boogey man to jump out and get me. In moments like these, I hoped he would. How's that for normal?

Poor Margaret. She made me promise to call as soon as I got home from the date. I could just picture her sitting in her comfy little house, knitting, waiting for me to call and tell her how magical the evening was.

I stared at my phone but threw it on the couch as I walked to my bathroom to get ready for bed. I didn't have the energy to let her down—I'd call tomorrow. I scrubbed my face and tore the brush through my hair—clearly still wound up.

Well, that was it for dating. I was done.

I glared up at the ceiling. I had settled into the middle of my large bed and was cuddled under the chocolate brown comforter. I could feel the cold air lingering around the exterior wall that my bed butted up against. I heard the rhythmic tick tock of the clock on the wall, reminding me that time was still dragging on. The dull roar of cars, trucks, and eighteen-wheelers speeding down the interstate only a few hundred yards from my house only worsened my already bad mood. I always wondered about the people driving by late at night. Were they working? Why were they driving across Oklahoma at two in the morning? Were they happy? All my unanswered questions didn't keep me from thinking of Bradley though. As always, it felt like hours before I was able to drift off to sleep.

I woke up the next morning and gravitated to the photo album I had placed on the built-in bookcase in the living room. I thumbed through the pictures and smiled as I felt the hope within me starting to replace the despair that had managed to drift in the night before. The memory of us was strong enough to get me back on track. His once potent love was capable of refilling my soul, even though it hadn't been reciprocated in well over a thousand miserable hours. I always wondered how much love it would take to make me whole. Now I knew.

CHAPTER 18

The days got colder as the last of the leaves fell from the oaks and Bradford pears, no longer beautiful shades of red and orange, but brown and dull. The daylight didn't last long enough. Too much darkness—too much nighttime. The sun seemed to be hidden by the gray clouds more often these days, but I didn't let the gloom take me under. Thanksgiving came and went, still without any response from Bradley. I hadn't given up yet. Maybe he had stashed my package away. Still too mad with me to deal with it then but safely stored away somewhere until he was ready. But I was thankful all the same. Thankful for the short amount of time we did have together. Thankful for the breath of life he breathed into me with his sweet kiss and loving words. Thankful that because of his love I was finally able to move on.

It was a bitterly cold December day. The local weathermen were predicting a white Christmas next week. Work was always slow for me around the holidays. I had also exhausted any type of research I could do when it came to the Oklahoma City market. I had tried to keep myself busy with that the past couple of months, but too efficiently, I suppose, because now I had nothing to do. So I was content to stay indoors with the wind out of the north blustering against the back of the house. I stared out my kitchen window as I watched the large, wet flakes that started to flutter through the air. They continued to fall gracefully and haphazardly floated where the wind blew. I sipped my hot chocolate and daydreamed about Bradley.

I was a little relieved when the postman had to bring my mail to the door so that I could sign for some certified mail. That meant I didn't have to get out at all today! But the return address on one of the letters took me by surprise. Not from New York— I'm not that lucky, but it was from my gran. A Christmas card maybe? I ripped open the envelope and pulled out the card— a "thinking of you" card. Just like my gran. Never missing an opportunity to lift my spirits. And more like her to write instead of call. My eyes quickly started to read the words written carefully in her pretty, yet shaky script:

Dearest Evie,

I just wanted to write you a quick note to let you know I'd be thinking of you on this day, December 19th. I know it would've been your daddy's birthday, and I know how you always get a little blue. But you know he'd be so very proud of the woman you are today, and he wouldn't want you to be sad for him. He wouldn't want you to be sad for you either…which leads to the other reason why I'm writing you.

Your momma told me about your movie star fella and what you did. I think I can understand why you did what you did, but I do believe I'm siding with your mom on this one. You need to be absolutely certain that you know what you're doing. I know not even you can deny the change he made in your life. I'll be forever grateful to him for bringing you back to life, for bringing back the happy, laughing Evie back to us. I know it's been a while, but you need to talk to him—see him in person and tell *him* why you walked away. He may not fully understand—he is a man, after all. He may have seen the candle you held for Josh and thought he'd never be able to live up to that—maybe that's why he's let you be. It's up to *you* to let him know that you've moved on—if in fact you have (and I'm fairly certain you have).

You know we all loved Josh. He was a great man. Everyone who met him could see that. But I sometimes wonder about the life you would've had with him. You two seemed perfect for each other. Maybe too perfect. You came from similar families, backgrounds, religious beliefs. Maybe too similar? Then I see your other love. I see how Bradley could challenge you and keep you on your toes—and give you a life you've never imagined. And the same is true for him—you'd be doing the exact same thing for him. Life, love, marriage—it's never easy, dear—no matter where you're born, no matter how big or small your home is, no matter what society you live in.

And *your* happiness isn't the only thing at stake here... Go now. Speak your peace. Find love again and grasp it with iron will.

Much love,
Gran

I had trouble reading the letter with the tears falling from my eyes. More than ever did I want to feel the warmth of Bradley's embrace, to see the flicker of light in his eyes and his killer smile. Something that had once been buried deep in my subconscious crept forward. The date. December nineteenth. Of course! It not only was my dad's would-be birthday, it *was* Bradley's birthday. I quickly remembered the tentative plans we had set for this day. To spend a day taking in all the magic of Christmas that was harbored in the New York City landmarks. When I closed my eyes, I could almost see us, holding hands walking through the bustling city.

I scrubbed the tears away with determination. I would tell Bradley I loved him. He would hear me say that I loved him even if he no longer loved me. I threw the most basic of needs into a small bag and headed to the airport. I didn't know when exactly I'd get to New York City, but it *would* be before midnight and I *would* find him.

After dropping a large amount of cash on a last-minute ticket and having to make three passes through the metal detector at security, I was able to board a flight heading toward New York City within a couple of hours. I tried not to let the winter weather worry me too much. Maybe it wasn't so cold and miserable in New York City. I plopped into my seat, buckled my seat belt, and within moments I felt the plane coming to life underneath me. I felt the familiar tug in my stomach once the plane left the ground and the shaking of the cabin as we soared upwards. I bounced up and down anxiously in my airplane seat. I just about drove the businessman sitting next to me crazy, and I think the airline workers were getting nervous. So I had to make a pointed effort to calm myself down. All I needed was to be pulled off the plane by TSA, patted down, and held in a little room for questioning.

Once on the plane and in a situation I couldn't easily escape, I started to have my doubts. *What am I doing?* No turning back now; it's time I found some type of resolve.

I rubbed a hand over my face, as I realized just how ridiculous this impetuous trip was, but I also knew that there was no going back now. In my haste to get to Bradley, I hadn't even told anyone of my last-minute plans. I didn't even call Gran to thank her for giving me the courage to do this. I twirled my phone between my hands practically the whole trip, debating on whether or not I should call or text Bradley. No. The element of surprise would be better. Plus, there was no guarantee he'd even respond to me. I had no clue where he'd be. Well, actually I only had one idea of where he would be tonight. I wished more than ever that I had gotten Mel's number at some point. Something told me he'd conspire with me.

I was glad I only had my one small carry-on bag. I wouldn't have to waste precious minutes at the JFK baggage claim. I rushed off the plane and got into a waiting cab as fast as I could. I gave him the only address that I remembered from my trip almost six months ago. "The G's" address. If he wasn't there—I'd have to get a better game plan together.

The foreign cabbie was driving much too slow for my liking. My heart was pounding out of my chest. My stomach was twisted and closer to my throat than usual. I was so close now. I could feel it. I felt like it would be faster to jump out of the vehicle and just run.

The buildings became more familiar to me, and I knew we were there. The cab came to an abrupt halt by slamming sideways into the curb.

"Ow! Cheese and crackers," I yelped as my head ricocheted off the glass window.

I rubbed the right side of my head, which was now tender. I glared at the driver—waiting for some kind of explanation.

"Sorry," he mumbled in a heavy accent. "A little icy."

Great. I glanced at the meter and tossed him some cash as I grabbed my bag. When I opened the door, the cold air pierced my skin, and I noticed a thin layer of ice covering the ground and took special caution when exiting the car. I didn't come all this way to fall and crack my head open only feet from where Bradley may be.

Now. A new problem. How would I ever get inside the restaurant without Bradley? Not only inside, but in the back room!

I vetoed several ideas while walking up to the front doors.

The whoosh of warm air felt good on my face when I walked through the doors, making my cheeks sting a little. I heard car doors closing at the curb as I walked inside. I was greeted by a pretty, young hostess. Her jet black hair smoothed back into a ponytail and narrowed, close-set eyes gave her an edgy look.

"Name?" she instantly inquired.

"Mercer," I lied, surprisingly effortlessly.

She scanned down the list with her thin fingers. I just stood there, trying not to fidget.

"No Mercer," she said flatly after lifting up a couple of pages and looking over them intently.

"Oh my! Maybe I have the wrong place." I made my tone light and cheerful, hoping she wouldn't sense any reason to pay much mind to me as I shifted toward the small waiting area just to the right of her hostess stand. I bumped into a small, white ottoman as I backed out of the way. I gained my balance and threw the hostess an apologetic smile. I fumbled in my purse so I could make a faux call. I pretended to dial...

"Hi, honey. They don't have our reservation down here. Where did you tell me again?" I said just loud enough for the hostess to hear. I didn't know how long I could hold up this fake conversation without her getting suspicious.

Luckily I heard someone coming through the front doors. I heard the couple give her a name that she immediately recognized and pulled two menus from a rack. I turned away as I saw them walking toward the main part of the restaurant. I slowly made my way back to the now empty hostess stand. It was late and several tables were empty. I saw the hostess leading the patrons through the room. I glanced down the hall. Empty.

Not only was my stomach in my throat, but now my thudding heart had taken up residence there. I swallowed hard in an effort to clear the passageway and urged my feet to carry me forward. I walked quickly down the hall and through the double doors. I looked behind me and didn't see anyone following me. Yet.

I made my way to the long, empty familiar hallway. Only the faint music from the main building was echoing against the walls. I walked slower now, closer to the door in the middle of the hall. I closed my eyes and focused on slowing my breathing. My fingers shook as they reached forward to find the doorknob. They froze when the sound of Mel's deep laugh penetrated through the door. Bradley *was* here.

My breathing became shallow as I realized that Bradley was just a few feet away. This is it. This is why I'm here. *Come on, Evie!*

I gritted my teeth and turned the knob. I opened the door slowly and poked my head in. It was a conventional scene. The same bartender at the bar. The same large half-moon tables. One of them filled with the usual motley crew, laughing, drinking and talking among each other. I closed the door behind me without turning my back to the room, dropped my bag, and managed to take a few steps forward before I was noticed.

I froze midstep as all eyes focused on me. I was a good ten paces from the table. Everyone was staring at me. Mel finally broke his gaze to look at Bradley. I watched as surprise and pain quickly flickered in Bradley's eyes. All too quickly they shuttered and all emotion was gone. It was then that I noticed the tall, thin, pretty girl sitting next to Bradley. The same girl, it looked like, from the magazine article.

My cheeks were hot from all the attention. It had only been a few seconds, but it felt like I had been planted there for days.

"I—I—I'm sorry to interrupt," I finally croaked out as I took a few more steps forward.

Mel was still looking to Bradley, probably waiting for some kind of secret signal that would prompt him to gingerly remove me from the room. Bradley had looked away from me. The girl next to him, along with the two other couples at the table still had their eyes glued on me.

I opened my mouth to speak again, but nothing came out. I slapped my hand to my throat in response. I was petrified. I didn't know what to say. I probably should've worked out some kind of speech on the way here. Because here I stood—like an idiot—not knowing where to even start. The room started to close in around me.

"What do you want?" Bradley's turbulent voice broke the silence.

"I needed to tell you something. I need to talk to you."

"Then talk," he ordered curtly, without making eye contact with me again.

My eyes flickered around the table. Even Mel's big brown eyes were back on me. His was the only look that didn't frighten me. My brain tingled, and my chest burned as I worked to pull coherent sentences together in my mind. It felt like my body was imploding: quaking violently underneath the surface.

"I," I started, but my voice was much too small. I cleared my throat and started again. It saddened me but made it a little easier to get through without Bradley's eyes boring through me. "I just had to tell you how sorry I am. I know it was months ago and you've probably forgotten all about it, but every day it haunts me," I quickly rambled.

He didn't as much as blink—from what I could tell. A couple of the others shifted uneasily in their seats, obviously uncomfortable being present during my soliloquy.

"You just caught me off guard. *I* caught me off guard," I corrected. "I didn't have a clue that you—" I broke off not wanting to say out loud that he had once said he loved me, "or even I... I mean I tried to explain later—with the text and package I sent you, but I didn't hear from you..." I saw his head snap up, but I kept going. "And I couldn't live with that. I had to come see you and make sure you knew before I moved on."

"You what?" he barked, making eye contact.

I just stood there—not knowing what part he wanted me to explain further. I shook my head.

"You sent me something?"

"Yes," I replied, shaken. "I texted you a couple of months ago to let you know that I was sending you something in the mail. I never heard from you, but I figured it was because you were still..."

His head slowly drifted to the woman sitting next to him as my words trailed off. Her eyes were no longer on me, and her head hung guiltily.

Ah. Foiled by an unknown nemesis. Okay. That made me feel a little better though. Bradley hadn't even known about my attempt to contact him in hopes to set things straight.

My body was still quivering. Every nerve was shot. I was starting to unravel, and I still hadn't even really gotten to my point. To make things worse, Bradley was looking at me now, and the only thing I could see in his eyes was emptiness. One of his eyebrows slowly raised—like "is that it?"

"Anyway." I shook my head in an attempt to re-group. "I came to tell you something. So that I could be sure you knew how I felt." I had to close my eyes or else I'd never get through it.

"I'm sorry, Bradley. Sorry for everything. Sorry that I wasn't a whole person when you met me. Sorry that you had to be the person to piece me back together and the person who had to pay for it. Sorry that I didn't believe that love was strong enough to bridge the gap between our worlds and real enough to drown out the past. But I'm mostly sorry for being so wrapped up in my own self-despair that I didn't see the most precious thing that had ever been given to me. *You*," I blurted out, all in one breath. My eyes were squeezed tightly shut, but I could feel the moisture gathering in the corners. After a moment of silence, I opened my eyes and blinked away the few tears that fell quickly.

"I love how you held every door open for me, even when there was someone else there to hold it open for *you*. I love that crooked, cocky grin of yours and the way you use it to get what you want. I love how you made me forget about all the destruction that a thunderstorm can bring and reminded me of the passion that could rumble within it." I paused as I thought about this last statement. "I love the rain again," I whispered tenderly as I stared at Bradley, hoping he knew just how much this meant.

Deer in headlights. Bradley's beautiful eyes were wide; both brows were raised—in surprise or embarrassment?

I cleared my throat softly as his expression returned to an emotionless mask. Nothing.

I turned toward Mel. His face was still stuck in surprise mode, but I figured I'd get more of a response out of him than Bradley. "I'm—I'm too late. Aren't I?" It was a rhetorical question if I'd ever heard one. I had already figured that much out. Mel's face drew up in pain. Like it hurt him almost as much to hear it as it was for me to say it. He was such a teddy bear.

I knew I'd regret it, but I turned away from the table without taking one last look at Bradley. I didn't want to see what expression his face had morphed into.

I grabbed my bag, went into the hall, shut the door, and took two steps to the right and braced myself against the wall. I slid down, hugged my knees, and the sobbing got more pronounced once I realized I never actually came out and told him that I loved him. I soaked the sleeves of my coat as I worked to wipe the salt water from my face. When I lifted my head slightly to catch my breath, I was caught by surprise by the pair of feet in front of me. I hadn't even seen or heard the door open.

Bradley was standing there. Sill no emotion on his face. Hands in his pockets. "What did you send?" he asked flatly.

"A-a CD," I said as I worked to gather myself off the floor.

"A song?" he correctly guessed.

I nodded. "And a letter," I added.

"What song?"

This angry tone was something new from him. If I wasn't hearing it now, I would have bet that his voice wasn't capable of such a menacing sound toward me. I thought I'd heard anger in his voice before, on the phone and in the car after I was mauled by the paparazzi. But nothing compared to the sound of his voice now. But even those anger-filled words he said to me now were music to my ears.

241

I fumbled through my purse to find my phone. I was pretty sure just giving him the title wouldn't tell him much. "I, uh, have it on my phone." I quickly scrolled through the songs and hit play when I found the right one. I prayed now, more than ever, that the words would go straight from his ears to his heart. I held my phone up in the space between us.

As the music began, there wasn't a single shift in his demeanor. It must be so nice to be a professional actor, to be able to stand there and not give away any type of emotion. I, on the other hand, was standing there knees shaking, palms sweating and voice breaking.

I'm sure he could have guessed what musician I would pick to explain my frame of mind, but I'm sure that it was a song he had never heard before. "Square One" by Tom Petty.

I was glad it wasn't a terribly long song because standing there avoiding each other's gaze was kind of awkward, especially when all I longed to do was throw myself in his arms. Neither of us said a word or moved. I struggled to keep the phone steady as the words started to fill the barren hallway.

"It took a world of troubles, took a world of tears. Took a long time to get back here."

On and on the song played and reinforced the thoughts and feelings that brought me here. It did take time, but I finally realized that I needed to start with a clean slate, at square one. The past is in the past but it made me who I am.

The chorus repeated and Tom Petty sang about finding higher ground and having fear to get around. A crease between Bradley's eyes was the only flaw of his otherwise smooth façade. I stood there for a few seconds after the song ended. After no response from him, I tucked my phone back into my purse.

"I don't get it. Why that song?"

The anger that was in his voice before seemed to have melted away, but I tried not to let that excite me too much.

"I, uh, yeah—I wrote a note trying to explain that," I recalled as I forked my fingers through my hair and stared at the cement floor between us. There was a reason why I chose a song to tell him this because obviously words were not my forte. "Well, I wanted to try to illustrate what I had to go through..." No, that wasn't the right word. "What I had put myself through and what I had to let go of," I continued. "In order to—to—to..."

"To love me?" Bradley queried, finishing my sentence.

I lifted my head slowly, and his soft gaze encouraged me. "To *let* myself love you," I murmured.

"Uh, boss?" Mel whispered as he closed the door behind him. I hadn't even noticed the door moving. "*She*," he inflected with chagrin, "wants to go now. What do you want to do?"

I was snapped back to reality. Right, the other woman who was obviously his date. Why did I think I could come here, play Bradley some stupid song, and think he'd fall back in love with me? I felt a cloak of insecurity and self-preservation wrap around me. I clutched my stomach.

I looked up, and Bradley's eyes were on me. They were still blank, but he could surely read my obvious embarrassment. "I'm sorry," I mumbled as I jogged down the hall, not even caring that I'd left my bag.

"Evie! Wait!" I heard Bradley order, but I had already flung the door to the main restaurant open.

Again! Again you turned your back on him! Maybe it was something about feelings being expressed in a hallway that held such an aversion to me...

I slowed to a brisk walk as people came into view and kept on going, not looking back.

The frosty air assaulted me once I stepped outside the restaurant. The honking, talking, and holiday merriment blurred together as I fought to catch my breath. I walked to the curb and felt the tears trailing down my frozen cheeks.

"Evie!" Bradley shouted.

I turned, my defenses crumbling, and I blinked trying to focus on him. Relief colored his face as I stared back at him. Then, in a flash, his expression changed. It took me a half second to process the change, but a half second too late.

It was horror. I felt a rush of anxiety sweep through my system. I broke our gaze and turned around just in time to see a sea of yellow metal rapidly closing the space between us. I didn't have time to react or even scream.

The cab hit me dead on and sent me flying through the air as the tires squealed to a stop. My head slammed against the cold concrete. Pain was reverberating through every cell in my body. The agony confused me. I knew that the ground beneath me was icy, but all I could feel was a flood of warmth in my abdomen. That couldn't be good. I tried to move, but my brain ignored my request.

By now a crowd had gathered around me. Then Bradley was on his knees next to me, hovering protectively over me as he ordered for everyone to back off and to go get help. I wasn't sure if it was the adrenaline kicking in or just his presence, but the agony became less…pointed. Instead of being able to separate the pain by sector (shoulder, ribs, leg, pelvis, head) all I could feel was a full body throb. Suddenly a single thought caused me more pain. Even though Bradley hadn't expressed his feelings or reacted to mine, I still had to tell him.

I opened my mouth to talk, but nothing came out.

"Evie! Evie!" Bradley cried, his hands moving cautiously over me trying to decide what injury to focus on first. "Where's the ambulance?" he yelled over his shoulder.

I concentrated harder. I had to tell him. I swallowed and started again. "Bradley," I tried to whisper, but it came out more like a gurgle.

"Shh, shh. Don't talk," he ordered.

I swallowed a mouthful of blood and winced at the metallic taste and the pain. "No," I demanded albeit weakly. He brought his face closer to mine. "Bradley—I love you," I managed to proclaim in a strained voice.

"Shh, shh. I know. I love you too," he replied instantly, voice breaking.

I stilled. Did he mean it? Or was he simply giving me peace before I went to meet my Maker?

His fingers were unnaturally shaky as he moved them across my face to wipe away tears.

I closed my eyes, and with determination, I tried to lift one of my hands. I wanted to touch him one last time. Sensing my wish, he lightly took my hand and placed it on his face. He kissed my palm as he closed his eyes. One perfect tear fell from the corner of his eye.

There was something else I needed to say. I coughed a few times as I tried to clear my throat to talk again. There was too much liquid in my throat. I could hear sirens in the background and I knew that I would be ripped away from Bradley in a matter of moments.

"Don't let me...be a reason...to be angry with the world, Bradley," I said brokenly.

He opened his eyes, and they narrowed as he tried to make sense of what I was saying.

I didn't want him to use my death as an excuse not to go on and have a full, happy life. A little egotistical, I know—thinking that my death would cause him the same grief that Josh's had caused me, especially if that "I love you" was just a phony. But I couldn't stand the thought of this moment ruining his hopeful existence.

"What? No. You're going to be fine, Evie. You're not going anywhere," he said, almost convincingly.

One of his hands was still holding my limp hand to his face while the other cupped my bloody cheek.

I closed my eyes tight. The pain of losing him was so much more unbearable than the pain of dying. "It's okay. I'll still keep an eye on you, and I'll see you again on the other side," I promised with the weakest of smiles. My words came out mushy from the blood rising back up my throat.

"No," he said again with a quiver in his voice. He brought his head closer to mine, and I cherished the feel of his lips on mine again. At least I would die a happy woman.

Everything started to grow dim. I could see Bradley, still beside me, rocking violently back and forth as more tears pooled in those ocean-colored eyes. I could hear a new sound, a familiar but out of place sound. I could see the lights of the ambulance flashing around in the distance but couldn't hear the sirens anymore. All the sounds in the background blended together into an incoherent hum. I thought I had already died as I placed the new, clear sound: guitars strumming a peaceful lullaby. Odd. I knew the song well. Josh used to play it for me over the phone after I had a bad day to help me go to sleep. Creed's "Lullaby."

I tried to push the gentle melody out of my mind to focus on Bradley. But the sound had already taken on a narcotic effect. I couldn't help but to be drawn to the notes no matter how hard I struggled to stay with Bradley. Just before I heard the world fade away, I heard Bradley's anguished plea breaking through. "Evie! No! Don't you dare leave me like this! Evie! I love you! *No!*"

I could no longer hear his voice, but I could feel a lot of… tugging. I didn't feel dead, but I feared I may be headed there as the words to the tranquil song continued to sooth me. "Hush, my love, now don't you cry. Everything will be all right. Close your eyes and drift in dream. Rest in peaceful sleep."

CHAPTER 19

I could still feel some phantom tugging, but all sound was still cut off—even the lullaby. Then I saw flickers of light around me, like old movie film coming to life in jilted movements. The images became clearer as the flickering faded. I struggled to make sense of what was happening. I felt...transported.

The scene was gravely familiar as I became part of the movie-like image. It was a hospital room, ICU to be more exact. I had to say good-bye to my dad in the exact same sterile, ultra-white type of room, a small room full of beeping monitors, life-supporting equipment, and the fog of resignation. It was unsettling to recognize that the body lying on the hospital bed was me. I wasn't hovering over the bed as a ghost but experiencing everything as a dream.

Bradley was in a chair on one side of the bed. He had both of his large hands wrapped around one of mine, his head bent over and resting on our knotted hands. I was lifeless, but I could see the waves and lights on the machines next to me working to keep me alive. My mom stood next to the bed, by my feet. Her eyes were heavy, and the dark circles under them did nothing to hide her pain. Bradley's head suddenly popped up, but I guess I missed what caused his reaction, and something told me I didn't get instant replay in whatever dimension (or dream) I was in now. I could feel everything going on around me, but it didn't feel like I was actually experiencing it. I was disconnected still, somehow.

Bradley's face was instantly at mine. Mom was closer too, and a smile had washed across her face. I tried to open my mouth but couldn't. I tried to move a muscle but couldn't.

The scene broke off abruptly, and I was left in darkness but still mentally alert.

I no longer felt the cold concrete under my back or the flooding warmth in my belly. Those were the last concrete sensations that I could remember along with the sound of Bradley's screams. The last thing I trusted that happened. The rest was a dream or some kind of subconscious effort to keep me alive—something to fight for.

A familiar feeling washed over me: exhaustion. I felt consciousness drift away, and a new dream started almost immediately. This one started off with a little less flickering. It promised to be a happier "flash" as I recalled the place. Uncle Bo's house in Cordell. All the kids and young adults were in place on the makeshift ball field. Just like always. I could almost feel the heat that filled the summer air of this new image. I smiled from the sidelines as I watched Bradley walk to home plate and pick up the bat. My brother Marcus had taken his place behind him as catcher.

Marcus threw up his hands. "Hold up," he yelled.

Bradley dropped the bat and took a few steps back. I scanned the other faces. They seemed to be snickering. I watched Marcus as he trotted behind a large oak tree that stood just a few feet from home plate. He disappeared. I scanned the other faces again. They were all laughing now. The musical sound that came to life tickled my ears. I didn't remember much sound from my last flash, dream…whatever that was. I looked back, and Marcus was in view now, wearing a large white and blue football helmet as he walked back up toward Bradley. Bradley was doubled over—laughing. He straightened and playfully tapped the side of Marcus's overly protected head with the plastic bat before getting back into his stance.

"Play ball!" Gran yelled from her usual ball-watching spot, with the other cheerleaders.

It felt like a memory, but I knew that's not how things went down when we were with my family just a few months ago. But it was just as intimate. I could feel every moment that was happening as I watched it being played out before me. It felt like I was *there*, but I wasn't. I was here—wherever here was—watching parts of my life being played out for me.

That flash ended just as abruptly, before I was ready for it to end. But I was anxious to see if another would take its place.

More flickering. Bradley and I were sitting next to one another in metal folding chairs. The image widened, and I could see that we were sitting on a stage with several men and women in uniform. There was a man dressed in a formal navy uniform standing at a podium. In front of Bradley and me was a large group of people, most in military fatigues or uniforms. There were listening to what was being said, most nodding intently.

"We're so very honored to have Bradley Matthews and Evie Castner with us today. They've done so much to help many of our struggling veterans and their families and to bring awareness to veteran's rights." I saw the speech giver motion toward us, and we stood. Bradley took my hand in his as we got up and walked over to the man.

I heard Bradley start to address the crowd, but my attention was diverted to something I noticed as we walked up to the podium. Behind the stage, on the wall, I noticed a sign. "DEC Foundation." Hum…that didn't ring any bells with me. Well, wait—DEC were my dad's initials. I read the few lines under the name of the foundation. It was the Teddy Roosevelt quote that I had recited to Bradley that stormy night at my house. I smiled as I concluded that we must have started a foundation in my dad's honor for veterans to get more assistance. I quickly began to scan the room again for more details and thought I recognized Bradley's parents in the crowd, but the scene abruptly snapped apart.

I was starting to get a little frustrated as I was "transported" to another point in time. What was all this—what did it mean? Was I unconscious? Dead? I felt detached from my body. I tried to make my brain give orders to move, blink or even feel pain, but couldn't.

All I could make out of the new flash was a large white tent that stood apart from the dark, starry sky outside. The image shifted perspective again, and I could suddenly see under the tent. A lot of well-dressed people. Another benefit perhaps? No, that didn't seem right. All of the people were lined up in rows, facing one direction. In my direction. I turned my head to look in front of me. Bradley. We were standing next to each other. I was in an elegant, white, off-the-shoulder dress, and he looked handsome as ever in a black tuxedo that molded to his muscular form. The tent was full of lights, candles, and flowers in the colors of a tropical paradise. They cascaded down the walls and hung from the ceiling. Our wedding…

I recognized Benjamin Russell standing in front of us. Talking. About love and commitment. About second chances. I saw Bradley move closer to take me in his arms as he kissed me. But again, as much as I wanted, I couldn't physically feel anything.

The crowd was clapping now as we walked down the long, petal-strewn aisle. The scene fast-forwarded in a blur of motion. We were now dancing, alone, in the middle of a square dance floor. The dance floor was surrounded by the guests arranged at tables. They watched as we gazed lovingly into each other's eyes.

For the first time, I actually felt something outside of the dream. It was sadness. Sadness that I had to *watch* my life being played out instead of getting to live it. It looked like such a happy life. And with Bradley. We must have found a way to make it work. All my worrying for nothing. But anger got the best of me. Why? Why this? What had I done to end up in hell? That's where I had to be. Satan was having a good ole time watching me suffer while I watched my would-be life displayed in front of me.

More flickering. Not only from the new scene taking shape, but from the light bulbs flashing intensely around us. Another red carpet event. I watched Bradley and me move through the crowd. I stood silently and proudly next to him as he was interviewed on camera about his latest film achievement. I kept my eyes on him or on the floor. I guess I was still uncomfortable with this part of his lifestyle—even after some time. Although time was not something I could put my finger on in this atmosphere. There was no real way of telling how much time had passed from the first flash till now. We didn't look all that older.

Then we were seated in a large auditorium. The two large, golden statues on either side of the stage in front alluded to our whereabouts. The Oscars. A new sense of pride was overwhelming. Bradley's face was serious, and his hand was bound tightly to mine. I reached over with my other hand to pat his thigh, in an effort to calm him down. I was concentrating solely on him.

"And the Oscar goes to…Bradley Matthews!"

Bradley bent down to kiss me briefly as he got up from his seat. I glanced around, and everyone was clapping and looking in our direction. As Bradley walked down the long aisle, I finally realized what had taken place. He won? He won! Thanks to the random fast-forwarding I had no idea what he had won for. Luckily, on the screen behind the stage where Bradley now stood were the words "best director."

I giggled. I was reminded of the night we spent talking in my small, ordinary kitchen. About how I'd joked with Bradley about him wanting to be a producer or director—something that didn't involve him being romantically involved with anyone on set—to avoid temptation.

"I want to thank the Academy for this great honor," Bradley began excitedly. "I had a great cast and crew, and they made it impossibly easy for me to direct them! I'm just so grateful,"

Bradley continued as he stroked the golden figure in his hands. "I'm in a room full of people who've spent years, decades, and even lifetimes perfecting this craft—to be held in your charge… is overwhelming. I definitely want to thank my family for their support and of course my amazing, beautiful wife who taught me all about fighting for what we want and for pushing me to become the man who's standing in front of you today. In every life a little rain must fall," he murmured as he stared in my direction. Bradley held up the statue triumphantly as he continued, "so here's to keeping your head above water!"

The crowd erupted in cheers and applause as he took a slight bow and said thanks again before walking off stage.

Another flicker distracted this warm would-be memory. It was a bedroom. A very foreign bedroom. A wall of windows framed the dark sky and tall, lighted skyscrapers outside. There was a large white bed in the middle of the room. I assumed it was Bradley's apartment. Though I never saw his room the one night I was there, the modern décor in this room matched the rest of the place. I could see a figure lying on the bed, but it was hard to make out who it was. It had to be Bradley. The long, muscular frame. His shirtless, tanned back. Lying on his side with one arm curled underneath his head while the other was in front of him, moving slowly up and down. The image was flipped, and now I could see what was cuddled in front of him. It was me again. Sleeping peacefully as Bradley stroked my swollen belly.

I felt another wave of hostility reverberate through me outside of the dream.

Enough! I screamed into the nothingness of my head.

I was alone now in the darkness. No pieces of my lost future to keep me company. My blood boiled. I was no longer part of a "flash" or "memory." I was trying once again to make sense of what was going on around me. Everything was fuzzy now. And the emptiness consumed me.

Why? Why would I be shown these wonderful, happy things? I'd much rather have died without knowing what all I would be missing. I didn't want to be left in this void with the new memories lingering.

I didn't know why I kept screaming to myself. It seemed like a natural reaction as I tried to fight my way out of the darkness boxing me in, holding me down and trying to consume me. I was alone, and now the tugging was gone as well. Was that it then? Had my life ended?

The faintest sound caught my attention. I tried to gain control over myself so that I could better evaluate. A sound, the real first sound, other than my blubbering and the strange images. Still very faint, but constant. Steady. Rhythmic. Strong.

Beep. Beep. Beep. Beep.

It echoed in my ears.

Hope broke through me, and my body quivered in relief. Not hell. No. No. No. This most definitely wasn't hell. It wasn't heaven either for that matter, but it was close. I was caught somewhere in between life and loss. I wasn't being shown images from my future that I couldn't have. I was being shown what I was supposed to be fighting for. This revelation made much more sense to me as the substantial beeping continued. I had allies. All of my loved ones who'd left me too early were on my side and doing everything in their power to give me the strength to fight, showing me what my life had in store for me if I could only find the will to keep the darkness from taking me over. Dad. Gramps. Grandpa. Josh. They didn't want me to join them just yet.

Excruciating numbness and the tingling that follows overwhelmed my consciousness, and I could tell that my environment was changing again.

The darkness that covered me wasn't new, but the fear of death quickly wore off as pain started to trickle through every part of my body. Slowly at first. Starting with my legs, then my abdomen, my neck, then my head. I didn't even think to moan. Just the movements of my shallow breathing made the pain worsen.

The beeping was much louder now. It almost ruptured my eardrums after the distressing lack of static from the outside world from before. But I welcomed the peaceful thump that I could feel in my chest that came with each beep.

I tried to brush off the flashes, but the similarity of the first one seemed to take over. I remembered seeing Bradley and Mom hovering near me, so I tried to find my hands through the darkness. I could feel warmth and weight in one of them. I tried to squeeze, but I was too weak. Like there were hundred pound weights lashed around my wrists holding them in position on either side of me.

I wanted so badly to tell Bradley that I was here—that I was still with him, but none of my body parts would cooperate.

So I waited, listening to my heart pulse on, thankful that it was there for me to listen to. The pain was more bearable now, the physical pain at least. The initial onslaught of agony must have been from my transition from dream world to real life. Real life was always much more troublesome and painful.

The torture of being so close to Bradley but unable to feel more of him with me than just his hand was eating away at me. I tried every once in a while to squeeze the strong hands that engulfed mine, to see if the weights had been lifted, but no response ever followed.

I fought against my closed eyelids too. Another battle lost, but I would not lose the war. I saw my future, no matter how delicately woven together it may still be, and I wanted it. I was fighting to keep the images intact knowing that someday they'd be no more to me than déjà vu. I thought of them over and over, keeping them alive in my mind. Bradley's flawless face and warm, loving eyes. The thought of marrying him and winning his love for an eternity. I let my imagination create the beautiful child that would one day blossom within me. If it was a son, a picture-perfect reflection of Bradley. If it was a girl, a pretty little tomboy who would no doubt be a daddy's girl. A wonderful life...

The new images that I created in my mind caused the corners of my mouth to pull upward into a smile. And for the first time it felt like my body was responding to something that my brain was telling it to do.

I tried one more time, timidly, to shed off the darkness, and my eyes blinked open. They shut just as quickly as they had opened. The blinding white light was too much to take in.

Excitement forced me to try again, even more slowly this time. After a few painful blinks, I was able to widen my eyes to take in the room. The life-supporting machines. The white tiled ceiling. Mom. And Bradley, sweet Bradley. Head down, just like in my memory. My eyes glinted around the room again, and when they got back to Bradley, they were met by his.

I felt my lips fold into another weak grin.

His face was instantly next to mine. Both of his hands wrapped gently around my neck as he struggled to muffle his tears.

I felt Mom's presence at my side but was consumed by Bradley's loving company.

"I love you," he whispered with a hoarse break in his voice.

I let those three little words absorb into my soul. More relief shot through me as I realized that I had made it. I was here. I was going to live out the life that I was meant to live. I was lucky—I got to finish my life. Not everyone did. Some had to leave their lives much too soon. Some had to leave their loves. Some had to watch from above and help others find their way back—to finish a life without them. And maybe, one day, that would be me, but for now—I would live.

Bradley slowly pulled his head back after my silence so that he could look into my eyes. Maybe he was wondering if I was the same person. Wondering if I even knew who he was. Or who I was for that matter! I had no idea what the doctors had told him about my prognosis; perhaps nothing good by the looks of his troubled face.

"I'm back," I croaked weakly with a smile.

He smiled back, his eyebrows furrowing just a little, probably trying to figure out where I was "back" from. "You know, I'm getting real tired of seeing you turn your back to me," he said painfully.

My cheeks flushed at his accusation. I had gotten into a dirty habit of turning and walking, more like running, away from him. "Thank you," I continued as I cleared my throat a little. It was dry and still sore from the tubes that had been down my throat.

Bradley shook his head a little in confusion, but his eyes glittered with relief.

"For not letting me let you go again," I murmured.

He chuckled softly as his lips found mine.

CHAPTER 20

The weeks of physical therapy were strenuous. I had suffered several broken ribs, a concussion, some internal damage, and a crushed right leg. But, hey, it wasn't anything that a little medically induced coma, a couple of pounds of surgical steel, and a couple dozen stitches couldn't fix. Mom and Bradley told me that right after I woke up, I talked about all these dreams that I had while I was in the coma. They said they couldn't make out much of what I said, and I still have no recollection of what they're talking about. But other than that, my recovery went well. I was stubborn and demanded that I live in my house instead of regressing and moving back in with Mom. So with help from a nurse, family, and friends, I was able to get back to normal.

Bradley stayed nearby for the first two weeks. He was amazing and made sure I didn't have to lift a finger. There were no mushy monologues. Neither of us felt the need to reassure each other that we were in love. His presence told me, and something in my countenance told him.

But the months that followed my rehabilitation were even harder as we struggled to maintain our long-distance relationship. I struggled with my insecurities and his career as well as the lack of quality time together. But after the accident I was strangely at peace with everything, something that Bradley never understood, mainly because I didn't want to try to explain the memories I thought I remembered from the six days I was in a medically induced coma. I just had a feeling that everything would work out as long as I had faith. But I didn't want to move in with him since we weren't married, and he understood. There was no realistic way he could live here and work either.

Bradley was so used to the other girls he dated that once we were actually a couple, there was some...adjusting. I didn't ask anything of him, materially. I was patient, not selfish, and trying to do everything in my power to make him happy simply because I loved him. He'd never known that before, and I really think he just kept waiting for the other shoe to drop. That I was too good to be true when in actuality, it was the other way around. Even though he was struggling at times, he still did all he could to woo me from a distance. He still sent me CDs in the mail, although now they were more of the romantic variety. Every Friday I had a large bouquet of flowers delivered to me. Any time we spent together, he made special and went out of his way to include my family when possible.

And any time we did spend together alone was both enjoyable and frustrating. Now that I was aware of my feelings for him, every touch turned feverish. My cells turned into bumper cars, and my nerves became live wires.

Bradley respected my boundaries when it came to our physical relationship, but he didn't hide the fact that it was hard on him (as it was on me). And I had to learn to deal with the fact that, as part of his job, he would more than likely be shown being intimate with an actress on screen in the future. That thought turned my spine to jelly and caused a flash of fire in my chest.

Bradley offered to cover all of my medical bills that piled up after the accident, but the cab company's insurance picked up everything. I took a settlement from them, not wanting to battle it out in court. And since the cab driver had hopped the curb and run into me on the sidewalk, he was clearly in the wrong, and I got a pretty nice chunk of change.

So several months later, I was sitting in my back yard enjoying a glass of tea. I hadn't talked to Bradley yesterday, so I was restless and had run out of little chores to do around the house. I almost did the jig when my phone rang with the familiar ring-tone telling me it was Bradley.

"Well, there's my cowboy. I was wondering what you were up to," I admitted right off the bat.

"Hey, baby. I miss you," he said on a sigh. I could instantly tell he was stressed, as he had been for most of the time we've been together.

Our first hurdle, apart from the distance, was the gossip magazines. The worst one came out first, and it was ridiculous, but hurt nonetheless. It indicated that Bradley and I had an affair while I was engaged to Josh and that Bradley hired someone to kill him and make it look like an accident. Outrageous, right?! The other filth focused on my rural upbringing and lack of social status. It didn't bother me too much since I had such a wonderful family who knew everything about me already and knew the substance of Bradley and mine's relationship.

"You okay?" I asked gently, fearing a storm.

He expelled a long breath and I braced myself. "Just another long day of fighting with my agent and publicist. Sorry. That's why I didn't get a chance to call yesterday. They've been on my tail."

"About what?"

"About all the scripts I've been reading over. They're pressuring me to make a decision."

"You don't like any of them?"

"Two of them are very good scripts. Good writing and great talent lined up for them."

"Okay, so what's the hold up?" I wondered aloud as I went back into the house and started to pace around the living room.

Silence.

"Bradley? You there?"

"Yes." He sighed again.

I waited. And waited.

"Tell me," I whispered.

"It's you," he spat abruptly.

It startled me, and I was about to question him but he interrupted me.

"It's you. Ever since we've been together, things have been different. I can't just look at a script and analyze it normal terms. Now I wonder how you'll react if I take it, and I wonder why I'm not okay with the horrible language, excessive drinking, and superficial sex scenes. I've never been so unsure of things in my life and—"

"Brad," I interrupted, "I've never asked you to change. I've never once given you an ultimatum—said it's me or your career, love me or love what you do. I don't work that way, but I'm not one for gray areas. It's either black or white. You love me or you don't. You want the commitment and are willing to fight for it, or you don't. But I won't apologize for whatever it is that has opened your eyes to see that there are obvious pitfalls to your job. I love you. I'm in love with you, and I'll do or say anything I can to help you. But I don't want to be an obstacle."

"That's not what I meant. You just don't understand," he said, a bit hotly.

I wanted to say, "No. No, I don't." But I kept my mouth shut, thinking I could easily say the wrong thing. I knew things weren't going well and I hurt for him.

"I think you're making this harder than you need to," I finally said.

He snorted. "Well, I'm sorry if I'm not perfect and that this relationship isn't as effortless as it was with Josh."

My legs wobbled, and I plopped onto the couch.

"Ouch, Bradley. Below the belt." I knew he didn't mean it, but that was a horrible thing to say. No silver-tongued suitor tonight. Yes, things with Bradley were more difficult, but the happiness that came from being together was fulfilling and life altering. If Josh and I were peas and carrots, Bradley and I were matches and gasoline.

"Evie, I'm sorry." I could picture him scrubbing a hand down his face or shoving his hand through his hair in exasperation.

"I know. What can I do?"

"I don't know," he answered honestly. His voice wasn't tight with frustration now but distant and, well, bleak.

"When will I see you again?" It had been nearly three weeks since we'd been together, and I thought that may be one of the reasons for this current feeling of disconnection.

"I don't know that either. I've got to figure things out with my agent tomorrow. Then I'm headed to L.A. for a while to see my parents."

"That sounds great. Tell them hi for me," I said to fill the silence.

"I will. I'll call you in a couple days. Okay?"

"Sure, babe. I'm sorry this is a hard time for you. I'm here if you need me."

"I know. Thanks, Evie."

I strummed my fingers along my thigh, waiting for him to say something more, but even though he remained on the line, he said nothing.

"All right. I'll talk to you soon, cowboy. Bye."

"Bye."

I sat up on the couch, brought my knees to my chest and curled my arms around them. I didn't like the feeling that settled in the pit of my stomach but brushed it off.

I shouldn't have brushed off that feeling so quickly. Bradley didn't call me the next evening. As I was settling myself into bed, I received a text. I situated the pillows behind me and grabbed my phone to read his text.

I'm sorry 2 do it this way, but I think we should take some time apart.

I cried out and buried my face in my hands. Was this a joke? Clearly not. I forced my short shallow breaths to deepen in order to remain conscious. What was I supposed to say to that? I wouldn't beg. I flew across the country and nearly got myself killed the first time I decided to pour my heart out. He knew I loved him, so there wasn't anything I could say now to change his mind. But I could only take so much. No matter how many dirty names and empty accusations I thought of, none of them seemed worth it. I had armored myself, but not well enough. His words were like a hollow-point bullet burrowing into my heart. I responded with the only phrase still turning over and over in my mind. My fingers shook as I typed the letters.

Oh Bradley.

Tears dropped from my face, and I wiped at them when my phone vibrated again.

I'm sorry.

That's it? That's all I got?

I'm sorry too.

After an hour of silence, I finally turned out the light and made myself comfortable in bed for what would no doubt be a fitful night's sleep.

The next day I mostly slept, making up for my inability to do so the night before. It was Friday, and when no flowers came, I knew that he had made his decision. It was over. I crawled back into bed and found refuge in unconsciousness. At least that way, I didn't have to process anything.

I couldn't shrug off the feeling of déjà vu even though I knew that wasn't quite the right feeling. That had happened to me a couple of months before. Bradley (along with his parents and sister) had flown down for a celebration for my little brain child: DEC Foundation, a foundation to help veterans. The whole day I had an odd feeling creeping up my spine, and the fine hairs on my neck were raised. I couldn't shake the feeling like I had lived through that experience before even though I knew I hadn't.

And now, I had an eerily calm sensation washing through me. I was devastated, but what I couldn't understand was a feeling that whatever was going on between Bradley and me right now wasn't final. But I had no concrete proof of why I felt that way. By all accounts, Bradley wanted a break, and I was giving him one.

After a whole day's worth of sleeping, I couldn't stay in bed any longer. My muscles ached from the hours of immobility. I managed to get myself into the shower and even got a little food in me. By late afternoon the skies were angry. It wouldn't be long before the storm made its way here. I turned on the television to see if we were in any kind of tornado warning. Not yet, but there was a distinct possibility. "Conditions are favorable for several tornado outbreaks, folks," stated the meteorologist.

Low rumbles of thunder came in intervals from the distance, shaking the earth and drawing me to the back window for a look. I watched as the drizzle turned into a dance of heavy drops. The sound of my doorbell made me jump. I walked through the house and opened the door as a loud crack of thunder pierced the air. I flinched and closed my eyes and gasped when I reopened my eyes.

"Hey," Bradley whispered with a tentative smile.

His hair was soaked, and a dark thatch fell across his forehead. My fingers itched to brush it away, but I clenched my hands into fists beside me. I watched a yellow cab back out of the driveway. I didn't speak. I opened the door and stepped back as he crossed the threshold. A million questions and emotions were scrambling my brain. He walked to the middle of the living room and dropped his bag. The dark blue sweater he wore clung to his well-defined chest. I walked closer, wrapped myself in my arms, and forced myself to stop from drinking in his looks a second longer.

"My song," he said suddenly. I noticed now how tired he looked and saw an uncertainty in his eyes that I'd never seen before.

I raised my brows, and he pulled out his phone in response. I longed to close the distance between us but convinced my muscles to remain locked into position. I was able to keep my eyes on him but refrained from looking at anything but his face. He quickly fiddled with his phone, and I could see the lights flickering. It looked like he was downloading something… After a few seconds, he held his phone out between us just as I had back in New York City months ago.

It was a song, and the first few chords knocked the breath right out of me. It was an instantly recognizable song, and I had to control my face to keep a smile from breaking. Bryan Adams's voice vibrated in my ears with "When You Love Someone."

I inhaled slowly and unsteadily. Bradley reached out for me with his free hand and grabbed my other hand after he placed the phone on the ottoman next to us. My heart fluttered wildly at the sensation of his touch, and it went even more out of control as he pulled me closer to him.

What did this song mean? What about our time apart?

Suddenly I didn't care. He had pulled me to his chest, my face nestled into his wet shirt. His left hand held mine as he curled it to his chest as well. His other arm was holding me tightly against him. My other hand shook as I ran it up his back and took a fistful of the soggy material.

As Bryan Adams's sultry voice continued to sing the words I longed for Bradley to say, I focused on burning this moment into my memory. He lowered his head to bury his face in my hair, and I took advantage. I took my hand from his and placed it gently on his face as I looked up to stare into his eyes. The electricity still sparked between us as we rocked gently from side to side to the music. He wove his hands into my hair and pressed his forehead against mine as he sang a few lines of the song.

"When you love someone—you'll sacrifice. You'd give it everything you got and you won't think twice. You'd risk it all—no matter what may come. When you love someone," he crooned.

I should've known that he'd have a lovely singing voice as well. The song ended, but neither of us seemed willing to budge from our position. We just held each other.

He sighed lightly as he moved to use one finger to pull my chin up. His face was blurry from the tears welling up in my eyes.

"I never should have let you leave me that night in L.A.," he whispered painfully.

I took both my hands and held his face firmly, enjoying the light that was now in his eyes.

"You shouldn't have ever seen me walk away. Either time," I admitted, just as pained.

That crooked smile of his that I loved eased into place. And in that moment, his lips were on mine, unleashing the pent-up passion from the past several months. My hands moved anxiously across his body as I worked to cover every square inch of him with my greedy fingers. He retaliated by pulling me up, and I instantly wound my legs around his torso. One of my arms locked around his neck while I moved the other so that I could knot my fingers in his thick hair, heavy with rain. He gripped my back and dug his fingers into my hair as well. After a couple minutes of losing my head, I slowly loosened my legs to slide down him. He was reluctant but held me close to him once my feet were planted on the floor.

"I thought you wanted time apart," I reminded him cautiously.

He chuckled. "I thought the song would explain it for me. Weren't you listening?"

I bobbed my head up and down.

"One day," he continued as he cradled my face in his hands. I wove my arms tightly around his waist. "One day is all it took for me to realize what a fool I am and how lost I would be without you. I thought I lost you once, and it nearly killed me. I don't know how I thought I could ever let you go. That wasn't just a song I played for you. It's a promise. Whatever it takes. No matter what the sacrifice. When you love someone the way I love you, anything is possible. I want you. Forever."

I melted into him as he commandeered my lips again. He wiped a tear that slipped down my cheek as he slid down onto one knee. I was shocked when he pulled out an emerald-cut diamond ring. My hands covered my face as I struggled to contain the sobs, and he pried them loose before speaking again.

"Evie, my love, marry me," he pleaded as he stared into my eyes. "Make me whole by becoming a part of me. Marry me."

I stared down into his hopeful eyes, and my heart lifted. The feeling of déjà vu materialized again, but I knew this moment had never happened to me before; I never even dreamed it. I was able to pinpoint that it wasn't *this* moment that felt like déjà vu. It was like something I'd seen before, something in my future, which hinged on this moment. It was like feeling the planets align and everything falling into place. Peace and happiness stole through me and filled me up. I fell to my knees in front of him and threw my arms around his neck with such force that I tackled him to the ground.

He laughed as he fell back then rolled on top of me with a wolfish grin. "That's a yes?"

"Definitely a yes," I said thickly. I smiled through the tears, pulling his lips to mine as the rain came down in sheets and the thunder applauded.